The
Windsor
Knot

The
Windsor
Knot

A Novel

SJ Bennett

WM

WILLIAM MORROW
An Imprint of HarperCollins*Publishers*

P.S.™ is a trademark of HarperCollins Publishers.

HarperCollins books may be purchased for educational, business, or sales promotional use. For information, please email the Special Markets Department at SPsales@harpercollins.com.

A hardcover edition of this book was published in 2021 by William Morrow, an imprint of HarperCollins Publishers.

FIRST WILLIAM MORROW PAPERBACK EDITION PUBLISHED 2022.

Library of Congress Cataloging-in-Publication Data

Names: Bennett, S. J. (Sophia J.), author.
Title: The Windsor knot : a novel / SJ Bennett.
Description: First edition. | New York, NY : William Morrow, [2021]
Identifiers: LCCN 2020023920 (print) | LCCN 2020023921 (ebook)
  | ISBN 9780063050006 (hardcover) | ISBN 9780063050013 (trade
  paperback) | ISBN 9780063050020 (ebook)
Subjects: LCSH: Elizabeth II, Queen of Great Britain, 1926—Fiction. |
  GSAFD: Biographical fiction. | Mystery fiction.
Classification: LCC PR6102.E66 W56 2021 (print) | LCC PR6102.E66
  (ebook) | DDC 823/.92—dc23
LC record available at https://lccn.loc.gov/2020023920
LC ebook record available at https://lccn.loc.gov/2020023921

ISBN 978-0-06-305001-3 (pbk.)

22 23 24 25 26 LSC 10 9 8 7 6 5 4 3 2 1

For E

And for Charlie and Ros,
who combine the pleasure of fiction
and the pursuit of truth

The
Windsor
Knot

PART 1

Honi Soit Qui Mal y Pense

Evil to him who evil thinks.

—MOTTO OF THE ORDER OF THE GARTER

April 2016

I T WAS an almost perfect spring day.

The air was crisp and clear, the cornflower sky slashed with contrails. Ahead of her, above the tree line of Home Park, Windsor Castle glowed silver in the morning light. The Queen brought her pony to a standstill to admire the view. There is nothing as good for the soul as a sunny morning in the English countryside. After eighty-nine years, she still marveled at God's work. Or evolution's, to be strictly accurate. But on a day like this, it was God who came to mind.

Of all her residences, if she had to pick a favorite, it would be this one. Not Buckingham Palace, which was like living in a gilded office block on a roundabout. Not Balmoral or Sandringham, though they were in her blood. Windsor was, quite simply, home. It was the seat of her happiest days of childhood: Royal Lodge, the pantomimes, the rides. It was where one still came at weekends to recover from the endless formality in town. It was where Papa was laid to rest and darling Mummy, too, and Margaret alongside them, though that had been tricky to arrange in the snug little vault.

If the revolution ever came, she mused, this was where she would ask to retire. Not that they'd let her. Revolutionaries would probably pack her off . . . where? Out of the country? If so, she'd go to Virginia, called after her namesake, and home to Secretariat, who won the Triple Crown in '73. Actually, if it wasn't for the Commonwealth, and poor Charles, and William and little George so nicely lined up to follow him after all the ghastliness, that wouldn't be such a terrible prospect at all.

But Windsor would be best. One could bear anything here.

From this distance the castle looked untroubled, idle, and half asleep. It wasn't. Inside, five hundred people would be going about their business. It was a village, and a vastly efficient one at that. She liked to think of them all, from the master of the Household checking the accounts, to the chambermaids making the beds after last night's little soirée. But today there was a shadow over everything.

A performer at the soirée had been found dead in his bed this morning. Apparently, he'd died in his sleep. She had met him. Briefly danced with him, in fact. A young Russian, brought in to play the piano. So gifted, so attractive. What a terrible loss for his family.

Overhead, a dull roar of engines drowned out the birdsong. From her saddle, the Queen heard a high-pitched whine and glanced up to see an Airbus A330 coming in to land. When one lives on a Heathrow flight path one becomes an expert plane spotter, though knowing all the current passenger jets by silhouette alone was a reluctant party trick. The airplane noise jogged her out of her thoughts and reminded her she needed to get back to her papers.

First, she made a mental note to ask after the young man's mother. She wasn't, to be frank, normally that interested in the absent relations of other people. One's own family was bad enough. But something told her this was different. There had been a very odd look on her private secretary's face when he gave her the news this morning. Despite her staff's endless endeavors to protect her from anything unfortunate, she always knew when something was up. And up, she suddenly realized, something most definitely was.

"Walk on," she instructed her pony. Beside her, the stud groom silently urged on his horse in unison.

UNDER THE ORNATE GOTHIC CEILING of the small State Dining Room, breakfast was coming to an end. The Queen's racing manager was sharing bacon and eggs with the Archbishop of Canterbury, the former ambassador to Moscow, and a few fellow stragglers from the night before.

"Interesting evening," he said to the archbishop, who was seated to his left. "I didn't know you danced the tango."

"Neither did I," groaned his companion. "That little ballerina rather swept me off my feet. My calves are killing me." The archbishop lowered his voice. "Tell me, on a scale of one to ten, how ridiculous was I?"

The racing manager's lips twitched. "To quote Nigel Tufnel, it was an eleven. I'm not entirely sure I've seen the Queen laugh harder."

The archbishop frowned. "Tufnel? Was he here last night?"

"No. *Spinal Tap.*"

The reluctant dancer grinned sheepishly. "Oh dear." He leaned forward to rub his lower leg under the table and caught the eye of the extremely beautiful, model-thin young woman sitting opposite him at the table. Her wide, dark irises seemed to stare into his very soul. She gave a faint smile. He blushed like a choirboy.

But Masha Peyrovskaya was looking through him, not at him. Last night had been the most intense experience of her life and she was still savoring every second of it.

"Dine," she practiced to herself in her head, "and sleep. Dine and sleep. Last week I went to a dine and sleep at Windsor Castle. Oh yes. With Her Majesty the Queen of England. You haven't been to one? They are so lovely." As if it happened every week. "Yuri and I had rooms overlooking the town. Her Majesty uses the same soap as we do. She's so funny when you get to know her. Her diamonds are to die for . . ."

Her husband, Yuri Peyrovski, was medicating an almighty hangover with a concoction of raw green vegetables and ginger made to his personal recipe. The staff was certainly efficient. Yuri had heard rumors the Queen kept her breakfast cereal in plastic containers (not that she was joining them this morning). He was expecting the old English shabby chic, which meant poorly maintained homes with inadequate heating and peeling paint. But he had been misinformed. This room, for example, had elaborate red silk curtains, two dozen matching gilt chairs around the table, and a pristine carpet of bespoke design. Every other room was equally immaculate. Even his own butler would find little to fault here. The port last night had been excellent, too. And the wine. And had there been brandy? He dimly remembered there had been.

Despite the pounding in his head, he turned to the woman on his left, who was the former ambassador's wife, and asked how he might go about procuring the services of a personal librarian, such as the one they had met after dinner. The former ambassador's wife, who didn't know but had lots of impecunious, well-read friends, turned up the charm to eleven and did her best.

They were interrupted by the sight of a tall, raven-haired woman in a pleated trouser suit, who appeared in the doorway in a dramatic pose, hand on hip, carmine lips pursed in alarm.

"Oh, I'm sorry! Am I late?"

"Not at all," the racing manager offered amicably, though she was, extremely. Many guests had already returned upstairs to oversee the packing of their overnight bags. "We're all very relaxed here. Come and grab a seat next to me."

Meredith Gostelow made her way to the chair being pulled back for her by a footman and nodded heartfelt assent to the suggestion of coffee.

"Did you sleep well?" asked a familiar voice to her right. It was Sir David Attenborough, as melodious and solicitous as he was on TV. It made her feel like an endangered panda.

"Mmm, yes," she lied. She glanced around the table as she sat, caught sight of the beautiful Masha Peyrovskaya half smiling at her, and almost missed her chair.

"*I* didn't sleep," Masha muttered huskily. Several heads swiveled to look at her, except her husband, who frowned into his juice. "I was thinking all night about the beauty, the music, the . . . сказка . . . How do you say in English?"

"The fairy tale," the ambassador murmured from across the table, with a crack in his voice.

"Yes, the fairy tale. Isn't it? Just like being in Disney! But *classy.*" She paused. This had not come out as she intended. Her English held her back, but she hoped her enthusiasm carried her through. "You are lucky." She turned to the racing manager. "You come here often, yes?"

He grinned, as if she had made a joke. "Absolutely."

Before she could investigate the cause of his amusement, a new footman, resplendent in a red waistcoat and black tailcoat, walked up to her husband, bending to mutter something in his ear that

Masha could not catch. Yuri flushed, pushed his chair back without a word, and followed him out of the room.

Looking back, Masha blamed herself for mentioning fairy tales. Somehow, this was all her fault. Because when you consider them, fairy tales always have dark forces at their heart. Evil lurks where we most desire it not to be, and evil often wins. How stupid she had been to think of Disney, when instead she should have remembered Baba Yaga in the forest.

We are never safe. No matter how many furs and diamonds we wrap ourselves in. And one day I shall be old and all alone.

2

S IMON?"

"Yes, ma'am?" The Queen's private secretary, Sir Simon Holcroft, looked up from the paper agenda he was holding. The Queen was back from her ride and sitting at her desk, dressed in a grey tweed skirt and a favorite cashmere cardigan that brought out the blue in her eyes. Her private sitting room was a cozy space— for a Gothic castle—filled with sagging sofas and a lifetime of treasures and keepsakes. He liked it here. However, there was an edge to Her Majesty's voice that made Sir Simon slightly nervous, though he fought not to show it.

"That young Russian. Was there something you didn't tell me?"

"No, ma'am. The body is on its way to the morgue, I believe. On the twenty-second, the president intends to arrive by helicopter and we were wondering if you'd like to—"

"Don't change the subject. You had a look on your face."

"Ma'am?"

"When you broke the news earlier. You were trying to spare me. Don't."

Sir Simon swallowed. He knew exactly what he had been trying to spare his aged sovereign. But the Boss was the Boss. He coughed.

"He was naked, ma'am. When he was found."

"Yes?" The Queen peered at him. She pictured a fit young man lying nude in bed under the covers. Why would this be unusual? Philip in his youth was known to spurn pajamas.

Sir Simon peered back. It took a while to realize she didn't see this as odd. She needed more; he girded his loins.

"Um, naked, except for a purple dressing gown. By whose cord, most unfortunately . . ." He trailed off. He couldn't do it. The woman would be ninety in a fortnight.

Her stare resolved sharply as she grasped his meaning.

"Do you mean to say, he was hanging by the cord?"

"Yes, ma'am. Most tragically. In a cupboard."

"A cupboard?"

"Strictly speaking, a wardrobe."

"Well." There was a brief silence while they both tried to picture the scene and wished they hadn't. "Who found him?" Her tone was brisk.

"One of the housekeepers. Someone noticed he wasn't at breakfast and"—he paused fractionally, to remember the name—"Mrs. Cobbold went to check he was awake."

"Is she all right?"

"No, ma'am. I believe counseling has been offered."

"How extraordinary . . ." She was still picturing the discovery.

"Yes, ma'am. But by the look of it, accidental."

"Oh?"

"The way he was . . . and the room." Sir Simon coughed again.

"The way he was what, Simon? What about the room?"

He took a deep breath. "There were ladies' . . . underwear. Lipstick." He closed his eyes. "Tissues. It seems he was . . . experimenting. For pleasure. He probably didn't mean to . . ."

By now he was puce. The Queen took pity. "How dreadful. And the police have been called?"

"Yes. The commissioner has promised absolute discretion."

"Good. Have his parents been told?"

"I don't know, ma'am," Sir Simon said, making a note. "I'll find out."

"Thank you. Is that everything?"

"Almost. I've called a meeting this afternoon to contain publicity. Mrs. Cobbold has already been very understanding on that point. I'm quite certain we have her absolute loyalty and we'll make it clear to the staff: no talking. We'll need to tell the guests about the death—though obviously not the manner of it. Because Mr. Peyrovski brought Mr. Brodsky here last night, he has already been informed."

"I see."

Sir Simon stole another look at his agenda. "Now, there is the question of where exactly you wish to welcome the Obamas. . . ."

They returned to business as usual. It was all very unsettling, though.

To have happened here. At Windsor. In a cupboard. In a purple dressing gown.

She didn't know if she felt more sorry for the castle or the man. It was much more tragic for the poor young pianist, obviously. But she knew the castle better. Knew it like a second skin. It was awful, awful. And after such a wonderful night.

IT WAS THE QUEEN'S HABIT to spend a month at the castle in spring, for the Easter Court. Away from the excessive formality of the

palace, she could entertain in a more relaxed, informal style—
which meant parties for twenty, instead of banquets for a hundred and sixty, and the chance to catch up with old friends. This
particular dine and sleep, a week after Easter, had been somewhat hijacked by Charles, who wanted to use it to curry favor
with some rich Russians for one of his pet projects that needed
a cash injection.

Charles had requested the presence of Yuri Peyrovski and his
preternaturally beautiful young wife, as well as a hedge fund manager called Jay Hax who specialized in Russian markets and was
known for being crashingly dull. As a favor to her son the Queen
agreed, though she had added a few suggestions of her own.

Sitting at her desk, she considered the guest list, where a copy
still sat among her papers. Sir David Attenborough had been
there, of course. He was always a delight, and one's own age, which
was rare these days. He had been very gloomy about the state of
global warming, though. Oh dear. And her racing manager, who
was staying for a few days and was never gloomy about anything
much, thank goodness. They were joined by a novelist and her
screenwriter husband, whose gentle, funny films were the epitome
of Britishness. And there was the provost of Eton and his wife,
who lived round the corner and were regular stalwarts.

For Charles's sake she had included various people with Russian connections. The recently returned British ambassador to
Moscow . . . the Oscar-winning actress of Russian descent, who
was rightly famous for her embonpoint and acerbic tongue . . .
Who else? Ah, yes, that star British female architect who was
building a rather grand museum annex in Russia at the moment, and the professor of Russian literature and her husband
(you could never assume the sex or sexuality of professors these
days—as Philip had learned the hard way—but this was a
woman, married to a man).

And somebody else . . . She looked back at the list. Oh of *course,* the Archbishop of Canterbury. He was another regular who could be relied upon to make the conversation go with a swing if some of the others became tongue-tied, as could unfortunately be the case. The other misfortune being if they all talked too much and one could hardly get a word in edgeways. For which there was little remedy, apart from the occasional stern look.

The Queen always liked to provide a little entertainment for her guests and Mr. Peyrovski had suggested to Charles a young protégé of his who "played Rachmaninoff like a dream." There were also a couple of ballet dancers who would perform cut-down solos from *Swan Lake* in Imperial Russian style to recorded music. The whole thing was set to be refined, serious, and soulful. In fact, the Queen had been rather dreading it. The Easter Court was supposed to be jolly, but Charles's *fête à la russe* sounded positively grim.

And yet. You never know what will happen.

The food was sublime. A new chef, keen to prove herself, had created wonders with produce from Windsor, Sandringham, and Charles's kitchen gardens at Highgrove. The wine was always good. Sir David, when not prophesying the imminent death of the planet, was impishly amusing. The Russians were not nearly as dour as one had feared and Charles beamed with gratitude (though he and Camilla had departed after coffee for an event at Highgrove the following day, leaving her feeling like the mother of a university student who comes home merely so one can do his laundry).

Slightly tiddly, they had joined a few other members of the family, who had been eating together in the Octagon Room in the Brunswick Tower, and all gone to the library to be shown some of the more interesting Russian volumes in her collection, including some nice first editions of poetry and plays in translation, which she had always intended to read one day and never quite got round to. Philip, who had been up since dawn, disappeared without fuss to bed and the Oscar-winning actress, whose profile had been much admired and whose views on Hollywood had been highly entertaining, was whisked off to a hotel near Pinewood, where she was filming at dawn. And then . . . the piano and the dancers.

Thoroughly relaxed, the remaining party had gone to the Crimson Drawing Room to listen to extracts from Rachmaninoff's Second Piano Concerto. This was one of her favorite rooms for entertaining, with its red silk walls, the portraits of Mummy and Papa looking glamorous in their coronation robes on either side of the fireplace, its vista of the park by daylight and extravagant chandelier by night, and the elegant view of the Green Drawing Room beyond. It was one of the rooms gutted by the fire in 1992— though you would never know it now. Restored to perfection, it was the ideal backdrop for evenings such as this.

The young pianist had been, as promised, quite magnificent. Did Simon say he was called Brodsky? In his early twenties, the Queen thought, but with the musical sensibility of a man much older. He seemed borne away by the passion of the piece, while she found herself reliving scenes from *Brief Encounter*. And he was so good-looking. All the women had been entranced.

Afterwards the ballerinas had done their solos—very nicely. Margaret would have enjoyed them. One secretly found them rather clip-cloppety, but that was probably just their shoes. And then, somehow, young Mr. Brodsky was back at the piano and playing dance tunes from the thirties. How did he know them? And she agreed the furniture could be moved back for dancing.

It all started out quite decorously, then someone else had sat at the piano. Who? The professor's husband, she seemed to remember, and he was surprisingly good, too. The young Russian was freed to join the assembled company. With impeccable manners he had clicked his heels and bowed down to his hostess with a look of real supplication in his eyes.

"Your Majesty. Would you care to dance?"

Well, as a matter of fact, she would. And the next thing she knew, she was fox-trotting across the floor with no thought for sciatica. She was wearing a light silk chiffon gown that evening, with plenty of swing in the skirts. Mr. Brodsky was an expert partner, reminding her of steps she had forgotten she knew. His timing was impeccable. He managed to make one feel like Ginger Rogers.

By now, most of the party were joining in. The music was louder and bolder. An Argentine tango struck up. Was it still the professor's husband at the piano? Even the Archbishop of Canterbury was tempted to cut a rug with one of the dancers, much to everyone's amusement. A few other couples gave it a go, but nobody could begin to match the Russian and his latest partner—the other ballerina—striding majestically across the floor.

She had retired soon afterwards, leaving the guests with the reassurance that they could continue as long as they liked. In her day, the Queen could outlast half the Foreign Office, but now she tended to droop after half past ten. However, that was no reason to cut short a good party. Her dresser, who got it from one of the underbutlers, informed her it had gone on until well after midnight.

That was the last she had seen of him: dancing around the drawing room with a beautiful young ballerina in his arms. Looking magnificent, happy . . . and so intensely alive.

PHILIP WAS FULL of the news when he arrived to share a coffee with her after lunch.

"Lilibet, did you hear the man was nude?"

"Yes, actually, I did."

"Strung up like a Tory MP. There's a word for it. What is it? Auto-sex something?"

"Autoerotic asphyxiation," the Queen said grimly. She had Googled it on her iPad.

"That's the bugger. D'you remember Buffy?"

One did indeed recall the seventh Earl of Wandle, an old friend who had been rather partial to the practice in the fifties, by all accounts. Back then it had seemed practically de rigueur among a certain set.

"What the butler saw, eh?" Philip said. "Had to rescue the blighter on many an occasion, apparently. Buffy was hardly an oil painting, even with his clothes on."

"What was he thinking?" she wondered.

"My dear, I try not to imagine Buffy's sex life."

"No. I mean the young Russian. Brodsky."

"Well, that's obvious," Philip said, gesturing around him. "You know what people are like in this place. They come here, decide it's the pinnacle of their bloody existence, and need to let off steam. The high jinks that go on when they think we're not looking . . . Poor bastard." He dropped his voice sympathetically. "Didn't think it through. Last thing you want is to be discovered in a royal palace with your goolies out."

"Philip!"

"No, I mean it. No wonder everyone's keeping it hush-hush. That, and protecting your fragile nerves."

The Queen threw him a look. "They forget. I've lived through a world war, that Ferguson girl, and you in the navy."

"And yet, they think you'll need smelling salts if they so much as hint at anything fruity. All they see is a little old lady in a hat." He grinned as she frowned. That last remark was true, and very useful and rather sad. "Don't worry, Cabbage, they love that little old lady." He rose stiffly from his chair. "Don't forget, I'm off to Scotland later. The salmon's spectacular this year, Dickie says. Need anything? Fudge? Nicola Sturgeon's head on a platter?"

"No, thank you. When will you be back?"

"A week or so—I'll be in good time for your birthday. Dickie's going to stuff up the atmosphere and fly me in his jet."

The Queen nodded. Philip tended to run his own diary these days. Years ago, she had found it rather heartbreaking when he disappeared off, with who knew who, to do God knew what, leaving her in charge. A part of her was jealous, too, of the freedom, the self-determination. But he always came back, bringing with him a burst of energy that cut through the corridors of power like a brisk sea breeze. She had learned to be grateful.

"Actually," she said, as he bent arthritically to drop a kiss on her forehead, "I wouldn't mind some fudge."

"Your wish is my command." He grinned, making her heart melt with clockwork precision, and strode to the door.

3

MEREDITH GOSTELOW HOBBLED out of the black cab that had brought her from Windsor to West London—at an extortionate fee—and stood catching her breath while the cabbie fetched her case from the space beside him.

She looked up at the pale pink stucco of her house and felt that she would never be the same again. Something had shifted, and she was terrified, and ashamed, and something she couldn't name. She wasn't sure what she was thinking, but a tear made its tentative way through the powder on her right cheek. Since the menopause had hit her like a freight train, moisture of any sort was hard-won these days. She was a young woman in an old woman's body, creaking and enfolded in a carnal carapace she could not control. Last night had made it worse.

And then, this morning . . . She would have sunk to her knees, if she hadn't known it would be impossible to rise up again.

"That it, missus?"

She glanced round, checking for her case and her handbag, and nodded. She had already paid him by card in the cab. Two hundred pounds! What had she been thinking? But then, who orders an Uber to pick them up from Windsor Castle? She should have gone to the station, of course, and caught the train to Central London like any sensible human who didn't drive—but at Windsor one thinks differently. Surrounded by liveried staff, one is expansive. One is there because one is successful. One did in fact spend twenty minutes last night talking to the Archbishop of Canterbury about a potential commission for a twenty-first-century church building in Southwark. And so, one orders a cab and hang the expense . . . and says goodbye to the price of a large tub of Crème de la Mer for the sake of getting stuck in terrible, utterly predictable traffic on the M4.

One was . . . *She* was . . . She must stop thinking as if she were a tightfisted version of the Queen. Mind you, HMQ herself was known to mind the purse strings. Anyway, she, Meredith Gostelow, was alone.

A partner would have had the train idea. A partner would have given her a moment to think. A partner would have prevented . . . whatever happened last night. A partner might have driven her here in a nice, big car. And would now be carrying her case for her up the small flight of steps to the front door.

And talking to her, and telling her what to do, and needing food cooked and beds made and attention paid, which would be a nightmare. Meredith had been through this mental rigmarole a thousand times and cursed herself for repeating it now.

But something had changed last night. Something deep inside.

Talking of which, she needed the loo, rather badly. She grabbed her case by the handle with one hand, holding her capacious bag to her chest with the other, and hauled herself up the steps. By the time she'd found her keys, opened the door, dumped the bags, and run down the hall, she made it to the loo seat with microseconds to spare.

Old ladies. No moisture when and where you need it. Gallons of it without warning when you don't.

MASHA PEYROVSKAYA SAT in the back of the Mercedes-Maybach, listening to the musical, rhythmical sound of Italian phrases as the car inched its way home. Her hands were folded in her lap and she watched the glimmering light show created by the facets of the yellow diamond, the size of a gull's egg, on her wedding ring finger. Across the seat, Yuri barked Russian obscenities into his phone. A muscle twitched in his neck.

It is astonishing how quickly the best day of your life can become simply another thing you did.

In her earbuds, Masha's Italian language app said something about the pleasure of being outside. Or was it wall paintings? She tuned it out.

Yuri had been quick to tell her how crass she had been, how common. How she ruined breakfast for him by mentioning Disney. How she'd ruined it for everyone.

But wasn't it he who had asked to bring his own chef (he couldn't), refused to eat anything that wasn't alkaline, and had insisted on applying his own Himalayan pink salt from a rock crystal pillbox at breakfast? The ambassador's wife had been watching at the time and Masha had seen the look she gave him.

The problem with Windsor Castle is that it is a dream. Real people only ruin it.

Today a trade war was brewing. The markets were down. Yuri

was incandescent that certain stocks hadn't been traded yesterday, when he had given the order. Eventually he ran out of bile and ended the call with a vicious stab of his thumb.

"Five hundred thousand. You can say goodbye to your gallery."

He glared at his wife, furious, wounded. At the word "gallery," she finally looked him in the face. Good. It was why he had said it. The things it took to get Masha's attention! God forbid she should support him while he was fighting to keep everything together for her, for them, for the future. All she cared about was art—collecting it, showing it off, and mixing with people who made her feel clever because she knew the word "Postimpressionism." That and being worshipped like a goddess. Well, he'd tried that for years, since he'd found her, aged seventeen, when she *was* a goddess in her tiny T-shirt and dirty jeans, and it was wearing him out. And it wasn't exactly as if he was the only one.

"By the way," he said casually, the way he'd rehearsed. "Maksim's dead."

"Uh?"

He watched her face freeze.

"Died this morning. Heart attack, probably. You liked him, didn't you?"

For a moment, she couldn't speak. When she did, her voice was barely there. "A little."

"All those piano lessons. So many. You must play me some of those pieces you learned."

He observed the way she stared at him, as if he was being shocking. As if he was doing something outrageous. The way she so often looked at him, saying nothing, from her high goddess pedestal, up in the stratosphere somewhere. When all he wanted was for her to step down and reach out to him. He wanted her to burn with shame and come to him, soft and humble, and hold him. Why couldn't she understand? *She* was the villain here. Why did she always make it all his fault? His head was still pounding. Why had she let him drink so much? Had she known what would happen next?

She took out her earbuds. The silence enfolded them like a shroud as she worked out what to say.

"I will play you something," she mumbled at last. "When we get home." Tears threatened to spill from those heavenly, glistening eyes, but she held them in.

She was made of ice, he thought. But one day he would melt her.

AT THE CASTLE, the Queen tried vainly to distract herself from thoughts of the poor misguided young man in the cupboard. She had spent the afternoon with her racing manager, going through her upcoming entries at Ascot. With the public safely shooed off the premises, she was on her way to inspect one of the tapestries in the Grand Reception Room, which was due for minor restoration, when a warder intercepted her to say Sir Simon needed to see her urgently.

"Did he say why?"

The warder tapped his two-way radio. "He said to tell you there's been a development, ma'am," he said impassively. She approved of his lack of curiosity. The last thing one needed was staff who practically nodded and winked as they passed on news. Such people never lasted long.

With a sigh she turned on her heel and headed back to her office. If Sir Simon was tracking her down this way it must be important. She retraced her steps through the Semi-State Rooms, where she had entertained the guests at the dine and sleep, heading back towards the Grand Corridor, where her private apartments were. As she reached the Lantern Lobby, she bumped into a small group of people coming the other way. This was where the fire had started and although it looked splendid these days with its new ceiling, the timbers spreading out like fans, she still felt the occasional shiver walking through it. The group, meanwhile, seemed quite astonished to see her here.

They were headed by a distinguished, square-jawed middle-aged man in a broad-breasted pinstripe suit and tie.

"Governor!"

"Your Majesty." General Sir Peter Venn clicked his heels and bowed at the neck briefly. He alone didn't look surprised, because he wasn't. As the current governor of Windsor Castle, he lived in a grace-and-favor apartment in the Norman Tower at the gate to the Upper Ward, and she knew him well. In fact, she could have named, in order, all his postings around the world and quoted from his commendations in half of them. She had known his uncle, too, whom she'd first met as a slip of a lieutenant at a party in Hong Kong aboard *Britannia,* and to whom she had awarded various medals for operations too secret to name. The Venns were a strong military family. If there ever was a revolution, she would want Peter at her back. Or, ideally, just a few paces out in front.

"You look busy," she said, as they drew close.

"Actually we're just finishing up, ma'am. Very useful meeting. I was about to give a quick tour."

She smiled with vague approval at the group, most of whom she had briefly met yesterday. She was about to go on her way, but Sir Peter had a look about him. If he wasn't a die-hard general, built to withstand all eventualities, she might almost have called it excitement. She paused a fraction and, seizing his chance, he said, "May I introduce you to Kelvin Lo? He's doing some interesting work for us in Djibouti."

"Interesting work" meant foreign intelligence. Sir Peter had been hosting a meeting on behalf of MI6 and the Foreign Office. A young man with Asian features, wearing some sort of dark hoodie over—Were they? Yes! Tracksuit trousers!—stepped forward and bowed shyly. He looked utterly overwhelmed by the honor of meeting her. She wished one didn't have this effect. It was really quite trying, although obviously chatterboxes and oversharers (Harry had taught her the term—a very useful modern description for bores) were worse.

"Were you here last night?" she asked.

"No, Your Maj— er . . . madam."

"Oh?"

He looked up from his trainers long enough to see that she was still staring at him.

"My plane was late," he managed to mumble.

She gave up. There was only so much time one could devote to the inarticulate youth of today, however brilliant. The other members of the group hadn't been much better last night, and nor were they today. One of the men trembled like an aspen in the Berkshire breeze and the young woman next to him looked positively unwell. She bade them goodbye. She wanted to know what Sir Simon had to say and hurried on to her office, where he was waiting.

OUTSIDE THE LAMPS WERE COMING ON, casting an opalescent glow across the lawns and paths leading down to the Long Walk. She was glad they hadn't closed the curtains yet. Inside it was warm and bright, and time for gin.

But first, work.

"Yes, Simon—what is it?"

Sir Simon waited until she had sat down at her desk.

"It's the young Russian, ma'am. Mr. Brodsky."

"I rather assumed as much."

"It wasn't an accident."

She frowned. "Oh dear. Poor man. How could they tell?"

"The knot, ma'am. The pathologist felt something wasn't right. The hyoid bone was broken. That's a bone in the neck, ma'am—"

"I know about hyoid bones." She'd read a lot of Dick Francis novels. Hyoid bones were breaking all the time. Never a good sign.

"Ah. The fracture doesn't necessarily prove anything because it can happen anyway, with hangings. But also the mark of the ligature round the neck was unusual. Even that wasn't conclusive. The pathologist has been working on the case all afternoon, because we wanted some reassurance. Anyway, she had a look at the photographs from the scene and . . . well, they're not very reassuring. There's a problem with the knot."

"Did he tie it incorrectly?" The Queen was alarmed. She imagined the poor pianist grasping at the cord with those elegant hands. Perhaps he meant to save himself and then couldn't. How awful.

Sir Simon shook his head. "It wasn't the slipknot around the neck that was the problem. It was the other end."

"What end?"

"Um, do stop me if . . . you don't want . . ."

"Oh, get on with it, Simon."

"Yes, ma'am. If you're intending to . . . tighten . . . for pleasure, or indeed otherwise, you have to attach the cord to something solid that won't give. It looked as though Brodsky chose the handle of the cupboard door and passed the cord over the rail above his head."

Now she was properly picturing the poor man inside this cupboard, the Queen struggled to make sense of it. "Surely there was no drop?"

"Apparently you don't need one." Sir Simon looked thoroughly miserable at his newfound expertise. "With a slipknot, you just need to bend your knees. A lot of people who . . . do it for pleasure . . . like to do it that way, I understand, because when they've had enough they think they can just stand up and loosen the noose, but it doesn't always work because they lose consciousness, or they can't loosen it after all and then . . ."

She nodded. It was what she had been imagining. Poor, poor man.

Sir Simon continued. "But none of that matters, ma'am, because that's not how he died."

There was a tiny pause.

"What do you mean, 'not how he died'?"

"If Brodsky had died that way, intentionally or otherwise, his body weight would have pulled against the knot attaching the dressing gown cord to the door. But that knot was still fairly loose: it hadn't been tautened by a falling weight. The pathologist has re-created the circumstances with a similar cord and it was fairly conclusive. The cord around Brodsky must have been attached to the doorknob after . . ."

A longer pause.

"Oh."

For a full thirty seconds the only sound in the room was the ticking of an ormolu clock.

First, she had thought it was accidental death, which was bad enough. Then deliberate suicide, which was dreadful . . . Now the Queen forced herself to entertain a new, unthinkable possibility.

"Do they know who . . . ?"

"No, ma'am. Not at all. Obviously, I wanted to tell you as soon as possible. There's a team setting up in the Round Tower. They're just getting to work on it."

SHE HAD HER GIN AND DUBONNET, and they made it a strong one. She missed Philip. He'd have said something rude and made her laugh, and known underneath how very upset she was and cared.

Not that the staff didn't care, or Lady Caroline Cadwallader, who was her current lady-in-waiting and who listened sympathetically as she relayed the whole story. The few who knew the truth had that terrible look of pity in their eyes that she simply couldn't bear. She wasn't unhappy for herself—that would be ridiculous:

she felt for the castle, the community, and the young man who had had his life taken so brutally, so ignominiously. She was also slightly unnerved.

There was a murderer on the loose at Windsor Castle. Or at least, there had been last night.

The Queen readied herself for dinner—a small affair for friends and family this evening—and put on a brave face. The best brains in the police and any relevant government agencies would be hard at work on the case tonight and all one could do was trust they would solve it as soon as possible. Meanwhile, she might just sneak a second gin.

4

Down in the servants' quarters, maids and housekeepers and butlers watched the police comings and goings with a mixture of curiosity and frustration.

"What're they still here at night for?" a deputy sergeant footman muttered to a passing kitchen pastry chef, who was a friend.

Mr. Brodsky, as a performer and not a guest, had been housed high up in overcrowded attics near the Augusta Tower, above the Visitors' Apartments, in the south side of the Upper Ward overlooking the town. That attic corridor was now cordoned off, causing great annoyance to all concerned, as there were hardly enough bedrooms to accommodate everyone who needed one as it was. Instead, it was occupied by various people in hooded white overalls and gloves, who carried bulky bags and didn't talk to anyone. News had spread, as it was inevitably going to do, about the way the body had been found. However, the additional information about the second knot had not.

"They're treating it like a bloody crime scene," the chef complained. "I mean, everybody has kinky secrets. The guy's dead. What happens in Vegas stays in Vegas, know what I mean? They should just stay out of it."

"Kinky how?" an underbutler asked, pausing in the corridor to listen. She had just come back from holiday and was still catching up with the gossip.

"Well, I got it from a security guy who's mates with one of the laundry maids who swore him to secrecy that he was wearing ladies' knickers and lipstick, and had a tie wrapped around his—"

They heard fast steps, saw a senior member of the Household staff approaching, and tried to look busy.

"How would he do that under the knickers?" the underbutler muttered, genuinely confused. The chef shrugged. This didn't do it for the underbutler, who was a stickler for precision. "Nah, I think he was winding you up."

"No, I swear!"

"But even if it's true," the footman persisted, "why are they prowling around the place at"—he slipped his phone out of his pocket and checked the time—"nine thirty P.M.? It's hardly going to bring him back to life, is it?"

"Maybe they think he was involved in a sex game with somebody else?" the underbutler suggested. She had a quick mind and a ready imagination.

"For God's sake, who?" the footman protested. "He'd just got here! He was only staying the one night. Have you seen those rooms? They're like little cells."

"That never stopped anyone," the chef observed. "He could've been getting it on with one of those girls who came. Did you see them? The dancers? Those legs?"

The off-duty ballerinas, confident of their physique, had worn the skinniest of skinny jeans and cropped-est of cropped tops. It was not typical Windsor attire and had been much admired by half the staff at breakfast.

"What—and they decided to go all-out kinky here, at Windsor?" the footman scoffed. He paused to think. "It would have to be both of them," he added, still skeptical.

"Oh, why?"

"Because the girls were sharing a room. We had a rush on. I had to help Marion work out the plan to cram everyone in, and we put them in a twin. Well, two single beds shoved in a room hardly big enough for one. If one of them was out doing the do and snuck back in, the other one would've known about it."

"Maybe it was the maid of a banker's wife," the underbutler speculated. "Or a bloke."

"What are you three doing huddled here?"

Three heads spun round to see the night shift head housekeeper standing six feet away, looking like thunder. She was known for her spectacular tongue-lashings and her ability to materialize from nowhere, like the TARDIS but without the warning sounds.

They pleaded their innocence, which she didn't believe, and she sent them on their way with dire warnings about what happened to staff who gossiped and speculated and didn't get on with what they were paid for.

ANOTHER MEMBER OF STAFF ARRIVED back from holiday that evening. Rozie Oshodi had been in Nigeria for her cousin's wedding, and was taking a moment to readjust. After the bright colors and funky Afrobeat of Lagos, the stones and silences of nighttime Windsor seemed surreal. In the Middle Ward of the castle, not far from the rooms where Chaucer once lived, Rozie looked through the mullioned window of her bedroom at the moonlight glistening on the River Thames far below and felt like a princess in a tower. A black princess, whose childhood braids would never have been long enough to let a prince climb up and rescue her. But then, Rozie had worked hard to get her job as the Queen's assistant private secretary; she didn't need rescuing.

Instead, she needed to find out what on earth was going on. Sir Simon had sent five messages for her to call him. Rozie had tried to as soon as her much-delayed flight had landed, but now his phone was going to voice mail. Super-smooth Sir Simon was not the sort of person to panic. And this week was supposed to have been extra quiet. It was why she'd been given the time off for cousin Fran's wedding. (To be strictly accurate, the wedding had been organized around this potential gap in Rozie's schedule—a fact she was too embarrassed about to linger on for long. The Royal Family always came first and if Fran wanted Rozie there, fresh from her star new appointment at the palace, this was the week it had to happen.)

For the tenth time, Rozie checked the news on her phone. Nothing unusual. She shivered in the cold. For a brief moment she flirted with the idea of climbing into her pajamas and collapsing into bed, knowing she would be up early tomorrow with a full day of work ahead of her and several days of partying to recover from. Sir Simon could update her in the morning, when she was fresh.

But that was the jet lag talking. Rozie knew things didn't work that way in the Royal Household and that's what you signed up for when you joined: you were always prepared, always informed.

So she unpacked, humming one of the tunes they had played in every Lagos nightclub. She smiled at the plastic key ring with the bride's and groom's faces grinning at her, to which she now attached her most precious possession: the key to her Mini Cooper. Then she sat on her narrow bedstead, fully dressed and still in her coat, scrolling through her phone to favorite the best photographs of Fran and Femi from the hundreds she had taken, waiting for Sir Simon's call.

IT FINALLY CAME at one in the morning, when his working day was over. Rozie made her way over to Sir Simon's quarters in the castle. He had a suite of rooms in the east side of the Upper Ward, not far from the Private Apartments. They were crowded with pictures and antique furniture, yet somehow immaculately tidy. Like Sir Simon's mind, Rozie thought.

He stared up at her for a moment, having opened the door to her. She stared back.

"Is there a problem?"

"Your hair. You've changed it."

She ran a nervous hand over the new cut, which she'd agreed to on a whim in Lagos. Since the army, Rozie had always kept it short and crisp, but the new look was sharper still, with asymmetric angles. She wasn't sure how her middle-aged, Home Counties colleagues would respond.

"Is it OK?"

"It's . . . different. I . . . Gosh. It's fine. Sorry, do come in."

Sir Simon could be awkward with her sometimes, but at least it was friendly-awkward. Rozie made him feel old, she thought, and short (in heels she was a good two inches taller than him), while he made her feel underinformed—about the royals, the constitution, pretty much everything. They made it work. However, tonight, they were both tired. As they sat facing each other on chintz-covered chairs, Sir Simon sipped from a cut-crystal tumbler of single malt to keep himself awake. Rozie, fearful that whiskey would have the opposite effect on her, stuck to sparkling mineral water. She made notes on her laptop as he brought her up to speed on the new police investigation.

"Bloody mess." He sighed. "Total nightmare. About fifty suspects and no motive. God, I pity those detectives. You can imagine the headlines when the *Mail* gets hold of it."

He had outlined the basics of the case, and Rozie could indeed imagine.

RUSSIAN IN DEATH SEX ROMP AT QUEEN'S PARTY

Or words to that effect. The headline writers would slaver at the chance to create the greatest clickbait of all time.

"Who was he, exactly?" Rozie asked.

Sir Simon ran through his most recent update from the investigating team.

"Maksim Brodsky. Twenty-four years old. Musician, based in London. Not a full-time professional—he was scraping a living playing in bars and hotels, teaching, doing the odd concert gig for friends in the business. It's not completely obvious how he paid his rent, because he shared a decent flat in Covent Garden. The police are looking into that. She wants to know about his parents."

"Who does?"

"The Queen. Wake up, Rozie! The Boss does. She wants to send her condolences. We're waiting for the embassy to give us the details."

Rozie looked sheepish. "Right."

"But so far no luck. His father's dead. He was killed in Moscow in 1996, when Maksim was five." Rozie's face flickered with surprise. "You were hardly born then," Sir Simon murmured. He gave her a lopsided smile.

"I was ten."

"Lord." He sighed. "Anyway, back in the nineties, murder on the Moscow streets was a daily occurrence. It was the time of Yeltsin, the Soviet Union had collapsed, capitalism was running amok. It was like Chicago in the twenties—gangs and thugs and corruption. Anyone with any money lived in fear of being bumped off by one side or another. I had friends in the City with family back in Moscow who lived in constant terror."

"What happened to Brodsky's dad?"

"Knifed outside his flat. He was a lawyer, working for a venture capital fund at the time. The authorities said it was a street gang that did it, but ten years later, when young Maksim was fifteen, he won a music scholarship to an English boarding school. The rest of the fees were paid by a company based in Bermuda. So was his holiday accommodation, according to what the police have unearthed. He spent Christmases and summers at an upmarket B and B in South Kensington."

"At fifteen?"

"Apparently so. A couple of Easter holidays were spent with a school friend who had a house in Mustique, but I'm more interested in Bermuda. The current hypothesis is that whoever had Brodsky's father killed made a mint, had an attack of conscience years later, and tried to save his Russian soul by giving the boy a break in the UK using money that couldn't be traced. Maybe one of the oligarchs who came over here to avoid getting on the wrong side of Putin."

"Peyrovski?"

"He made his billions at the turn of the millennium. He wasn't one of the tough guys in the Yeltsin years."

Rozie thought of the Queen's potential question tomorrow morning.

"What about Maksim's mother?"

Sir Simon gave a snort of a sigh. "The embassy claims they can't find her. She had mental health issues. Maksim was brought up by a series of relatives and neighbors until he came to England. Last they heard, she was in some sort of hospital in the Moscow suburbs, but she isn't now."

"So he was effectively an orphan?"

"Apparently."

Sir Simon eyed his whiskey tumbler ruminatively, and Rozie thought how much Maksim Brodsky's early life resembled a classic spy biography. Did real spies actually grow up like that? She decided not to show her ignorance by asking a stupid question.

"Possibly," Sir Simon said.

"I'm sorry?"

"You're wondering if he's FSB. It's possible. He's not on our list."

Rozie simply nodded and tried to keep her expression neutral. But she was new to this job and she was thinking how incredible it was that a year ago she ran a small strategy team at a bank and now here she was, casually discussing whether or not somebody was a Russian spy with someone who knew. Or at least, was supposed to know. The Official Secrets Act was a scary thing, but she had sworn to obey it and now the secrets just seemed to tumble out on a daily basis. She was still getting used to it.

"And what about the other killer? The one last night, I mean."

Sir Simon took another sip of Glenmorangie. "That's where the bloody nightmare begins. A team of top detectives; one nude Russian found dead in a castle surrounded by armed guards. After sundown nobody gets in or out without security verification, not even you or me. Everything is monitored and recorded. Everyone's vetted and new visitors have to show their passport on arrival, which they all did. They thought they'd have it sorted by teatime, and yet . . ." He shrugged. He looked very tired. Rozie knew how relentless his job was.

"Brodsky was brought down here by Peyrovski," he continued. "So it seems most likely it was someone in his entourage. There's the valet, who had the room next to Brodsky. He went up to the Peyrovskis' room after the party at their request, which isn't unheard of. He hardly knew Brodsky, from what the police have ascertained. There's certainly no rumor of any relationship or quarrel. Mrs. Peyrovskaya brought her lady's maid, who did know him quite well, but the woman is tiny, apparently. Doesn't look as if she'd have the strength to wring out a hankie, never mind subdue and strangle a fit young man. And from the shape of the ligature it looks as though he was strangled first, lying down, then strung up afterwards. I'm sorry. Not a nice way to say it. It's been a long day."

Rozie looked up from her laptop. "Not a problem. There are other suspects, then?"

"Well, two ballet dancers performed after the dinner. Strong as oxen I should guess, but they claim to have only met him in the car on the way down from London. The girls were sharing a room and one of them was FaceTiming her boyfriend half the night and all of them swear neither of the girls left the room except to go to the loo or have a quick shower—neither of which would have given them enough time to have a sex romp with a stranger, kill him, and stage an accidental suicide."

He rubbed his eyes and went on. "At a pinch any of them could have done it, but it's not obvious. A couple of dozen other people were sleeping in the visitors' quarters that night, scattered about the castle. There were conferences and meetings and all sorts going on. It was Piccadilly bloody Circus. I mean, is there a visitors' Tinder I know nothing about? And did I mention the two o'clock cigarette?"

Rozie looked up from her laptop, frowning. She shook her head.

Sir Simon lifted his glass to the lamplight and stared into the amber glow.

"One of the policemen on duty found Brodsky smoking a fag on the East Terrace, practically under Her Majesty's bedroom. He said he went out to enjoy the night air and got lost. How do you get lost at Windsor Castle with the Queen in residence? Oh, and don't forget the hair."

Rozie looked up again. "The hair?"

Sir Simon's expression was very thoughtful. "They found a single, dark hair, trapped between the dressing gown cord and Brodsky's neck. About six inches long. Doesn't obviously match any of the Peyrovskis' entourage. Obviously a DNA gold mine. Tell her about the hair. That might cheer her up."

"Will she need cheering?" Rozie asked. The idea of an unhappy Queen made her edgy.

"Yep," Sir Simon said, before glugging back the last of the whiskey. "I think she probably will."

$$5$$

THE QUEEN WAS NOT CHEERED by the news of the hair. She wasn't cheered by any of it. A young man had died—died horribly—in an ancient castle that was supposed to be a modern fortress. Yet over twenty-four hours had gone by and nobody seemed any the wiser as to who had done it or how. It did not make one feel entirely safe. However, it did not do to give the impression that she was nervous and upset, so she carried on as normal as the week wore on, nodding grimly as Rozie or Sir Simon passed on the persistent lack of developments.

Sir Simon and the communications team had done a good job with the press, at least. The story that "leaked out" was bland and unremarkable: a visitor to the castle, not one of the Queen's guests, had died unexpectedly at night. The thoughts of Her

Majesty were with his family. Initial rumors that he had had a heart attack in his sleep were not contradicted. A few sordid web-based news rags carried unsubstantiated gossip that the dead man had been found in a sexually compromising position with a member of the Household Cavalry—but these seemed so outlandish and, frankly, predictable for the online sites in question that no respectable news agency picked up on them.

Meanwhile, four detectives and two officers from MI5, the Security Service, beavered away under glowering skies, high up in the Round Tower. In the opinion of King George IV, the medieval version of that great tower was not impressive enough, so he had added a couple of extra stories and some Gothic battlements. The internal space thus created was normally reserved for the royal archivists, but they had been moved downstairs temporarily to create an incident room. Whiteboards had been erected in front of floor-to-ceiling glazed cabinets containing boxes of royal files. Computers were set up with high levels of security. A request for a kettle was politely denied because the steam could do untold damage to ancient documents, but a hotline to the kitchens was installed, and endless rounds of sandwiches readily supplied to the detectives and their new colleagues from MI5.

Increasingly senior people came and went across the drizzle-soaked paths. Gossip around the castle was rife. According to the Queen's dresser, most bets were on Mr. Peyrovski's valet and a secret gay love affair gone wrong. Her racing manager, however, who got it from the grooms, informed her that unofficial sources were giving odds of seven to four that it was accidental suicide all along and the police were simply being cautious.

They didn't know about the second knot, the Queen thought to herself. It was always dangerous to give generous odds if you weren't up to speed with the stables. It was all in extremely poor taste, but one had to acknowledge that betting was in Windsor's blood. It was only seven miles to Ascot, down a road created for the purpose, and the races were not far off.

People were people, she considered. They did what they did. In Tudor times, attending public executions used to be a regular cause for celebration. The odd wager was tame by comparison.

IT WASN'T UNTIL FRIDAY, three days since the discovery of the body, that the Round Tower team finally emerged from their stuffy, windowless room. They met with their bosses' bosses, who would in turn report to Her Majesty. An hour before lunch, the Queen was getting ready to walk the dogs when her equerry told her a delegation would like a word.

"Tell them to put some wellies on," the Queen said. "It's muddy."

It was a sorry band who arrived at the East Terrace ten minutes later, in borrowed raincoats and boots. There were three of them and the most junior, who was introduced to her as Detective Chief Inspector David Strong, looked as if he hadn't slept for days. He was the man who'd been leading the police team in the Round Tower. There were blue-grey bags under his eyes and cuts to his sallow skin where a recent shave had been too hasty. He needed daylight and exercise, the Queen judged. The walk would do him good.

The other two were on better form and needed no introduction. Ravi Singh was an experienced and competent commissioner of the Metropolitan Police who had come in for a lot of stick recently for various incidents that were outside his control. The Queen had the urge to put a hand on his and commiserate, but obviously she didn't.

The third man was Gavin Humphreys, appointed last year as the new director general of the Security Service, known generally as MI5 and in government circles as Box. There had been two excellent, highly qualified candidates for the job, whose keen supporters had lobbied hard on their behalf. In the way of these things, bitter infighting had allowed a third, uncontroversial candidate to emerge from the shadows, and that was Humphreys.

Uncontroversial, because no one had taken a deep enough interest in his personality or leadership credentials to care. Humphreys was one of the new breed: a managerial technocrat. The Queen had met a few technical experts who were spellbinding when they discussed the ins and outs of cyberspace—but Humphreys, whom she had met various times in his anodyne rise to power, was not among them. He was grey of hair, suit, and mind. He was also convinced that, at eighty-nine, one had no possible means of understanding the complexities of the modern world. He didn't seem to grasp that she had lived through all the decades that had created it, and she had perhaps a more nuanced understanding of it than he did.

In short, she didn't like him. Thank God for the dogs.

"Willow! Holly! Come on, come on."

The last remaining corgis, as well as two friendly dorgis, scurried around her ankles and the group set off.

"I'm sorry it's taken so long," Humphreys said, as they headed downhill towards the gardens. "This case has turned out to be much more complicated than you would think. We've been up all night putting the pieces together."

The Queen stole a glance at DCI Strong, whose pallor suggested late sessions in front of a computer screen. Humphreys's dewy glow did not.

"And I'm afraid it's bad news."

The Queen turned to look at him. "Oh? Who's responsible?"

"We don't know that yet, exactly," Ravi Singh admitted. "But we know at least who ordered it."

"Ordered it?"

"Yes," Humphreys confirmed. "It was a government hit. An assassination."

She stopped in her tracks, calling briefly to the dogs, who were keen to keep going. "Assassination?" she repeated. "That seems unlikely."

"Oh, not at all," Humphreys said, with an indulgent smile. "You underestimate President Putin."

The Queen considered that she did *not* underestimate President Putin, thank you very much, and resented being told she did. "Do explain."

They headed off again, Humphreys walking slightly too fast for Holly and Willow, two nonagenarians in dog years, with the commissioner right beside him and poor, exhausted DCI Strong lagging slightly behind. The drizzle formed a fine mist against the horizon through which the tall trees loomed from the park below. Their footsteps crunched on gravel, then sank into the damp grass as they followed the younger dogs down the slope. The Queen usually loved these walks—but she wasn't loving this one.

"Brodsky was apparently a very good pianist," Humphreys began.

"I know. I heard him."

"Oh, right, of course. But that was just a front. We discovered he was the brains behind an anonymous blog attacking Putin's Russia. A blog is a kind of website. It's short for 'weblog.' . . ."

The Queen frowned. She was certain she reminded him of his doddery granny. It was tempting to remind him that she had signed several state papers this morning and could recite all the countries in Africa in alphabetical order, and the kings and queens of England from Ethelred up to herself. But she didn't. She set her face grimly to the drizzle and prepared to be patronized.

"Brodsky ran it under an avatar—a fake Internet name, if you will—so we didn't spot it straightaway, but analysis of his laptop quickly confirmed that he was a big Putin-basher. He kept a record of every journalist who's died in suspicious circumstances in the ex–Soviet Union since Putin came to power. The most famous is Anna Politkovskaya, of course, who was killed ten years ago, but it's a long, long list. Brodsky had done some quite intelligent research, for an amateur. He thought of himself as one of them, highlighting their cause. But it's a very dangerous thing to do, even from London. Putin isn't averse to killing Russian nationals on foreign soil. They made it legitimate ten years ago. He's done it here before."

"Not in one of my palaces."

"It looks like he's upping his game, ma'am. Perhaps he wanted to send us a message," Humphreys persisted. "'Look, I can get them anywhere, anytime.' It's just like him. Brazen. Brutal."

"Even here?"

"Especially here. Right in the heart of the British Establishment. It's classic Putin."

The Queen turned to Mr. Singh. "Do you agree, Commissioner?"

"I admit I took some convincing. But the motive is strong. And Putin is unpredictable."

"Candy! Stop that!"

The elder dorgi looked up sheepishly from the muddy puddle she had been wallowing in and padded back to their side. She shook herself energetically all over Humphreys's trousers. The Queen hid her approval with sangfroid.

"I'm so sorry."

"Think nothing of it, ma'am." He bent down and brushed off a few filthy drops of water with his fingers. He really was rather soaked around the knees. "And, of course, you know what that means," he added, straightening.

"Do I?"

"The thing is, we've been through the lives of Peyrovski's staff and those ballet dancers with a fine-tooth comb and there's no indication they're agents, never mind of the caliber you'd need to pull this off. No—it's more likely, I'm afraid, that the killer has been here for a while."

"Before anyone knew Brodsky was coming?" The Queen threw a questioning glance across at Mr. Singh. But the commissioner got no chance to reply as Humphreys warmed to his theme.

"They wanted to be ready for anything. It's how these people work, ma'am. They're planted years in advance. Sleeper spies, just waiting for instructions when the right moment comes. Imagine it." He gestured around them. "A killing here at Windsor Castle, right under your nose, so to speak. 'Nobody's safe now.' The message has gone out."

"A sleeper spy," she echoed, unconvinced.

"Yes, ma'am. An insider. Here among your staff. At least one, but maybe more. It's possible the killer was another visitor, of course, but to pick this venue it seems more likely they'd have tasked someone who knew it well."

"I'm sorry, but I don't think that's likely."

Standing under the shelter of one of her favorite beech trees, he gave her a pitying look.

"I'm afraid it is, ma'am. We need to face facts. It wouldn't be the first time."

The Queen pursed her lips and turned for home. The sodden little group of men followed, while the dogs appeared from the undergrowth and ran ahead.

"What are you going to do?" she asked eventually.

"Track him down. It won't be easy. We'll be discreet, of course."

Singh added a detail that his colleague, in his Putin mania, had omitted.

"We think Brodsky arranged to meet up with his killer after the party, ma'am. At about two A.M. a man of his description was spotted smoking outside and escorted back to the visitors' quarters. It must have been some sort of rendezvous. I'm sorry to be the bearer of such bad news."

Singh did indeed seem genuinely sorry. Unlike Humphreys, he did not give the impression of treating this place like the location for an exciting game of spies, but as a home, where a lot of people would now be living under suspicion, and that never did anyone any good.

"Thank you, Mr. Singh."

"And we'll keep you informed."

"Please do." She would have liked to invite him to stay to lunch, but that would have meant inviting Humphreys, too, and she couldn't do it.

What hurt most were those six little words: "It wouldn't be the first time." They were quite correct, but the Queen found them unforgivable.

6

THAT EVENING, Sir Simon needed to consult the Queen about some of the finer details of the Obama visit. The White House team kept finding new security issues to worry about. He found Her Majesty unusually downcast. He might have blamed it on the weather if he didn't know she was impervious to wind and cold.

Maybe the murder's got to her at last, he thought. She was tough as old boots, but there were limits. Perhaps he shouldn't have told her those gory details. She had asked, but it was his job to protect her as much as to serve her. At least Box was on the case. He gently reminded her about Gavin Humphreys's progress, but she didn't seem as reassured as he hoped.

"Is Rozie here?" she asked.

"Of course, ma'am."

"Can you send her in? There's something I'd like to talk to her about."

"Ma'am . . . if there's anything Rozie's done . . ." Sir Simon was aghast. He'd thought Rozie was coping rather well, for someone so new to the job. He certainly hadn't noticed any issues and instantly blamed himself, whatever they were. "If I can help in—"

"No, no. It's a small thing. Nothing to worry about."

Rozie arrived ten minutes later, looking puzzled.

"Your Majesty? You wanted to see me?"

"Yes, I did," the Queen said. She fiddled with her pen for a moment, deep in thought. "I was wondering if you could do something for me."

"Anything . . ." Rozie offered, with more passion in her voice than she'd intended. It was true, though. Whatever the Boss wanted, she would do. Rozie knew most people in the Household felt this way. Not because of what she was, but because of *who* she was. She was a special human being who had been given an almost impossible job, and had taken it on and never complained, and done it brilliantly for longer than most people in the country had been alive. They adored her. They were all terrified of her, obviously, but they adored her more. Rozie felt lucky she was still going.

"Can you get someone for me?"

Rozie was snapped out of her reverie. The look accompanying the Queen's request was an odd one, as if this time the answer might be no. Usually, they were simply polite instructions. This one seemed more philosophical.

"Of course, ma'am," Rozie said brightly. "Who?"

"I'm not sure, exactly. There's a man I've met before—an academic from Sandhurst or Staff College, I think. An expert on post-Soviet Russia. He has scruffy hair and a ginger beard and his first name is Henry. Or William. I'd like to invite him to tea.

Privately. Actually, I think he'd like to meet my friend Fiona, Lady Hepburn. She lives in Henley and I'm sure she'd be happy to host. She can invite *me* to tea, and him, too, and we can talk."

Rozie stood in front of the desk, trying to decode what was happening. She wasn't sure exactly what she'd been asked, but that was a detail: she'd work out how to do it later.

"When would you like?"

"As soon as possible. You know my schedule." There was a pause. "And, Rozie—"

"Ma'am?"

The Queen gave her another odd look. This one was different from the last. That had been uncertain; this one was challenging. "A *private* conversation."

BACK AT HER DESK, Rozie went over the whole encounter in her head.

What did "private" mean? Of course tea at Lady Hepburn's house would be private. Was the expert—and Rozie thought she knew the man the Queen was referring to—supposed to keep quiet about meeting Her Majesty? Rozie would make sure he did, but why not just say so? Her relationship with the Boss had been pretty straightforward until now: she simply did whatever the Queen told her, and if there was any doubt, she checked with Sir Simon, who had nearly twenty years' experience and knew *everything*, and . . .

And suddenly Rozie knew what the Queen meant. And why it had been impossible to say it out loud. And why this was a test, though one she sensed the Queen didn't want to give her.

It was all rather frightening and just a little bit exciting.

She logged on to a government database of experts and set about finding a particular man to invite to tea.

THE QUEEN SAT up in bed, writing her diary entry for the day. She never wrote much, and certainly not what she was thinking now. Many historians would be itching at the opportunity to get their hands on the pages she dutifully composed in longhand each night, which one day would be deposited in the Royal Archives in the Round Tower, alongside those of Queen Victoria. But such historians would almost certainly be disappointed. Whoever read this document in the twenty-second century would find it a detailed source of racing information, observations on the dullness of certain prime ministers, and minor family anecdotes. Her deepest thoughts she kept between herself and God.

And God knew, Vladimir Putin was an infuriating individual, definitely a cruel one, but not stupid. You didn't become the richest man in the world, as rumor had it, by making lazy mistakes. Nor was he the sort of person to ignore the unspoken accord among the ruling classes, among whom he was so proud to count himself these days: princes simply did not tread directly on the patch of other princes. One might spy, certainly, if one could. One might seek to undermine one's enemies in negotiations or elections. But you did not commit lèse-majesté and cause havoc in their palaces. If you did—who knew?—perhaps one day they might do the same in yours. Even dictators understood this.

Technocratic heads of MI5, it seemed, did not.

The Queen had not bothered to try to correct Mr. Humphreys. He seemed so certain of himself and so little interested in her opinion, even though she had met Putin and ruled alongside him, temporally speaking, for decades.

Dogs. They knew. Like Candy this morning. The corgis had hated Mr. Putin on sight and tried to nip his ankles during a state visit. Even a minister's guide dog had barked, she remembered. Dogs have such natural instincts. Putin used them to his advantage. He knew that Angela Merkel was afraid of them. Was that because she was brought up in East Germany, the Queen wondered, where they were more likely to be trained as guard dogs rather than pets? Armed with this information, he had ensured the German chancellor was met by two aggressive German shepherds when she came to visit him in the Kremlin. The poor woman. It was a mark of the smallness of the man. The Queen did not always agree with Mrs. Merkel's politics, but she was fond of her. Merkel had managed to stay at the helm of a great democracy for a decade. She was a woman in a man's world—as it most certainly had been when she started. As it still was, if one went by the photographs at meetings of heads of state: Merkel's, the only trouser suit in a sea of trousers. The Queen knew very much how that felt—although of course she did not share Merkel's rather Teutonic sense of fashion.

She realized she hadn't written anything in her diary for about ten minutes and tried to get back to the sentence she had left half finished, but her mind continued on its train of thought.

Putin was absolutely the sort of man who would seek to make a woman like Merkel uncomfortable. He was a bully, an ex–KGB officer with an unhealthy fondness for control. His attitude to canines, and theirs to him, said it all. Yet this did *not* mean he would have a very junior young expat killed on one's own turf. When such a thing was so unnecessary.

According to Humphreys, this cold and calculating man had established a spy in her Household *just in case* one of his enemies should come to visit—a very junior enemy indeed—so that he could show off the extent of his power. And when that moment had come, this "sleeper"—who had presumably been in place for years, simply waiting—had set up an elaborate attempt to suggest suicide and had failed to check the simplest of knots. Why suggest suicide at all if you wanted to make a statement about yourself? Was the idea that the police would realize it was murder after all?

If so, surely there were more subtle ways of doing so than to make the whole sordid affair look so ham-fistedly botched. She liked to think that if one *did* have a traitor in one's midst, he would at least be half competent. Oh, the whole thing was unutterably ridiculous.

And yet, "It wouldn't be the first time. . . ."

Well, no, it wouldn't. And that had seemed impossible, too.

Anthony Blunt was her first surveyor of pictures, having worked for her father before her. What an erudite, cultured man, so at home among the courtiers. A Cambridge don, he was an art historian, an expert on Poussin and the Sicilian Baroque, and a member of MI5 himself. He had saved her uncle Edward from embarrassment by rescuing some of his letters during the closing stages of the war.

He was also, as he later confessed, a long-term committed Communist and a Soviet agent. He and his friends had caused untold damage to the people she held most dear. He had remained at work at the palace for years after she was told, to spare the shame and embarrassment of admitting how far he had come—until Margaret Thatcher let the cat out of the bag and Blunt had to go. He seemed repentant for some of it, but one could never be sure.

She couldn't pretend that all her servants were above reproach. There had even been a play by Alan Bennett, and the BBC had made a film of it, with a comic actress who portrayed her as a prig and a frump. Not the Crown's finest hour in any sense.

Gavin Humphreys's words brought back unpleasant memories and made her doubt herself, which was not something she particularly liked to do. Nor did she enjoy having to rely on Rozie Oshodi when the girl was so new and so young. But one did what one had to. And hoped to be pleasantly surprised.

She wrote another paragraph about something else entirely and drifted off, with difficulty, to sleep.

PART 2

The Last Dance

7

W HAT'S THIS in the diary for tomorrow?"
Rozie looked up from her keyboard at Sir Simon, who
had popped his head round her office door. She tried to keep any
hint of nerves from her voice.

"The afternoon, you mean?"

"Yes. She's supposed to be visiting her cousin in the Great Park
after lunch. It's been in for weeks."

"I know. But unfortunately Lady Hepburn's brother died recently and the Queen wanted to see her. When the invitation to
tea came, she asked me to accept."

"When?"

"Yesterday."

"You didn't tell me."

"It didn't seem important."

Sir Simon sighed. It wasn't important, in the great scheme of things, but he was a control freak and that's why he was so good at his job. He tried to relax and delegate. If you didn't trust your subordinates, where were you? Even so, something rankled.

"How did Her Majesty know? About the invitation, I mean? I didn't see anything."

Rozie paused for half a second. Sir Simon saw every email, every log of every phone call, every message of any sort. And if he didn't, he could check it out. He probably wouldn't bother, but what if he did?

"I heard about Lady Hepburn's brother from Lady Caroline." She was improvising as she went. Sir Simon was not close friends with the Queen's lady-in-waiting. She simply had to pray he wouldn't check with her. In fact, Rozie *had* had a brief conversation with Lady Caroline about Lady Hepburn first thing this morning, but it had been the other way around: Rozie had engineered it, having noticed that they had houses near each other in Henley. She had wondered whether it might be presumptuous to assume rich, titled neighbors knew each other—but, no, that turned out to be a thing, and they were friends.

"Lady Hepburn's brother died a few weeks ago, didn't he? Heart attack in Kenya." Sir Simon knew *everything*.

"Yes. And Lady Caroline said that Lady Hepburn was still very upset about it." (She hadn't.) "When I mentioned it to the Queen, she asked me to pass on her sincere condolences and when I did, Lady Hepburn invited her to tea and Her Majesty said yes."

Was this even possible? Did such things happen? Rozie held her breath. Her heart hammered in her chest so hard she was sure Sir Simon would see it under her dress.

Sir Simon frowned to himself. This was most unusual. The Queen liked to visit Fiona Hepburn, but not on a whim. The Boss was not a whimsical person. How very odd. Perhaps it was a sign of advancing age. Not dementia, surely? No, that didn't make sense at all. But there was something about Rozie that didn't quite—

He stared at her for a moment. Rozie wouldn't make anything *up*, surely? What would be the point? He made a mental note to double-check with the Queen that she really did want to go on this consolatory visit, and went back to his desk.

About an hour later, Rozie's heart stopped hammering. She didn't know whether to be very proud of herself or deeply ashamed. She had just lied to her immediate boss about the words and deeds of two lady aristocrats and the British monarch. In the privacy of the ladies' loos, she sent her sister a Snapchat of various goggle-eyed expressions. Fliss would have no idea what it was about, but it helped.

THE WEEKEND WAS a difficult one. The Queen was already starting to notice the first ripples of a pebble dropped by MI5 into the Household pond.

The maid who delivered tea and biscuits to her bedside did so this morning with a doubtful expression and a biting of lip, suggesting huge discomfort and a need for reassurance. Had the Queen not known better, she would have asked a question and enabled a conversation. Usually, one could quickly solve the problem if one nipped it in the bud. But today she had no reassurance to offer.

Similarly, the page who later poured her Darjeeling in the breakfast room did so with a querulous look. She had known the man for years (Sandy Robertson; started as a beater at Balmoral; widower with two children, one of whom was at Edinburgh University studying astrophysics) and could easily read the unspoken message in his eyes: *They've questioned me. And not just me. We're all worried. What's going on, ma'am?*

The look she gave him back was just as easily translated: *I'm sorry. It's out of my hands. There's nothing I can do.* He nodded sadly as if they had actually exchanged words, and otherwise behaved with his usual calm efficiency. She knew he would report back to the servants' quarters and the social club, though, and the news would not be good. Something was rotten in the state of Denmark and even the Boss could not guarantee it would blow over soon.

For the rest of the day, she felt the shadow of fear and uncertainty fall over the castle. She and her Household operated on a code of absolute loyalty: both theirs to her, and hers to them. They did not blab, did not sell stories to the *Sun* or the *Daily Express,* did not ask for or expect the exorbitant salaries they could command from the likes of Mr. Peyrovski, did not ask impertinent questions, or allow the inevitable belowstairs ructions or personal concerns to punctuate the smooth running of her affairs—or not often, anyway. In return, she respected and protected them, valued the sacrifices they made, and rewarded lifetimes of service with medals and other honors that were treasured far more than gold.

Foreign dignitaries, presidents, and princes marveled at the precision and attention to detail accorded to every aspect of their visits by these men and women. One's family was jealous, frequently tried to steal some of the more exceptional stars, and occasionally succeeded. From Balmoral to Buckingham Palace, Windsor to Sandringham, the army of servants, hundreds strong, *were* family. They had nurtured her through ninety complicated years, been the buffer against the tides of disaffection that it sometimes pleased her subjects to display, and worked tirelessly to make a really rather difficult job at times look effortless. They worked on mutual trust, and now the Security Service was undermining it, one insidious interview at a time.

Still, the question remained: *Had* a member of the Household killed Brodsky? And, if so, why? Until she could answer it herself, she had to let Humphreys conduct his investigation in his own way.

ON SUNDAY, the Queen was very pleased to escape the doom-laden atmosphere and accept Lady Hepburn's kind invitation to tea at Dunsden Place, her small estate a few miles west, at Henley-on-Thames. They had been friends for decades, through Fiona's tempestuous marriage to Cecil Farley in the fifties and sixties, her fascinating single years in the seventies, when she traveled the world on the arm of various eligible men, her quiet second marriage to Lord Hepburn in the eighties, and now her gentle widowhood.

Fiona was a good ten years younger than the Queen, but these days friends of one's own age were like hen's teeth—certainly those who retained their marbles—and it was a boon to talk to anyone who had lived through the war and shared the values that had pulled the country through.

She was also a gardener. The house—elegant Queen Anne with a spot of Jacobean folderol at one end and an unfortunate Victorian extension at the other—was in need of a little updating, but the garden was lovely. Fiona walked them through the house, looking pretty as ever with her white-blond hair piled high in a loose chignon, and a pair of baggy trousers showing only the faintest traces of soil.

Today, on a blustery weekend in April, vast pots of daffodils and narcissi glowed yellow and cream ahead of them against a verdant backdrop of box hedging and billowing topiary yew, through which one got the occasional glimpse of the river. Most people would have considered the day too cold to sit outside, but Fiona knew her guest, and had ordered homemade scones and prize-winning raspberry jam to be served on the terrace overlooking the parterre, with thick Kashmiri blankets for their knees and plentiful supplies of hot tea.

The Queen's driver waited in the kitchen and her protection detail blended into the background, just out of earshot, refusing all offers of refreshment. The only other people outside were Fiona herself, Rozie Oshodi, and a bearded man in his midforties, in a tweed suit and tie, seated at a large teak table on the terrace. He rose to his feet as soon as they arrived.

"I invited Henry Evans," Fiona said cheerfully, as if the idea had been her own. "I believe you know each other."

Mr. Evans bowed. When he straightened and smiled, the Queen suddenly remembered what a sweet, boyish expression he had, and how charmingly innocent he seemed, given his specialist subject. "We do indeed. Good afternoon. How nice to see you."

"And you, Your Majesty."

"I hope it wasn't too much trouble to get here."

"On the contrary. A positive delight. Especially to come to Henley. You have a beautiful home, Lady Hepburn."

"Oh, Henry. You charmer." Fiona grinned. "Have a scone."

They chitchatted with friendly politeness, while Rozie sat at a nearby table, pretending to be engrossed in her notes. She was impressed that Henry Evans managed to talk animatedly about the journey from the Royal Military Academy at Sandhurst, where he worked as a lecturer, without showing the slightest concern about why he'd been summoned in the first place. Rozie hadn't been able to explain much on the phone—beyond mentioning how much she, personally, had enjoyed his lectures when she had done her officer training there. That wasn't relevant to today's meeting, though, so she made do with a brief smile of recognition and kept herself apart.

After a while Lady Hepburn made some excuse about checking

with the lady from the village who was helping out in the kitchen, and they were alone.

"Now, Mr. Evans, I wanted to ask you something," the Queen said, almost without pause.

"Yes?"

"The suspicious deaths of Russians on British soil. You've been studying them for a while, haven't you?"

"A couple of decades, ma'am."

"You contributed to that report I got last year. I remember you accompanying the minister to the palace."

"That's right."

"And you believe the Russian State has been murdering its enemies here in Britain with impunity?"

"Not exactly the Russian State, ma'am. Putin and his allies, specifically. I know he can be seen to embody the State these days. It's all a bit murky."

"Did the list include any journalists?"

"Only Markov, who worked for the BBC. He was the Bulgarian dissident writer, killed with the ricin bullet fired from an umbrella in seventy-eight. Before Putin's time, of course—but it set a precedent."

The Queen nodded. "On Waterloo Bridge, I remember."

"Exactly, ma'am. It seemed almost too le Carré to be true."

She nodded at the reference. People assumed she didn't read—God knows why, she probably read more papers in a month than most people in a lifetime, and she was fond of a good spy story. Henry Evans understood her better than many of her ministers.

"How many deaths have there been since then?"

"On British soil? Five or six. The first was Litvinenko in 2006. He was the ex–FSB agent poisoned with polonium-210. Horrible business."

"Quite. And yet no one was arrested or charged for any of them."

"No, ma'am," Evans confirmed. "Not since that agent we tried to extradite for the Litvinenko poisoning."

"The Americans often tell my ambassador how furious they are with us."

He gave a wry smile. "They're welcome to supply the evidence."

There was a pause while he took a quick sip of tea. Rozie noticed how naturally the Queen took the teapot to refill his cup. She was a remarkably practical person for someone with hundreds of servants to call on, and, in fact, an army. (As Rozie knew from experience, the British Army specifically pledged allegiance to her, not the government, and meant it.)

After another warming sip he went on. "Putin's good these days. Since the slipup with Litvinenko, which was sloppy, all the subsequent deaths have been very professional. And there's still a question mark over whether Boris Berezovsky was murder or suicide."

"What do you think?"

"Oh, murder, definitely. The color of the face, the broken rib, the shape of the ligature . . . But one could of course argue, as they did, that he was found in a locked bathroom, and he was certainly depressed. Berezovsky's a tricky case. He was the most high-profile of Putin's critics, the richest, until the Abramovich lawsuit bankrupted him, the man most obviously in Putin's sights. All I can say is whoever staged the suicide, if it *was* staged, did a damn good job of it. And the others were harder still to pin on Moscow."

"Go on."

"Well, Perepilichnyy died of a heart attack while out running four years ago. They found traces of a poison in his system, but no proof of how he came by it. Gorbuntsov was the victim of an assassination attempt in Mayfair the same year. He survived it, but the would-be assassin got away. Scott Young—he was the one with links to Berezovsky—was depressed when he fell onto railings. It's not that we don't suspect Russian involvement. It's that we don't want to start a diplomatic war without incontrovertible proof of why we're doing it."

"Naturally. They all died in their homes or public places?"

"Yes." He seemed surprised that she would ask.

"And they all had high-level links to people in Moscow? I believe your report said as much."

"Absolutely. These were quarrels about whistleblowing or money. That's where their threat to Moscow lay."

"Tell me, what do you think of the idea of these people killing someone purely to send a message?"

"What kind of message?"

"Just to say they can. Someone low-level. The wrong person in the wrong place, so to speak."

Henry Evans considered the question. He stared out at the gunmetal-grey clouds, whose outline mirrored the billowing yew beneath. He was considering over two decades of research into suspicious deaths behind the old Iron Curtain, and later here at home, since he had first become interested as an A-level student at school in Manchester.

"It's not Putin's style," he said eventually. "I can't think of another example. Do you have someone in mind?"

The Queen ignored his question. "Imagine they've changed tack. That it's not about *who,* it's about *where.*"

Evans's brow furrowed. "I don't understand."

The Queen tried to channel Gavin Humphreys as objectively as she could. "They've used poison in the past, have they not? Sometimes rare, radioactive poison, as if to make it clear that they are the perpetrators, even if they can't be brought to justice."

"Yes, but that's for revenge. Revenge on individuals for specific acts, and to send a message to other individuals not to do the same. I can't see how that works if it's just the *location* that matters." He still looked perplexed by the Queen's line of reasoning.

"What if the location were very . . . specific? Designed to show how brazen they can be when they want to?"

"It just . . . I . . ." Evans trailed off. He was frustrated. He genuinely wanted to support his sovereign, to follow her argument and agree with it if he possibly could. He'd never known her to spout what in other company would be robustly referred to as "bollocks," so he was very surprised by what she was suggesting. Whoever heard of an assassination based on *location*? What was she on about?

"And you said the Litvinenko murder was sloppy," the Queen added. "Agents don't always behave as professionally as they should. Do they sometimes panic? Have you come across this?"

Again he stared at her and tried not to seem rude. "Panic, ma'am?"

"Yes. The Berezovsky case, too. You said there were problems with the ligature."

"Well, apparently it was the wrong shape: circular, not V-shaped, as one would expect from a hanging. But whoever did it, *if* they did it, managed to leave the bathroom door locked from inside, which doesn't smack of panic, exactly. . . ."

"And Litvinenko?"

"They didn't panic there either, I wouldn't say, ma'am. They poisoned the man in a hotel tearoom, in cold blood, and walked away." He shrugged. "The sloppiness came earlier, leaving radioactive traces in various places they visited beforehand. They probably weren't familiar with how trackable those things are. Polonium isn't exactly typically on the weapons training syllabus. . . ." He realized that he was piling up counterevidence to her argument again, and this was hardly polite. He slowed to another halt, still perplexed.

"Thank you," she said. Which confused him even more.

"I'm sorry, ma'am. I don't think I've—"

"You've been more than helpful, Mr. Evans."

"I really don't think—"

"More than you know. Might I just ask . . . ?"

"Of course."

"Well, it's been very nice to see you again. But this is a very sensitive issue and I'd be extremely grateful if, when you're asked about today . . ."

She paused to choose her words carefully, and before she could find the right ones, he butted in. "Nothing happened, ma'am."

"Thank you."

"I wasn't here."

"You're very kind." She nodded and smiled gratefully. From her nearby seat, Rozie noticed an unspoken agreement pass between them. From her own experience, she could translate it now: Henry Evans would say nothing, regardless of who asked him, even the commandant at Sandhurst and his contacts in MI5 and MI6. This conversation was absolutely private.

Rozie wondered for a moment why it had been so easy for Mr. Evans to make this silent pact, when for her it had seemed more complicated. But she reflected that for her it *was* more complicated. Evans simply owed his ultimate loyalty to the Queen and that was that. The man Rozie had to hide this conversation from—lie to, if necessary—was the Queen's own right-hand man, and that made her secrecy so strange and uncomfortable. It wasn't that the Queen didn't trust Sir Simon, Rozie felt sure of that. She had seen the warm, long-standing relationship between them at firsthand. It was something else. . . . What? She didn't know.

Meanwhile, by some telepathic trick, Lady Hepburn returned right on cue with a fresh-brewed teapot and a coffee-and-walnut cake that she had made herself that morning. The conversation turned to the cricket, where England were doing well in the Twenty20 World Cup in India. The Queen, who had seemed perfectly herself before, looked to her friend now as if a giant unsuspected weight had lifted off her shoulders. She positively sparkled.

"Would you like to see the pots?" Fiona suggested. "I've got some rather lovely narcissi from Sarah Raven's catalogue that are doing awfully well."

They were joined by her golden retrievers, Purdey and Patsy, who flowed down the terrace steps to the parterre beyond. Henry, whose wife and mother were gardeners, took a surprising interest in the niceties of "lasagne" planting. Rozie, whose mother could kill a balcony tomato plant at ten paces, did not. But she perked up when Lady Hepburn turned to the Queen with a sudden smile and changed the subject.

"I heard you had a lovely time on Monday evening."

"Oh?" The Queen looked surprised.

"Caroline told me. We were on the phone about Ben's memorial service. Oh goodness, which reminds me—of course there was that young man. I heard something . . . a heart attack, was it? The next day? Nothing to do with the dine and sleep, I hope? I assume it wasn't a guest? No one you knew?"

"No, no," the Queen said carefully. Her friend was not fishing, merely trying to avoid putting her foot in it without meaning to—as she unfortunately had. However, it was strictly true to confirm that young Brodsky wasn't a guest. And one couldn't claim to have known the man. Not exactly.

"Oh thank goodness for that. It's awful how these fit young people seem to die these days for no reason at all. Or at least, unsuspected cardiac trouble or whatever it was. Perhaps they always did, and one didn't hear about it so much. Anyway, on a happier note, Caroline said the evening was a smashing success. Lots of super dancing after supper. I do so enjoy a good dance, don't you? I can't remember the last time I properly did it. And apparently there was this dishy young Russian who danced with all the ladies."

"Yes, there was."

"Did he dance with you?"

"He did, actually."

"Oh, how wonderful! Was he as good as Caroline said?"

"Well . . ." The Queen wondered how effusive her lady-in-waiting's description had been.

"Ha! I can see from your face he was. And then he absolutely swept that other woman off her feet."

"Which woman?" the Queen asked. "He danced with a ballerina, I remember."

"Caroline said he danced with two of them. To perfection—just like something off *Strictly Come Dancing*. But then he got together with another lady, a guest, and they simply went *mad*. It might have been after you went up. She said it wasn't the dancing, exactly. They did the tango, but it was something between them. Electric." Lady Hepburn twirled her wrists and spread her fingers. "Almost too personal to watch. Like Fonteyn and Nureyev."

"Oh, I doubt that!" the Queen scoffed.

"Well, almost. Caroline might not have mentioned Nureyev, come to think of it, but that's what I like to imagine."

"Your imagination always amazes me, Fiona. Look, the tips of poor Mr. Evans's ears are burning."

Flustered, Henry tried vainly to deny it.

"It's the only thing that keeps me going, these days," Fiona opined. "That and the garden. And visits from delightful academics. Do say you'll come again, Henry. You're always welcome."

"Thank you, Lady Hepburn."

"We must go."

The Queen had spoken these words to Rozie, who glanced at

her watch and saw that exactly sixty minutes had passed since their arrival. She hadn't seen the Boss consult a timepiece once, but her punctuality was legendary.

"I'll get the car, ma'am," she said, and soon they were on their way home again, the Queen sitting upright in the back of the Bentley, hands neatly resting in her lap, eyes fluttering closed in the very definition of a power nap.

8

IN THE MORNING, Sir Simon was in a cheerful mood when he arrived with the battered red boxes that contained the government paperwork for the Queen to review that day.

"You'll be pleased to hear they'll be finishing the interviews with staff today or tomorrow, Your Majesty," he said, placing the boxes on her desk.

"That's excellent news. Are they changing the line of inquiry?"

"No, ma'am, not at all. Apparently they've uncovered two members of staff with surprising links to Russia who were sleeping in the castle that night. It's lucky, in a way, this happened—I know it's tragic for poor Brodsky, of course. But who knows what havoc they could have wreaked, in time."

"Oh dear. Who are they?"

Sir Simon took a small folder from under his left arm and consulted his notes.

"Alexander Robertson, your page, and an archivist called Adam Dorsey-Jones. Both based at Buckingham Palace, but Sandy Robertson is here with you for the Easter Court, of course, and Adam Dorsey-Jones was visiting the Round Tower to consult the library. He's working on the project to digitize the Georgian Papers. I believe he joined about five years ago. I can check if you like."

"Yes, please."

"Ma'am." He made a lightning note and continued. "They've been relieved of their duties and put on extended leave while the police test their alibis and Box does more background checks. There are a few more people they want to question, just to be on the safe side, but Mr. Humphreys is pretty sure they have their man."

"Not Sandy!" she exclaimed, exasperated. "You know him, Simon. His father was a ghillie in Balmoral. They've been with us since Andrew was small."

"Yes, ma'am. But that might make him an ideal sort of person to target. Apparently his wife was very ill for a long time. Big medical bills."

"What about the National Health Service?"

"Perhaps she went abroad for it? I don't know. That's all there was in the report Humphreys showed me. It's all rather early days. And Adam Dorsey-Jones"—he peered at his notes again—"studied history and Russian at university and his live-in partner deals in Russian art."

"I see."

"He asked to come to Windsor at the last minute to look at some letters, and the theory is he might have been instructed to get himself down here when they discovered Brodsky was going to be in the Peyrovski party."

"'They' being his Russian handlers?"

"Yes, ma'am."

"Did you say Mr. Dorsey-Jones joined five years ago?"

"Indeed."

"Five years," she mused. "Simon, don't you think it rather odd that a young musician with an unknown website should be the target of such a drawn-out plot?"

Sir Simon gave the comment a good few seconds' consideration before replying.

"It's above my pay grade. Box knows what it's doing. We have the best world experts on Russian statecraft."

"Yes, but is Humphreys *consulting* those experts?"

"I'm sure he is, ma'am. If we have an insider at work, he's doing whatever it takes to find him."

He worked hard to reassure the sovereign, though he sensed her resistance. It was understandable: she was devoted to her staff. It must be a shock to realize treason could exist so close to home—though goodness knows, it often had before. Sir Simon was an avid historian and could name two dozen treacherous English courtiers down the ages at the drop of a hat. The Queen felt safe because she had people like him to serve and protect her. He thought, not for the first time, how delicate she seemed, like fragile porcelain. He would happily lay down his life to save her. Gavin Humphreys, too, he was sure.

Fired up, and rather wishing for opportunity of a puddle, so he could throw his cloak over it (would a Savile Row jacket do?), he spent another five minutes explaining the emerging plans for more comprehensive background checks on future servants. But he sensed the Queen wasn't really listening. Far from reassured, she looked brooding.

"Can you send Rozie in to collect the papers?" she asked. "I won't be long."

"I can always come and—"

"I'm sure you're busy, Simon. Rozie will do."

"Ma'am."

Alone at last, the Queen looked out of her sitting room window at a plane on its landing path, against a watery blue sky. She was furious and frustrated, and a few decades ago she might have railed at her helplessness. But not anymore. One learned one's lessons. She couldn't always do the right thing, but at least she could try.

ROZIE WAS GROWING ACCUSTOMED to the feeling of her heart hammering against her rib cage. It was getting dark. She stared out past the raindrops battering the windscreen of the Mini, looking for a sign that read KINGSCLERE and praying she was not about to make the biggest mistake of her life.

She had told Sir Simon that her mother, back in the family flat in London, had fallen out of bed and broken a hip. With immense grace and kindness, he had told her to dash to the hospital bedside, do whatever was necessary, and not think for a moment of rushing back. Which in royal circles meant she had about twenty-four hours.

Her mother was still safely in Lagos, visiting the extended network of aunties and uncles, and fit as a flea. A part of Rozie wondered whether Sir Simon would check the flight manifests for the last few days and find that out. She chided herself not to be so paranoid. Sir Simon was lovely, the ideal boss in many ways. It was not his fault that she was habitually making up stories to get round him. But enough was enough: she needed to know at least *why* she was doing it.

This morning the Queen had asked her to do some further research into the night of the dine and sleep. She had three interviews lined up in London for tomorrow. And none of this was to be mentioned to Sir Simon.

Her mind was racing. The Boss was up to something. Surely

such tasks should be left to the professionals, not entrusted to an ex-banker with three years in the Royal Horse Artillery to her name? The Queen had the whole of MI5 and the Metropolitan Police to call on. Or the prime minister. Or, if she liked to keep it close to home, Sir Simon himself or her equerry.

So why me?

And then she had remembered an offhand comment from her predecessor during the handover a few months ago. Katie Briggs had been the assistant private secretary for five years, before succumbing to mental health issues that were never fully discussed. Rozie admired the fact that Katie's privacy had been maintained throughout, that Sir Simon and the Queen were never anything but kind when talking about her, and that she had been quietly provided with accommodation on the Sandringham estate so she didn't have the stress of worrying about somewhere to live while she got better. During the final handover day, when they were briefly alone, Katie had said, "One day, she'll ask you to do something strange. I mean, *every* day will be strange, but you'll get used to that. One day it will be super strange. You'll know it."

"How?"

"You just will. Trust me. And when you do, go to Aileen Jaggard. She was APS before me. Her details are in the contacts book. She explained it all to me and she will to you, too."

"I don't get it. Can't you tell me now?"

"No. I asked the same thing. It has to come from her—from the Boss, I mean. When it does, track down Aileen. See her in person if you can. Just say 'It happened' and she'll know."

At that moment, Sir Simon had interrupted them to invite them for lunch and Katie had made a point of pretending they had been talking about the calendar entry system. Whatever it was, Sir Simon wasn't a part of it.

The rain outside beat harder, bouncing off the bonnet of the

car. Ahead, Rozie's headlights briefly caught the sign she was after. The Mini's satnav swore blind there was no turning here, but
a fork in the road proved otherwise. Rozie turned off the main
road and followed the narrower, unlit one up a gentle hill until she
reached the residential streets of the village of Kingsclere. Aileen's
cottage was halfway down the main street, within sight of a squat
stone church tower. Rozie parked the car opposite the church and
was surprised to find, walking back, that the address she had been
given was that of an art gallery. Peering through nets behind old
Georgian windows, she could just about make out modern paintings against crisp white walls. She rang the bell and waited.

"Ah, you came."

The woman who opened the door to her was tall, very slender,
and much younger looking than the sixty-one it said on her Wikipedia page. Her highlighted hair was swept into a bun held in
place with a pair of chopsticks, and she was wearing what looked
like cashmere yoga pants and a baggy T-shirt. Her face and feet
were bare.

"I hope I'm not disturbing you," Rozie said, aware that she
must be.

"No, it's good to see you. Come and join me for a glass of wine.
You must need it after that drive. So, you're the new girl. Let me
look at you."

Rozie stood in the narrow hallway while the older woman
paused for a moment, smiling quietly to herself, taking in the
short, sharp hair, the immaculate eyebrows and contouring game,
the athletic body clad in a pencil skirt and figure-hugging jacket,
the high-heeled shoes.

"Things have changed since my day," she said, still smiling.

"For the better?" Rozie batted back, with more than a hint of
challenge in her voice. She'd driven a long way in the rain and
the dark and the last thing she needed was a bit of Establishment

racism—which, to be fair, she wasn't used to getting from the Private Office. The tabloids had published a couple of articles about the Queen's "distinctive new assistant," taking care to point out her "exotic looks." At the royal palaces she was used to the odd startled raised eyebrow and some exaggerated politeness, but no one within the Private Office had commented on her appearance, other than when Sir Simon had pointed out she might find it difficult to walk at speed in a tight skirt. (She really didn't.) Aileen was the first person to say something outright.

"Definitely for the better," the older woman agreed. "Come on up. Careful on the stairs in those heels—just don't let them catch on the matting. I live above the shop. Funny, really, that's what the Queen used to say. Here we are."

They stood in a long, low-lit room, furnished in white and cream and hung with the same sort of pictures as downstairs. The television was showing Netflix with the sound off. Without asking, Aileen padded across the floor to a kitchenette in one corner and poured a third of a bottle of red wine into an enormous glass, which she handed to Rozie.

"As I was saying, things have changed. And about bloody time, if you ask me. Anyway, how are you finding it?"

"Fine, until now. Great, actually. Then it suddenly got complicated. Katie Briggs told me to say 'It happened.'"

Aileen's eyebrows shot up. "Tell me everything." She gestured to a corner of a squashy cream sofa, sitting cross-legged on the floor nearby, nursing her own glass of wine.

"I'm not sure how much I can say."

"Look, I joined the Royal Household in the year dot," Aileen said, "and I did the job for over a decade. There's nothing that's happened in any of those residences that I don't know about. No scandal, or divorce or disaster. And I know about the other stuff, too. The things she doesn't tell Simon. She's on a case, isn't she?"

"She . . . What?"

Aileen grinned. She gestured to a side table temptingly laid out with bowls of Doritos and guacamole. Rozie suddenly realized how hungry she was. "Look, help yourself. You came to me because she's asked you to do a bit of digging about, hasn't she?"

Mouth full of Dorito and avocado, Rozie nodded.

"You kind of know you're not supposed to tell anyone, but it feels horribly wrong?"

Rozie nodded again.

"Is it that dead young man at Windsor Castle?"

Rozie swallowed. "How did you know?"

"Actually, I hoped it wasn't," Aileen admitted, taking a swig of merlot. "I saw a very low-key news report about a heart attack and hoped it was just that. But when you called me this morning . . ."

"He didn't die naturally."

"Damn! At Windsor!"

"Why at Windsor, particularly?"

"Because it's her favorite place. How are the police getting on?"

"They don't seem to be doing much. It's MI5 who— Look, are you *sure* we can talk about this?"

Aileen gave Rozie a sympathetic look and shrugged. "You called me. We're not being bugged. Katie warned you something odd would happen, yes?"

"Yes."

"And it did, and here you are. You have to decide if you want to trust me, but I'm you, remember. If we can't trust each other, who is there?"

Rozie had already thought about this. She quelled the panic that the Official Secrets Act always induced and took a deep breath. "The head of MI5 thinks Putin ordered a hit, but the Queen's going in a totally different direction. The victim was an entertainer at a dine and sleep. She wants me to talk to one or two of the guests."

"And Box?"

"They suspect the Household staff. Sleeper agents."

"Oh God, she'll *hate* that!"

"I think she does."

"And let me guess, Simon's fine with it."

"He seems to be, yes. I mean, it's a nightmare organizing the interviews with them all, and the atmosphere is terrible and that's upsetting, but he's getting on with it."

"He would," Aileen said, with some finality.

Rozie was confused. "I mean, yes. Why wouldn't he?"

Aileen stared into her glass for a moment. "I don't know, exactly. But I do know that if the Boss thinks it's a bad line of investigation, it probably is. Has she tested it out?"

"Um . . . well, yes, she has." At last the meeting with Henry Evans made proper sense. "She met with a man who's studied the subject for years," Rozie explained. "The death at Windsor didn't seem to fit the pattern at all. The victim wasn't high-profile or well-connected, like they usually are outside Russia. He wasn't in his own home. And the murder was sloppy. She seemed to know the details didn't fit."

Aileen laughed.

"Yeah. She doesn't just trust her instincts—she trusts her experts. And she's the best at knowing which ones to pick. You would be, after seventy odd years, wouldn't you?"

"I guess," Rozie said. "Sixty-five years, I suppose. Officially."

"Oh, she's been doing this much longer than that."

"What do you mean?"

An enigmatic smile stole across Aileen's face. She closed her eyes briefly and rolled her shoulders. Then she put down her glass and fixed Rozie with a steady gaze. "The Queen solves mysteries. She solved the first one when she was twelve or thirteen, so the story goes. On her own. She sees things other people don't see— often because they're all looking at her. She knows so much about so many things. She's got an eagle eye, a nose for bullshit, and a fabulous memory. Her staff should trust her more. People like Sir Simon, I mean."

"But he trusts her totally!"

"No, he doesn't. He thinks he does, but he also thinks he knows best. All her private secretaries do. They always have. They think they're brilliant, which to be fair they usually are, and they think the other men in their clubs are brilliant, and the heads of the big organizations who went to Oxbridge with them are brilliant, and they're all being brilliant together and she should just sit there and be grateful."

Rozie laughed out loud. She was really very fond of Sir Simon, but this described his style exactly. "OK," she agreed.

"They should trust *her*. But they don't. She's one of the most powerful women in the world, supposedly, but she spends her whole bloody time having to listen to them and they don't listen back. It drives her bonkers. I mean, she grew up with it. She was a girl in the thirties; male domination was normal. God, even now I bet you get it, too, but at least we know it's wrong. She's had to work out for herself how good she is, what she can do. And what she can do is notice things. See when something's off. Find out why. Unpick the problem. She's a bit of a genius at it, actually. But she needs help."

Rozie bit into the last green-laden Dorito and looked regretfully at the empty bowl. "Female help," she said thoughtfully.

"Uh-huh. The help of someone who isn't trying to constantly buck her up. Someone discreet. A listener. *Our* help. Oh, look, you're still starving, aren't you? Let me get the pasta on."

They moved to the kitchen corner and Rozie put together a small salad from the leaves and tomatoes Aileen set out in front of her, while her hostess whipped up a dish of smoked salmon, cream, and tagliatelle in what seemed like no time at all.

"Did you help her a lot?" Rozie asked as they sat down on either side of the kitchen bar and Aileen lit a candle and topped up their glasses.

"A few times. Thank God mysteries don't crop up every day. But Mary—she was my predecessor's predecessor back in the seventies—she could tell you a dozen hair-raising tales of missing ambassadors and stolen jewelry and goodness knows what. They were a real team, those two. The Queen must miss her. It must be odd when your fifties were forty years ago, don't you think?"

Rozie shrugged. Her fifties were nearly twenty years ahead. She couldn't begin to imagine them, really, never mind life beyond. Also, she was wondering about something else. "So how come, if she's solved all these mysteries, nobody talks about it? I mean, even at the palace? Not a whisper."

Aileen's face lit up. "Ah, good! I'm so pleased. It's because that's her style. My favorite part. She'll get you running round like a mad thing, finding out details, lying like a trooper where you have to, and then, when it comes to the big showdown . . . it never happened."

"What do you mean?"

"You'll see. You have to savor the moment."

"But I—I really don't understand."

"You will. Trust me. Ah, I envy you a little." Aileen reached for the thin stem of her glass and lifted it until the bowl glowed bloodred in the candlelight. "Here's to the real queen of crime."

Rozie lifted hers, too. "The real queen of crime."

"God save her."

9

THE QUEEN SURVEYED the outfits laid out for her today. After lunch she would change from her comfortable skirt and shirt into a raspberry wool dress and diamond brooch, because later there was a Privy Council meeting to attend. Windsor was not all fresh air and fun.

Her thoughts were in London, though, where she felt the answer to the death of Maksim Brodsky lay. If Henry Evans was right, there had been no castle-based plot to murder Brodsky—so he must have been killed by one of the people he traveled down with, surely? Or someone he met at the dine and sleep. Fiona Hepburn's comments about that late-night dance had given her pause for thought. Did Brodsky perhaps already know this woman? Did they meet up later? It was an interesting idea. She wanted to know more.

And what about Peyrovski? He had rather insisted to Charles about bringing Brodsky down with him that night, even though it was most unusual for a guest to suggest the entertainment. Almost unheard of, in fact. Could it be a coincidence that the entertainer in question had ended up dead? What was Peyrovski's relationship with him? There was so much she needed to find out, and she had hoped that Rozie could help discreetly on that front, but last night Sir Simon had sent a message to warn her the APS was off for a day's compassionate leave, because her mother was unwell.

It was so frustrating! What bad timing. But it couldn't be helped. She would have to see what the girl could do when she got back.

AT EIGHT THIRTY in the morning, a week after the discovery of the body, Rozie parked in a loading bay outside a small row of shops near Ladbroke Grove. Normally she wouldn't dream of dumping the Mini somewhere so obviously begging for a ticket, but she didn't have twenty minutes to spend circling for a proper space. And this was her manor. She grew up round here, knew every side road—and knew that at this time on a Tuesday morning such spaces were as rare as invitations to a dine and sleep.

With a quick check in the mirror that the scarf she'd wrapped around her head to protect her hair from the rain was immaculately in place, she got out and ran across to Costa Coffee, where her cousin Michael was waiting for her at a table. He caught sight of her immediately and grinned.

"Hi, baby girl! Long time no see. You baff up good."

She smiled, a bit embarrassed, as she slunk into a free chair at his table. "Have you got it?"

"Of course." He took a small, cheap black plastic phone out of his backpack and handed it over. "Locked and loaded. Fifty quid on it. Plus the fifty to buy it." He watched as she swiftly stashed the phone in her handbag. "I s'pose it's not worth asking what you want it for. A nice, well-brought-up girl like Rosemary Grace Oshodi? Ex Her Majesty's armed forces. Ex la-di-da Posh Boys Investment Bank? You dealing or what?"

"You got it," Rozie deadpanned. "The Queen's got me pushing tea round the back of Windsor Great Park."

"I don't think that's the lingo, fam. What programs have you been watching? I took time off work to get this for you." He looked slightly pained, mostly teasing, and Rozie realized how much she had missed him.

There were three levels of cousin in Rozie's life. In the outer ring were the family in Nigeria and America. Newly married Fran was among them, running a yoga studio in Lagos while her new husband, Femi, managed several of the nightclubs where Rozie and her sister, Felicity, had danced the night away on the wedding trip. In the middle ring were the Peckham crew, who grew up in South London, where she and Fliss were born. And then there were Mikey and his brother, Ralph.

They were the inner circle and Rozie thought of them more as brothers. Her mum and his had always been close. They'd moved together from Peckham to Kensington when Auntie Bea married Uncle Geoff. That was a cataclysm for the family. Uncle Geoff was not a member of the Church; he was not a native of Peckham; he didn't speak Yoruba. And he was white. But he was a great artist and musician, he adored Auntie Bea, and when Rozie's mum had uprooted her own young family to be with them, Rozie learned what love and loyalty meant. Growing up in the mean streets of Notting Hill, Mikey and Ralph had watched out for her and Fliss, and saved Rozie once or twice, before her self-defense skills matched up to her gift for sass.

He'd changed his hair, too, Rozie noticed: three sharp lines were shaved into a close-cropped cut. Rozie felt jealous. In her pre-army days, she was known for dyeing the top of her hair gold. Now it was back to its natural color and, despite the new cut, she missed the drama.

"Thanks for doing this for me. It's good to see you, Mikey." She took out her wallet and extracted five twenty-pound notes, withdrawn from the cashpoint outside the minimart in Kingsclere that morning. "Here you go."

"Nice one."

"How's work?" she asked, breathing a bit more calmly.

"Scintillating. Yesterday I spent four hours in a windowless room talking about sales targets."

"Ouch."

"When I got promoted I thought it would be all minibreaks in posh hotels. Not four hours looking at PowerPoint slides in some rank basement off Earls Court Road. Then I get back to the store and this guy asks me about a smart TV that you can plug into your PC and play games off and stuff. So I spend half an hour explaining everything, then he actually goes on Amazon and orders it right in front of me on his phone. Right in front of my face! So he could save a hundred quid. Nice, man. You go right ahead and use me like a walking Wikipedia."

"I'm sorry, Mikey."

"Not your fault. I bet you at least go outside before you get stuff off Jeff Bezos."

"I—"

"I'm kidding you. But you didn't need me for that." He indicated the cheap phone stashed in Rozie's bag. "I mean, anyone can buy a pay-as-you-go phone. You could have got it yourself, you know."

"I didn't want it to be traced to me."

"So you asked your *cousin*? Who works for PC World?"

"I was in a hurry." Rozie knew it was hardly perfect tradecraft—

but at least a call to Michael wouldn't look unusual on her phone records. "You should be flattered I trust you."

"With your *burner phone*."

He raised an eyebrow and flashed her a grin. Rozie decided it was time to change the conversation. Mikey was studying for a part-time degree now, and had a girlfriend she'd never met, because they couldn't afford to fly out for Fran's wedding. She had so much to catch up on.

"How's . . . ?" she asked, hesitantly.

"Janette?"

Was that the girlfriend's name? She nodded.

"She's cool. Always busy. You'd like her."

"I'm sure I would."

"And Fliss?" he asked. "She doing OK? How's Germany?"

Rozie fought to keep her smile in place. Her sister's recent move to Frankfurt hurt like an open wound. "She's doing great. She loves it."

It was true. Fliss worked as a family counselor and therapist. Last year she had fallen in love with a German on one of her courses. Her skills were in such high demand that she could work almost wherever she wanted, despite her rudimentary grasp of the language at the time—although by now, being Fliss, she was nearly fluent.

Rozie remembered how the world had spun around her the day Fliss told her of the plan. "But you got your new job," Fliss had insisted. "Your fancy career. You'll hardly notice I'm not here." This was at Christmas, two months after Rozie started at the palace. The worst Christmas she could remember. The long and short of it was . . . she noticed. She also noticed that Mikey hadn't asked just now if Rozie herself was hooked up with anyone. And he was correct not to bother: it was never going to happen. Not in this job.

Mikey was staring at Rozie's hands and she realized she was fiddling with her car keys.

"I got one of those, too," he said. "Fran sent it to me, to remind me of their perfect love." With a sickly smile, he fished in his pocket and showed Rozie an identical key ring to the one she was using, featuring the heart-shaped shot of the happy couple on their big day. Rozie remembered the Mini. She made a face and got up.

"Sorry, I've gotta run. The car's on a double red. Give my love to Auntie Bea. I wish I could stay, but—"

"Duty calls," he finished for her with his best fake-posh accent. "Queen and country."

She nodded.

Mikey pulled her in for a bear hug. "Give Her Maj and the Duke a high five from me."

"Will do."

Back in the car, Rozie thought of the phone in her bag, in the passenger footwell, like an unexploded bomb.

A burner phone! For goodness' sake! She was turning into Jason Bourne.

She had discussed the idea with Aileen late last night, wondering how the "helpers" had coped without getting caught by their own Sir Simons, before the age of prepaid phones. It was easier then, apparently. The various residences were full of rooms you could nip into, unobserved, all with a landline you could use, and no one to say for certain who'd made the call. Not anymore. Smartphones were great, but you paid the price for convenience with traceability.

By now, Rozie had already done as much as she dared on her office mobile, which was the only one she had. If questioned, she could just about cobble together an excuse for each call she'd made so far, but any more would look beyond suspicious. And if questioned, she knew, she would never drop the Boss in it. She would take the rap, and *then* who would look like the sleeper agent to MI5?

She navigated expertly through familiar roads, past building sites, flash new blocks of flats and old ones dressed up in fancy cladding, mentally running through the list of calls and messages she needed to send before her first proper meeting. This was not the job Sir Simon had so graciously explained to her that glorious day in Buckingham Palace. She might joke about being a weed dealer to Mikey, but that's how it felt. Rozie had tried all her life to do the right thing and stay out of harm's way. Now . . . she was literally using her family to stay one step ahead of the Security Service.

No wonder the Queen had given her that strange look, that day in her office when she had first mentioned Henry Evans. She had known it would inevitably lead to days like this.

WESTBOURNE GROVE WAS not far from Ladbroke Grove geographically, but it would never have occurred to Rozie to meet Mikey here. Coffee shops adorned their midcentury modern chairs with sheepskin rugs, the single charity shop was full of designer cast-offs, and all the independent boutiques set out to appeal to the ladies who lunched and lived in pastel-colored multimillion-pound houses around the corner. The number of black and brown faces among the white ones diminished with each passing street. From that point of view, it was a bit like being back at work.

Rozie found a parking space eventually—a proper one, this time—and checked her watch. Ten minutes to spare. She rubbed her hands with some shea butter and consulted the bright ankara notebook she had bought as a souvenir on a shopping trip with Fran and Fliss in Lagos.

After a few pages of bad poetry to put a casual reader off the scent, all information relating to the Brodsky case was captured old-style, in pencil on the notebook's ruled paper, for fear of leaving a digital trace. Luckily, Sir Simon had no such concerns back in the office, and all the names, addresses, and contact numbers for people who had been invited to sleep at the castle that night were faithfully recorded on a spreadsheet the master of the Household had been asked to provide to the police. Rozie had accessed the file and copied them out yesterday morning. She called one of the numbers now (there had been no response yesterday) and spoke to a young man who agreed to meet her late in the afternoon. It would be her fourth interview of the day. Then it was time to head to Meredith Gostelow's flat in Chepstow Villas.

The woman who met her at the top of the steps looked nervous and distracted. She was wearing an emerald-green floor-length robe above oversize retro trainers. Wild wisps of hair poked out of an extravagant red half turban. Her only makeup was a slash of matching red lipstick. But there were bags under her tired blue eyes, laced with traces of yesterday's mascara, and she avoided Rozie's gaze while ushering her in.

"Come this way. I haven't . . . I didn't know what you wanted."

She led the way down a black-and-white tiled hallway to a small, untidy kitchen overlooking a shady garden.

"Tea?"

"Lovely. Whatever you've got."

Meredith pulled a couple of spotted mugs from a shelf, fished out a couple of tea bags from an old dented tin, and sloshed in water from a kettle. Milk came from a fridge whose shelves exuded the odor of something long past its sell-by date. Rozie steeled herself for the interview to follow and was not remotely surprised when she felt something rub at her ankle and looked down to find a tortoiseshell cat staring back up at her with impassive green eyes. Of course the mad old bat would have cats.

The architect took a mug and wandered back down the hallway.

Rozie picked up the second one and followed on, just in time to catch the emerald robe disappearing through an open doorway. She followed and stood . . . amazed.

The room was long and wide, with windows framed in lavish pink silk curtains. The walls were painted a delicate china blue, but they were almost hidden by a patchwork of paintings, lithographs, and textiles in mismatched frames; a vast antique mirror; and floor-to-ceiling shelves of books, immaculately arranged. Furniture was simple and geometric, but clearly expensive. A couple of console tables displayed collections of jade and little bronzes. The effect was breathtaking, and it was something to do with the hidden lights, the artful use of color, the way the eye was constantly drawn to different details, and the confidence and perfect finish of it all.

Meredith Gostelow simply did not care about kitchens, Rozie realized. Or making tea. She cared about entertaining spaces, and she was a bit of a genius at creating them.

"Excuse the mess," she said, picking up a paperback from a sofa seat—the only object out of place—and installing herself among its comfortable cushions. The tortoiseshell came to sit beside her. Rozie sat down on the matching sofa opposite and put her tea on the table between them—itself a work of art in bronze and glass.

"This isn't what I expected," she admitted.

"Oh? What did you expect?"

"I don't know exactly. I don't know any architects. Something white and minimalist?"

Meredith sighed. "Everybody does. As if architecture stopped at Norman Foster. It's so boring. What about *maximalist*? Clashing cultures, vivid memories. Isn't it joyful? It's what my clients pay me for." But she didn't look joyful. She looked bleak.

"Are you working on something at the moment?" Rozie asked.

"Several things, as always. Mexico . . . Saint Petersburg . . . You're lucky you caught me in the country. I'm off to Heathrow at seven. Look, let's get this over with, shall we? I assume you're here about Maksim. Are you MI5?"

"Definitely not," Rozie assured her, rather startled. "Quite the opposite, really."

"You said you were from the Queen's private office. . . ."

"Yes."

"So who sent you?"

This was a perfectly legitimate question, and Rozie saw that she was probably going to be asked it quite a lot—if she was lucky to continue in the job beyond tomorrow. She needed a clever answer.

"Her Majesty." There was no clever answer. All she had was the Boss's magic dust.

"Bloody hell." Meredith sat up straighter. "D'you mean it? Really?"

"Yes." Rozie saw Meredith's skeptical gaze transformed by wonder.

"Why does she want to talk to *me*?"

"I can't answer that directly, but I can say that anything you tell me is in absolute confidence. She wants to know what Mr. Brodsky did after the party. I gather from the way you were dancing, you might have got close to him. Perhaps he talked to you that evening. Or did you already know him?"

The architect's expression was a tangle of mixed emotions. Eagerness fought with wariness, then both were followed by something calmer. The planes of her face settled. She leaned back in her seat.

"No, I didn't know him. As I told the nice policeman who questioned me after he died. We danced the tango, that's all."

"But it wasn't all, was it?" Rozie asked gently.

"No, it wasn't."

There was a brief silence while Rozie wondered what to say. She thought back to Lady Hepburn.

"I gather it was an amazing tango."

"Thank you." Meredith took it as her due. "I learned it in Argentina. I thought so."

"It was much admired."

"The Queen wasn't there, though, by then. She'd gone to bed."

"True," Rozie agreed.

"So why does she . . . ? Why does it matter?"

"I can only say it matters very much. She wouldn't ask you if it didn't."

Meredith got up, walked over to a wall of artwork, then across to the window and looked out at the cherry blossom view. "If I tell you, do I have your word that it goes no further?"

"Did you kill him?" Rozie felt as if she was living in an alternate universe. How could such a sentence seriously pass her lips?

"No, of course I didn't!" Meredith exclaimed. "This has nothing to do with his death. Don't be ridiculous!"

"Then you have my word. No further," Rozie said. She allowed the ensuing silence to fill the room.

Meredith stood for a moment, framed by the light.

"Do you dance, Miss—?"

"Oshodi." She pronounced it like they did at home: O-show-dee.

"D'you dance, Miss Oshodi?"

"A little," Rozie admitted.

"Well, I dance a lot. Not often, but when I do, I dance with my very soul. I studied ballet as a girl, took all the exams. I wanted to be a ballerina, but then, who doesn't? Then I grew these"—Meredith gestured to her bosom—"and also too tall, and, and, and . . . We all have our excuses. I went abroad, traveled through South America, met a man. . . ."

Rozie nodded, but Meredith obviously thought she wasn't paying enough attention. The architect's voice resonated with intensity as she walked across the room and sank into a seat beside her visitor.

"He taught me tango. And, Miss Oshodi, I'm very good. I'd forgotten how good I was, over the years, trying again with different partners and never quite capturing the flick, the drama, the spark." Meredith gestured with one arm and Rozie could well imagine her on stage, commanding an audience. "I gave up. My feet were still. And then there was Maksim. Of course he was *gorgeous*—everyone must have told you that. And he danced with these beautiful young creatures and they were perfect, but they didn't *feel* the dance to their very souls, didn't give themselves up to it entirely. And, I don't know, Maksim must have seen something in my eye. He asked me onto the floor of that Crimson Drawing Room and I said no. How could anyone follow those ballerinas? But he insisted and insisted, and someone said something encouraging beside me and the next thing I knew he was holding me and saying something to the pianist, and whoever that was struck up a *brilliant* version of 'Jalousie,' and we were off."

"I wish I'd been there."

"I wish I *hadn't*," Meredith rasped. She got up again and started pacing the carpet. "That dance brought out the eighteen-year-old in me, and at the same time something ageless in Maksim. You'd think he'd lived a thousand years, not twenty-four, or whatever he was. You see? I don't even know his age! We hadn't even spoken during dinner. Even then, our bodies did most of the talking and, yes, when they say dancing is the vertical expression of horizontal desire . . ."

Rozie sensed where this conversation was heading, but couldn't quite believe it. She fought to keep her expression neutral. Would it even have been possible in that place . . . ?

"You became very close?" she ventured.

"We became absolutely intertwined. You get very physical with the tango; together and apart. When he pulls you in . . . It was obvious he wanted me. Of course, I wanted him. I mean . . . it's absurd, isn't it? I can see from your face you think so."

"I'm sorry. I didn't mean—"

"A fifty-seven-year-old woman and a twenty-something man. A woman like me." Meredith glanced down disdainfully at her breasts and belly. Rozie had seen flair when she first saw the emerald robe and trainers, but Meredith only saw the three stone in weight she had put on since the menopause. She moved more slowly, ached more frequently, had to work harder every day not to feel invisible.

"I just meant . . . How did you do it? At the castle?" Rozie asked.

"Sleep with him?" Meredith's smile was both wry and triumphant. "Have you ever had one of those moments, Miss Oshodi, when you absolutely need to be with someone, and it makes no sense and it's probably wrong, but nothing else matters?"

Rozie swallowed.

"You know. You know! Well, Maksim and I both realized, on the dance floor, that this tango was just the start of something. We had to continue it. It was utterly, utterly mad and the most exhilarating feeling I've had in years. He whispered filthy things in my ear and when I whispered filthy things back, he laughed. He didn't see our ages, my . . . *this* . . . it just didn't matter. He asked where I was sleeping, and when I told him where the guest suites were, he said he'd sort something out. He had a word with that fabulously beautiful Peyrovski woman, who he obviously knew quite well, and I saw her smile and mutter in return. Then he told me he'd meet me in my room within the hour. Just to wait for him there."

"Um, so it was your room you went back to, not his?"

"Yes?" Meredith said. She sounded puzzled, rather than anxious at being caught out in a lie.

"And did you go to his room at any point?"

"No, of course not! Mine was much nicer. I had this gorgeous suite with Regency furniture and I imagine he had a rabbit hole somewhere. Why would we go to his?"

"I'm sorry, I interrupted you. You went back to your room."

Meredith nodded. "I said good night to everyone and ostentatiously went up on my own. I was sure the feeling would wear off as soon as I was alone, but it didn't: I just fizzed. Here I was in Windsor Castle and every cell in my body was alive. I wanted to laugh and make love all night. I felt . . ." Meredith paused to find the right words, and bleakness stole back across her features. "I felt like me. *Les neiges d'antan.* Like I hadn't done for a very long time."

"And he came?"

Meredith threw Rozie a look and screwed her face into a smile. "You could say that. He knocked at the door about thirty minutes later. He was clutching a spare bottle of champagne. We drank some of it and, as you say . . ."

Rozie gazed down at the piled-up art books on the coffee table. She couldn't catch Meredith's eye. "Mmm-hmmm."

Meredith laughed. "He stayed for about an hour. Or two—I have no idea. And that is all I am going to tell you. I hope it's enough. His phone went at some point. A text. He rolled over and looked at it and reluctantly said he must go, and he did. I smiled and said nothing. I was certain I'd see him again. Not as a long-term lover, don't misunderstand me, Miss Oshodi. I didn't think it was the start of a beautiful relationship. A friendship, perhaps. But the next thing I knew, he was dead and it was all . . ." The bleakness was back. She looked hollow. "Over."

"Do you know what he did while you went up to your room?"

"Not exactly. But he was wearing different clothes, come to think of it, when he came in with the champagne. A suit. I remember thinking it was a shame, because he'd looked so gorgeous in his dinner jacket, but then, he wasn't wearing the suit for long."

"Did you have the impression that he was meeting someone after you?"

Meredith sucked in a cheek while she considered. "No, not really. He might have been. He just said, 'Don't tell anyone about this,' but he said it laughing, not as if he was ashamed, but as if he wanted it to be our secret."

"Thank you for being so honest."

"I know I should have told the police, but as far as I know those were his last words. And I didn't promise not to tell anyone out loud, but in my head I did. I keep my promises to the dead."

And yet she had told the story now. It was the Queen's magic dust that did it. Rozie felt powerfully the trust that Meredith had bestowed on her. She didn't see how it helped explain Brodsky's death, but perhaps the Boss would spot something she had missed. She got up and thanked the architect once again.

"Actually, you've helped *me*," Meredith said. "I couldn't really make sense of it until I said it out loud. I thought I'd done a terrible thing and been punished for it, but really, it was lovely."

Rozie smiled. "I'm glad."

"Apart from the cystitis."

There was a second's silence while their eyes met and Rozie tried to bottle up the laugh bubbling in her throat, but she couldn't do it. Then Meredith laughed, too, throwing her head back and hooting.

In the end they hugged each other. Meredith accompanied her guest affectionately to the hall. "God, imagine you telling the Queen about my sex life," she said, opening the door.

"I'll do it gently," Rozie promised. "Only the salient details."

"Do it with brio," Meredith urged instead. "Do me justice. Don't forget about that tango."

10

THE COUNCIL MEETING was long and dull. The privy coun-
cillors themselves, carefully chosen over the years, were a
decent bunch whose wisdom and support had proved invaluable
in difficult times. The Queen was a ruthless chairman who conducted the meetings standing up and never liked these things to
overrun; but unfortunately there were myriad arrangements for
the celebration of her upcoming birthday, and somehow they had
found themselves on the council's agenda. Really, all she wanted
was a visit from the great-grandchildren, a few nice letters, and a
decent ride in Home Park. Instead there would be the lighting of
beacons; endless events of various descriptions, most of them on
foot; and, on the official day in June, a service under television
cameras at St. Paul's Cathedral. One was used to it, of course. And
glad of a grateful nation. But honestly.

Meanwhile, her thoughts kept straying to Rozie. Would she return tonight, as she had told Simon? When she got back, there would be a lot for her to do, and the Queen still didn't know if she was ready for it. She had done well with Henry Evans, but that wasn't unduly difficult. And if things got complicated, she might not have time to follow up on all possible ideas anyway.

There was always Billy MacLachlan, of course. After working on her protection team, he had made it to chief inspector. He had helped often enough before; and as well as being utterly discreet, he was hugely inventive. He was good at asking questions without anyone really remembering he was there. She knew he was finding retirement dull. He might appreciate a job like this. Even if Rozie turned out all right, he could always help. Something to bear in mind, at least.

ROZIE'S NEXT CALL was to the honey-toned bar of a bland, upmarket Mayfair hotel. She nursed a coffee in a quiet corner, behind a display of white orchids. The woman who arrived ten minutes later had attempted to disguise herself with mannish sunglasses, a baggy black hoodie, and a baseball cap; but anyone who knew her would instantly recognize the trademark pout, the sculpted jaw, and skinny thighs in Lululemon running gear.

Masha Peyrovskaya slid into the opposite seat and glanced back at a distant table where two bulky bodyguards were making themselves comfortable.

"You are the woman who called me?"

Rozie nodded. "I am."

The Russian took off her sunglasses and stared at Rozie for a moment, tilting her head to one side. Rozie maintained her even smile for such situations. The one that said *Yes, I am the lady from the Queen's private office. Perhaps I'm younger than you expected?*

"So," Masha said eventually, with a tiny shrug. "I told them you were interviewing me for a blog about art." She gestured back towards the bodyguards. "Make this quick. I need to be home in thirty minutes."

Rozie had wondered how you make small talk with billionaires. Perhaps you just didn't.

"All right. It's about the night of the dine and sleep."

Of all the visitors that night, Masha and her maid seemed to be the best acquainted with Maksim Brodsky. Rozie had arranged the meeting to find out if Masha or her husband could throw any light on what had happened to him. But now, she knew for certain that Masha was involved. She wanted the whole story.

"From what I understand, you knew Mr. Brodsky quite well. . . ."

"*Quite* well. He taught me piano."

"You helped him that night."

"I did not," Masha responded, with a flash of challenge in her eyes.

Rozie waited to see who blinked first. She had played this game since primary school. "You say you don't have much time," she observed. "And I'm not asking if you helped Maksim; I'm saying you did. You arranged for him to see Meredith Gostelow without the castle staff and police finding out about it. And you saw him afterwards yourself."

Masha blinked hard. She had been playing it cool so far, but now she bridled. "It's not true!" she expostulated. "Who tell you that?"

"You called for him; he came."

Rozie was fishing, hoping for a reaction, but this was not the one she had expected. Masha half stood, leaned across the table, and hissed in Rozie's face.

"You know absolutely nothing! Did the old woman say it to you? She lies! She's jealous! She thinks I sleep with Maks, everybody does. Even my husband. Do you understand? He could kill me!"

She slumped back down again and started to scratch the table angrily with the stone in her magnificent engagement ring, muttering as she did so, "And yet I take a risk for Maks, as a friend, and for that bitch. Because they wanted each other. He was laughing; he was desperate. He said, 'You can get me up there, to her bedroom, I know you can. Make it happen.' And I did."

"How did you manage it?" Rozie asked, more gently than before. This was a woman who needed to feel appreciated, she realized. She adapted her style to fit.

Masha's eyes glittered. "I think of the plan in moments. I tell him to go back to his room and change into clothes such as Vadim might wear. Vadim is Yuri's manservant. He wears smart suits—smarter than Maks's, but your Queen's staff do not know that, I think. Maks must say he is Vadim, and go to the bottom of the stairs leading to the guests' sleeping quarters, where I will meet him and say to the servants I need his help. I give him some champagne I find. We go up the stairs together. Yuri is outside with his friend Jay at this time, smoking cigars and drinking port and talking about his space trip and all the things they talk about—"

"His *space trip*?" Rozie interrupted, unable to help herself.

"Yes. He wants to go into orbit. He has paid for a flight in two years' time. It cost ten million dollars." Masha looked at Rozie as if this was the most obvious, boring part of her tale, like saying Yuri wanted to get a puppy or a flight to New York. "But I did not know for how long they talk, and maybe he call for Vadim for real when he come upstairs, so I said to Maks I will warn him when Yuri comes to bed. And I did. That is all." She practically snarled this last sentence.

"And Maksim took this as his cue to go back to his room?"

"I suppose so."

"Wasn't there a danger he might pass Vadim on the stairs? What would he have said?"

"That was his problem." Masha shrugged. "He have plenty of time to think about it."

"Did Vadim come, in the end?"

"Yes. Yuri was so drunk he could not undress himself." Masha looked matter-of-fact about her husband's inebriation. "But he did not call him for a while. He try to make love to me first."

She maintained her deadpan look, as a challenge to Rozie, who deadpanned back. "I see."

"I did not stop him. He came towards the bed and said all the usual things and quoted Russian poetry to me. Pushkin—do you know him?"

"Not really."

"You should. Lermontov, also. I let him say those lines, and take down the straps of my nightdress, but then he look at me as if he is suddenly disgusted, and he turn away. That's when he called for Vadim."

Rozie had the odd feeling that she was somehow being used as a makeshift therapist by this hostile, angry woman. She wanted to reach out and take her hand and ask what was really wrong. Instead, she asked, "Do you think it was something to do with Maksim? Did he suspect something?"

Masha's eyes blazed. "There was nothing! Why should he?"

"I believe you, but—"

"Yuri does not trust me. And yet he is surprised when I find someone who treats me like a human. But that is all I do. I *play the piano* with this man. Rachmaninoff. Satie. Debussy. We laugh, because he is kind. There is always someone in the room with us, *always*. Ask those men over there. They are with me every minute. If I was unfaithful, they would know. . . . I go now. I'm late."

"Wait!"

Masha was getting up, putting her sunglasses on. "What?"

"Do you know anything about what Maksim did afterwards?"

"Of course not, I told you."

"And Yuri?"

"He fell asleep beside me. Snoring like a pig. What else could he do?"

"Vadim—wasn't he questioned about his trip to your room that night?"

"I guess so. I tell him to say to them he had gone up two times. I didn't want the police talking to Yuri about it. One good-looking young Russian look the same as another in a servant suit, yes? Vadim is gay, so at least Yuri think I am safe with *him*."

And with that, Rozie realized, Masha had outfoxed the protection arrangements for the overnight guests of one of the most guarded monarchs in the world, in a thousand-year-old castle bristling with tech and layers of top security. With a swish of her ponytail Masha turned and left, threading her way back through the tables, her baggy hoodie signally failing to hide her sexy strut.

It seemed hard to imagine that Yuri was not somehow behind what happened to Brodsky later, though if Masha was telling the truth, he couldn't have done it himself. He might have ordered it beforehand. Would a man kill for a woman like Masha Peyrovskaya?

Yes, Rozie thought. A certain kind of man probably would.

11

THE FOLLOWING MORNING Sir Simon was due to be in charge of the Queen's office schedule, but she asked him to liaise with the Cabinet Office about a difficult diplomatic issue regarding the Sultan of Brunei, and so it was Rozie who came in to collect the boxes.

"I gather you were away yesterday," she said, looking up. "I was very sorry to hear about your mother."

"My mother's absolutely fine, thank you, Your Majesty."

"Well, I'm pleased to hear that."

"I had quite a busy day in London. I wondered whether you might be interested to hear about it."

The Queen was absolutely delighted. So the sick parent had been a ruse! She had underestimated Rozie. This prompted an idea, before they got down to business. "I wonder whether you might perhaps like to meet one of your predecessors—Aileen Jaggard. I sense you might have a lot in common."

"I met her two nights ago, ma'am. Katie recommended her to me. And, you're right, we do."

"Ah. I see."

The Boss's smile lit up her face with girlish excitement. Rozie had seen it before, but never had it focused exclusively on her. She basked in it for a moment. It was difficult to be businesslike again, but Rozie knew they didn't have much time.

"I had a conversation with Mr. Brodsky's dance partner and discovered what he did that night."

"Go on."

Rozie recounted her discussions with Meredith and Masha, skirting over the sex but noticing that the Boss wasn't remotely fazed by any of it, though surprised and at times amused.

"They were very generous with their time," the Queen observed. "Do you believe what they told you?"

"I do, ma'am. I'm no expert, but they didn't *need* to tell me anything. I think they wanted you to know the truth. Meredith swore me to secrecy. She wanted me to tell only you."

"And you promised?"

"Yes, ma'am."

The Queen frowned. "This makes things a little difficult."

"Oh, does it? I'm sorry. I—"

"We'll deal with that later. Go on."

"I met up with the ballerinas after rehearsal. They didn't really add anything to what they'd already told the police. One of them had met Brodsky before socially, but didn't know him well. Again, I'm no expert, but I didn't get the sense they were lying. They were both very upset at his death, understandably."

"And the young man himself?" the Queen asked. "Apart from his penchant for tango, did you learn anything more about him?"

Rozie had tried. Late in the afternoon she had visited his flat in Covent Garden and talked to his flatmate, whom she had managed to contact on the burner phone. The flat was on the top floor of a building above a restaurant not far from the Piazza. It was a brilliant location, with windows looking out on the buzzing streets below and sounds of buskers and theatergoers wafting in on the breeze. The interior was basic, though, painted white and furnished with secondhand finds and badly made pieces from Ikea, untidily strewn with clothes and pizza boxes, smelling of musky men. It did not reek of offshore money and hidden bank accounts, as she had half expected it to.

Rozie had said she was from the Russian Embassy (warming to her role by now), keen to understand if Mr. Brodsky had any debts, such as rent, to pay, with a view to helping, if possible, in such difficult times. But the flatmate, Vijay Kulandaiswamy, assured her the rent was in his name, paid for by his job in the City. In fact, he was looking for someone to replace Brodsky to cover the extra costs, though he'd often paid those himself, too. Maksim had been hard up as long as he'd lived with him.

Rozie was surprised. "According to our records he went to an expensive public school."

Vijay had laughed. "So did I. Same school—it's how we met. But it doesn't necessarily tell you much. He had the fees paid for him, I think. But that all stopped once he left. And whoever paid them didn't hang around. Some boss or mate of his dad's, I think. He didn't talk about it much. I got the impression he was kind of grateful, kind of furious. He liked his life here and he loved the music, but he felt dislocated, like he didn't really belong anywhere. It made him kind of restless."

Maksim thought maybe one day he'd become a writer, Vijay said, but meanwhile he was trying to make it as a professional musician, supplementing his income with piano lessons and tutoring rich teens in maths and computing. He spent a lot of time on the Internet, as they all did.

No, Vijay hadn't known he ran a blog, until the police told him about it. Maksim wasn't a hacker, or super tech savvy either. You didn't need to be, to teach secondary school computer science: the syllabus was still in the dark ages. Vijay had friends at work who were big tech guys, and they said he wasn't remotely in their league.

Maksim hadn't talked about Russia much, except in the context of Putin and his cronies. He was definitely political. Even at school, where he was a couple of years below, he was known for his rants about the suppression of opposition politicians in Moscow and the deaths of dozens of journalists. He was compiling a spreadsheet. Truth was a dangerous game in Russia, he'd said. "If a tree falls in the forest and there is no one around to hear it, does it make a sound? And if a journalist falls from a window . . . does anybody care?" He used to get pretty depressed about it.

At this point in their conversation, Vijay remembered he was talking to a member of the embassy and had clammed up. Rozie, too, had been jolted back to her cover story.

"Listen," she had asked, "is there anyone else we should get in touch with? A girlfriend, for example? Did he have anyone special? Someone we should talk to about this unfortunate incident?"

Vijay had shrugged. There were various girls, but nobody who stood out. Maksim was a popular guy, but he had split up from a long-term girlfriend a couple of months before and he was too brokenhearted, and too damn nice, to get deeply involved again so soon.

"I miss him, you know?" Vijay had said. "I just . . . He was good to have around. I miss the sound of the piano. I miss the peanut butter running out just when I need it. I miss girls calling and having to tell them he's busy because he isn't interested. He owed me, like, a few hundred pounds in utility bills and stuff, and I just don't care. He'd have paid me eventually. It didn't matter anyway. He was . . ." Vijay sighed deeply, looking a bit lost. "Like I say—he was a good guy. No one deserves to go like that. He looked after himself; he seemed so healthy. I had no idea about his heart."

It came home to Rozie then that a real human being had gone that night, not just a "case." She didn't know if envoys from the Russian Embassy gave people consoling hugs, but she decided that in this case they did.

Rozie reported the basics of this conversation back to the Queen.

"I was trying to find out who in Brodsky's past, or his home life, might have wanted him dead," she said. "Apart from maybe Mr. Peyrovski. But I didn't find anything, ma'am. Unless you think I missed something?"

"No," the Queen agreed. "From that point of view, I fear Humphreys is right, and the motive is here somewhere."

"Sir Simon told me this morning that Mr. Robertson and Mr. Dorsey-Jones have been sent on leave and put under a sort of house arrest. That must be difficult for them." Rozie remembered the Queen's conversation with Henry Evans, and what she obviously felt about Humphreys's theory.

The Queen merely nodded. "I imagine it is. I have another job for you, Rozie. Do you mind? I do understand this is not in your job description. It might mean working on your day off."

"Whatever you want, ma'am."

The Queen gave her swift instructions. The new girl was working out even better than she had hoped. She couldn't be another Mary, surely? Mary Pargeter had been in a class of her own when it came to these little mysteries. But Rozie Oshodi—who was a good ten years younger than Mary had been when she started—promised very well.

12

LATER, THERE WAS AN INVESTITURE in the Waterloo Chamber. The Queen always enjoyed holding them at Windsor. Though the chamber was vast, dominated by portraits of the kings and statesmen who came together to defeat Napoleon, it was more informal than the ballroom at Buckingham Palace. Anything was more informal than the palace. Nevertheless, there was the appropriate pomp as she awarded honors to the great and good under the loving eyes of their families, attended by her Gurkha orderly officers and the yeomen of the guard.

After it was over, she was grateful for tea and a slice of chocolate biscuit cake in her private sitting room, while catching up with the racing results on Channel 4. Sometimes she liked to take a little nap before the evening's activities, but today she had other things in mind. She asked the footman to warn the housekeeper of her plan. One could do what one liked in one's own castle, but staff did not appreciate surprises in areas they considered their own. She gave them a few minutes to spruce things up.

It had been a while since she had last set foot in the attic corridors above the Visitors' Apartments. She took the younger dogs, who were keen to have the exercise and padded along ahead of her, sniffing at doorways. The journey down the Grand Corridor, from the Private Apartments to the Visitors' Apartments on the south side of the quadrangle, took a good ten minutes, going at dorgi speed.

She knew the main guest rooms well, popping in quite often to check on the state of the furnishings, or to ensure everything was in place for a particularly honored visitor. But the attics were another matter. They had once housed sparrows and a family of jackdaws, along with abandoned furniture and assorted Victorian fancy dress costumes. Philip had been instrumental in getting them cleaned out fifty years ago, when it became clear the family would be spending most of their weekends here. When one is the Queen, and one's home is one's castle, it comes with an awful lot of servants, and they need space. Servants, and guests' servants, too, and other visitors who are not servants at all but are important to the running of the castle and can't be housed in any of the other properties on the estate. The more rooms they made available, the more people it seemed they needed to make room for. And somewhere, they had found room for Maksim Brodsky.

The time had come: she wanted to see it for herself.

The top-floor corridor was whitewashed and hung with various Edwardian etchings deemed unsuitable for the downstairs rooms. Bedrooms were spartan and functional, recently decorated in greens and creams, with the odd touch of purple in a blanket or a seat cover. Philip, when he popped in to see the refurbishment, had said they looked like something out of a motorway hotel (how would he know?), or Gordonstoun, or—given the color scheme—Wimbledon. She wasn't sure there was a problem with any of these analogies, though they had not been given as a compliment. Either way, visitors wouldn't mind.

Along the way, she passed various chambermaids, footmen, and a fender smith, all busy with a task or on their way to one. One footman, carrying a covered tray, was rudely assaulted by the dogs but took it well, nimbly twisting out of reach with barely a break in stride. The head housekeeper, Mrs. Dilley, was waiting for her in the section of the corridor containing Mr. Brodsky's room. To her left there was a door with a sign indicating a shower room. Behind her, the Queen could hear the sound of convivial chatter coming from another room. She was glad that whoever was inside was unaware of her presence: wherever she went all conversation stopped, and sometimes it was nice to hear the staff just being themselves.

"This is the room, ma'am," Mrs. Dilley announced, leading the way. She inserted a small key to open the door with a push. It was a perfectly plain door, varnished a rather horrible fake mahogany color, and sporting the number 24 etched into a small brass plaque. There was a laminated-paper notice on the front, saying something about DO NOT ENTER. The last time the Queen had visited, she was sure such rooms were locked from within using an old-fashioned bolt, if so desired, but many of the doors had stood open. The castle of old used to assume that the inhabitants would respect each other's person and possessions, and it was rather cozy that way. Now, everyone assumed the worst, and doors closed with the click of a latch; valuables were safe, but the air of informality had gone.

Brodsky had probably known his killer, she reflected as she entered the room. Unless he left the door on the latch, he would have had to open it to him. Why do so in the middle of the night to a stranger?

Mrs. Dilley went to stand near the head of the single bed, waiting patiently while the Queen looked round. There wasn't much to see. A small window to the right of Mrs. Dilley's head showed only a thin grey patch of sky between open purple curtains. All the bedding and any extraneous objects had been stripped out. There was a bare mattress on a wooden base to her left, against the wall beside the door. Next came the wall with the window, under which sat a side table and a hard-backed chair. They faced a wall with a small chest of drawers missing half their handles (one must get that fixed). And in between, against the wall opposite where she was standing, was a narrow, modern wardrobe that stood open to reveal . . . nothing. There were no stains, no sign of life, or death, no sense that anything important had happened in this place at all.

The Queen stole a closer look at the open wardrobe door, whose D-shaped handle had housed the second knot. The whole thing looked flimsy—hardly strong enough to hold a man, never mind hang him. What sort of person would look at such a thing and think *instrument of murder*?

She cleared her throat. "It must have been very difficult for the housekeeper who found him."

Mrs. Dilley looked up. "Mrs. Cobbold? Yes, awful, ma'am. She couldn't get in at first. She had to go to the office and get the master key. Then she opened the door and there he was, right ahead of her with that cupboard door open and his legs sticking out. She nearly fainted. But she's much better now, ma'am."

Everyone always sought to *reassure* one. Except Philip: he was the only person she could trust to be perfectly straight. Back tomorrow, Sir Simon had told her. And not a moment too soon.

"I'm glad to hear it. Is she back at work already?"

"Oh, no, ma'am. Next week, possibly." But Mrs. Dilley looked doubtful.

So, not as much better as all that. Well, not surprising.

"Thank you, Mrs. Dilley."

"Ma'am."

"I hope it hasn't been too much of an inconvenience, with the police here at all hours?"

"No, ma'am. Just rather dreadful. For all of us."

Mrs. Dilley caught the Queen's eye and held it, woman to woman, and there was huge sympathy there. She knew how much it must mean to her, this tragedy so close to home. The Queen looked away and called to the dogs, who had been milling about in the corridor. They padded in now, circling her legs and giving the room a brief semblance of normality.

"Candy, Vulcan—time to go."

The walk downstairs and back along the Grand Corridor seemed twice as long this time. She took it slowly. She was unprepared for the shock she felt, not by what had been in the room but what *hadn't* been, which was any sense of the life that was lost. Brodsky had vanished from the world, it seemed, without a trace, and one felt somehow responsible.

Sir Simon would have told her not to go, had she consulted him, which was of course partly why she didn't. He would have said it wasn't necessary, which was quite untrue, and that it might be upsetting, which was so infuriatingly right. The thought of it pricked her, even though she had not given him the chance to say it. She batted it away. As Queen Mary had always insisted to her as a little girl, it did not do to dwell.

Instead, she thought about the door that could not be opened from the corridor without a key. Brodsky had been away until the early hours of the morning, so whoever he let in, or whoever came in with him, must have lingered until late to do him harm. A spy could have had a master key cut, she supposed. All part of this big plan Humphreys insisted on imagining. And yet the failure to tighten the second knot suggested it was an improvised attack. It couldn't be part of a long-running feud, as Brodsky didn't know anyone here. Nor did it seem likely to be based on sex. The young man had had enough of that downstairs and there were only so many unorthodox lovers one could take at Windsor Castle in one night. Even Philip would think so, surely?

And so . . . who had done it?

Not Putin. Gavin Humphreys was an imbecile with an obsession, and every bone in her body told her so.

Not Charles, who had gone back to Highgrove that night with Camilla. (She was trying to be objective and consider all possibilities, and Charles had after all arranged the evening.) Similarly, the provost of Eton had gone back to his house at the school, half a mile away. But Brodsky's adventures with the architect woman had proved that, with a little ingenuity, it was possible to move between staff and guest quarters without impediment. At this point the suspect list became almost comic, including as it did Sir David Attenborough and the Archbishop of Canterbury. No—honestly, no. If one could not trust these men, one might as well give up.

Nevertheless, even excluding them, the range of possibilities remained disconcertingly wide. There was no reason to suspect the former ambassador, but it was not impossible that his life in Russia had created links to young Brodsky that she was not aware of. The police had uncovered no connection between the young man and the novelist or the professor—but Blunt had been an academic. Of course, most of them were pillars of the Establishment, but one never quite knew. . . . Then there was the architect herself—the woman who had danced the last tango. The Queen pondered for a minute, trying to create some kind of motive from what she knew from Rozie's account, but everything in the tragic story suggested quite the opposite. The poor woman had been besotted. That left Peyrovski, his wife, his hedge fund manager friend, and their servants. *This* was where the police should be focusing, surely?

At this point in her walk, she passed a policeman guarding the entrance to the Private Apartments and in nodding to him the Queen was reminded of the madness of this location. If you were in day-to-day contact with a man you hated, for whatever reason, why choose the castle for his murder? True, within its perimeter, tight security—apart from around herself—was not an area of concern normally. Once inside, what guests chose to do with their staff, or each other, after hours was up to them. True, too, the perpetrator had got away with it so far. But it was the highest-risk strategy there was. Once foul play was discovered, every high-ranking detective and spymaster in the land was bound to descend on the case. Why strike here, when an enemy could do it so very much more easily in Mayfair or Covent Garden?

In that case, it made sense for the murderer to be someone who *didn't* know Brodsky well—and that opened up the list of suspects back to everyone in and around the Upper Ward that night.

She had reached her own rooms at last, and sensed she had made little progress in her thinking at all. If anything, she had gone backwards, with more uncertainties than ever.

Something odd had happened the evening of the dine and sleep. Not during the event but beforehand. A memory lurked in the corner of her brain and tugged at it occasionally. As the dogs preceded her into her sitting room, it almost came back but was lost.

She made a mental note to ask Rozie for a full list of last Monday's overnight visitors throughout the castle. And to chase the Russian Embassy for more news of Brodsky's family. It pained her to think he had disappeared so completely from this life, having been so fully engaged in it—and had nobody to mourn him.

Sir Simon was waiting for her with a slim sheaf of papers to sign. At his elbow was a footman with a tray containing a tumbler, ice and lemon, a bottle of Gordon's, and another of Dubonnet. She glanced at one with brisk efficiency and the other with a little longing. Five minutes more and then, for a little while at least, one could relax.

13

MORNING, CABBAGE. Everything under control?"
Sitting at the breakfast table on Thursday morning,
Philip looked as if he had never been away.

"I thought you were arriving this morning."

"Got in last night. Quick dinner with some friends in Bray.
God, you look ghastly. Have you been sleeping?"

"Yes, thank you."

She tried to say it crossly, but he had such a grin on his face.
There was always the hint of a joke in his eyes, unless he was furious with someone. He was perfectly dressed for the day, as always,
in a check shirt and knotted tie. The radio was on, there was toast
on the table again, and already it felt as if the place had come back
to life. She couldn't help smiling.

"Did you bring me the fudge?"

"Damn. Forgot. Have you seen the pictures of William and Catherine in the papers? Cover to cover, practically. I told William he'd enjoy India. Did you see them at that safari park with the elephants and rhinos? Lucky buggers. Beats sticking medals on breast pockets."

The Queen refused to rise to the bait. "How was the salmon?"

"Bloody impressive. Caught four. I brought them down with me in an icebox. Thought the chef could do something with them for your birthday."

"Thank you."

"Mind you, they probably decided the menu six months ago."

They had.

"But they can always change it," he mused.

"Mmmm."

That wasn't going to happen, but she would think of something. She was really very touched that he had been thinking of her birthday. And that he had thought four large fish an appropriate present—which they absolutely were. Salmon was always being recommended for one's diet. Good for the brain, apparently. And it was a nice reminder of days out by a fast-flowing river.

Companionable silence reigned for a while, apart from the radio in the background, until he looked up from his toast and said, "That bloody Russian. Tom said it was foul play."

Philip's equerry, Lieutenant-Commander Tom Trender-Watson, was good friends with Sir Simon and usually up to speed on all the details of the castle. He was also reliably discreet, thank goodness.

"Have they found the bugger that did it yet?" Philip asked. "I haven't heard anything."

"No, they haven't," she said. "The Security Service thinks it was Putin."

"What? In person?"

"No. In the guise of a royal servant."

"Bloody idiots."

"That's rather what I thought."

"Have you got someone in mind?"

She stared into her tea and sighed. "Not exactly. The place was full that night, but I can't see why anybody here would want to kill him."

"Half the ladies would have wanted quite the opposite, from what I heard."

"Mmmm. Yes." She was tempted to tell him about Brodsky's after-midnight shenanigans with the architect, but she knew he would love the story and share it widely with his staff who, equerry excepted, were bound to spread it like wildfire. At the moment even she wasn't supposed to know about it, so she kept her counsel.

"Well, they need to sort it out sharpish," Philip observed. "Does nobody any good, worrying about consorting with murderers. And, by God, it needs to be fixed before the press get their hands on it. They'd have a field day."

The Queen, who knew all of this, merely obliged him with another "mmmm."

"You should have a word with whatever police johnnie is in charge of it. Ignore Box. Putin! Pah!"

With that, he pushed back his chair and opened the paper. The Queen was, in equal measure, mildly infuriated by being told to do what she had been about to do anyway, and relieved that he was home, so she could be reassured by words like "Putin! Pah!"

He honestly kept her sane.

RAVI SINGH WAS REMINDED, more than anything, of the time he won the Year Nine debating competition at school. His hands trembled slightly in exactly the same way, and he could feel his blood pulsing in his head. It was the only time he had been called in to see Mrs. Winckless, the headmistress, who lurked in a paneled office down a long, tiled corridor at the posh end of his grammar school's rambling site. She had a bowl of flowers on her desk, he remembered: pale, mop-headed things he had subsequently learned to recognize as hydrangeas. And an electric-blue dress that encased a larger expanse of bosom than a teenage boy was entirely comfortable with.

The Oak Room, where the Queen had granted him an audience, was not the same as that paneled room, of course. It was bigger, and oddly shaped, owing to its position in a sort of tower. It had white walls, comfortable sofas, and a roaring fire, alongside unexpected details such as one of Her Majesty's TVs. But the sense of meeting a powerful woman one was, without knowing exactly why, slightly afraid of, and feeling guilty, even though he had as far as he knew done something good, was identical.

I am the Met Police Commissioner, he reminded himself as he sat down. *I have reached the top of my profession. She is not going to tell me off.*

The Queen sat opposite him on a small sofa near a large, elaborate window overlooking the quadrangle he'd just come from. She was indeed all smiles and the offer of a biscuit to go with his tea. The dogs made themselves at home near his feet. He wasn't in trouble.

He thought of the sharp look Humphreys had given him when he'd heard about the requested meeting. "Make sure you tell me everything. Word for word. We need to know what she's thinking." But the Queen, blandly polite, just seemed to want to catch up with the investigation in general terms. Which was only fair—it was her castle.

"Obviously, MI5 have their specialist checks going on, but the overall suspect list remains long, I'm afraid, ma'am. A lot of people had access to that corridor that night. Oh, you've seen it, have you? We've conducted interviews with all of them. Obviously, it's difficult when you don't want to let them know it's a definite murder investigation. It also makes it harder to do a DNA match with the hair we found on the body. Obviously, once we have a firm suspect, we will."

He realized he had said "obviously" three times. And he was perspiring under his jacket. Her Majesty was a lovely woman who hadn't asked a single difficult question, but this was worse than doing the *Today* program on Radio 4.

"I'm sure you're doing everything you can."

"Of course, ma'am. Obv— I mean, we're clearly focusing on the people who knew Brodsky or had Russian links. The manservant, who had the room next door; the maid; the ballerinas, though their computer records suggest their FaceTime alibi checks out. There's a librarian who's an expert on Russian history, but she lives in rooms halfway across the site. The archivist—well, Mr. Humphreys can tell you more about him, I imagine."

"And Mr. Robertson? Is there any news of him?"

"Nothing yet, ma'am. Nothing certain. It turns out he does have an explanation for some payments that were of concern, but the investigation is ongoing."

"I see. And is that all? Who else have you talked to?"

The commissioner consulted his notes. "The communications team was having a bit of a conference, ma'am, so there were about five of them visiting from the palace, plus those who already work here. Various staff who stay on a regular basis. A group of guests of the governor."

"And my guests on the floor below."

"They're out of the picture, ma'am. You can't get between the guest suites and the visiting staff quarters without passing two sets of security, and they didn't see anything."

The Queen gave him a smile which, if it hadn't come from Her Majesty, he would have called playful. "Oh, there have been some rather surprising stories over the years, Commissioner. Philip was reminding me only this morning about a famous time when the French ambassador managed to smuggle a cabaret artiste up to his suite, disguised as a housemaid, for a bet."

"Not this time, ma'am," Singh assured her, making a mental note to share that one with the lads back at New Scotland Yard.

"Well, that's a relief."

The Queen knew that at this point it was her duty to tell him what Rozie had learned from Meredith Gostelow and Masha Peyrovskaya—but equally, Rozie had promised secrecy. The Queen felt this had been unwise. One never knew what one might be required to do or say. However, telling Mr. Singh anything would bring Rozie into the story—and ultimately herself—which of course one must avoid at all costs. If the commissioner was primed with the possibility of staff and guest shenanigans, perhaps he could find out for himself. For now, she graciously accepted his reassurance. "And is there any news from the embassy?"

"Ma'am?"

"About Brodsky's family? Has someone come to take the body?"

Singh paused for a moment. Nobody had asked that question recently. "No, ma'am. I imagine it's still in the morgue. Would you like me to find out what we know?"

"Yes, please. That's very kind. And do tell me, how are the new stab vests working out?"

With that, following her lead, Singh pivoted on a sixpence and talked instead about the new uniform his staff had been issued, about which the Queen was remarkably well-informed. *She misses nothing,* he thought. Now, she reminded him of his great-grandmother Nani Sada, who was, if anything, more terrifying than Mrs. Winckless in her paneled office. But at least he could tell Gavin that she was happy with the way the investigation was progressing.

14

T HE BLOCK OF FLATS was long and low, four stories of reddish-brown brick with matching balconies and modern plate-glass windows. It might have been built in the 1960s, Rozie thought, though she was no expert on architecture. It was not a prepossessing building in itself, but what marked it out was the view: beside the River Thames, overlooking the massive hulk of Battersea Power Station through the trees.

This was Pimlico, home to many an MP's London pad, and an odd mixture of posh, stucco-fronted houses and postwar flats, like these. It would be about half an hour's walk to Buckingham Palace from here, she reckoned. A nice one, on a sunny morning. And not a bad place to come back to, with that view.

She maneuvered a wicker hamper marked with Fortnum & Mason's distinctive "F&M" from the back seat of the car. It had been a hair-raising drive from Piccadilly, racing through the morning rush hour traffic, knowing she had two deliveries to make and must still be back by three. A "day off," in the Queen's private office, really meant half a day, and lateness was not an option. She closed the car door with her knee, locked it with the key fob dangling from her fingers, and carried the hamper to the nearest entrance.

The inside door to flat 5 was opened by an unshaven man with salt-and-pepper hair, wearing baggy gym shorts and a sweaty T-shirt, with a towel around his neck. He had only answered on the third ring of the bell. At first, she was horrified to think how he had really let himself go, but then she realized he'd been exercising. This was encouraging.

"Mr. Robertson?"

"Yes?" He was staring at the hamper, which was as large as could fit in the back seat of the Mini and seemed out of place in the narrow communal corridor where she was standing, with its strip lighting, peeling paint, and missing carpet tiles.

"I'm here from the Private Office." He would know which one. "This is for you."

"What?" He rubbed the side of his face with the towel. "You'd better come in."

She followed him across a little hallway that somehow managed to seem immaculately tidy despite containing two road bikes, a coatrack, several framed photographs, and a shelf of running shoes. The room beyond it was the kitchen, which was half the size of Meredith Gostelow's in Westbourne Grove but had the benefit of uninterrupted views towards the abandoned power station's iconic chimneys. Surfaces were white or stainless steel, and gleamed.

"Can I offer you something?" he asked.

"No, thank you. I'd better be quick."

She put the hamper on the counter next to the sink and smiled at the royal page. "My name's Rozie. I— The office wanted to give you this as a token of our understanding of everything you're going through. I really must emphasize that it's from the *office*. Not Her Majesty personally."

Lady Caroline, in passing on the Queen's message, had been very specific about this. Also, she must not apologize. One did not say sorry for the things one's public servants, such as the Security Service, did in one's name. That would be hypocritical and wrong.

Sandy Robertson rubbed the side of his head again, looking perplexed. "You must emphasize that, must you?" he echoed. His voice was deep, with a gentle Scottish burr, and very pleasant to listen to. Rozie imagined him offering drinks to the Boss, pulling out her chair, ensuring everything was just as she wanted it. He seemed the sort of person you would want to have around. "Well, let's have a look at it."

He unbuckled the hamper and lifted the lid. Inside was wine and whiskey, jars of thick-cut marmalade, and eau de nil–blue tins of shortbread and ginger biscuits. There was also a card, blank and unsigned, featuring a watercolor image of a white camellia.

Sandy looked up sharply at Rozie, who said nothing, then down again at the provisions. He ran his fingertips over a marmalade jar, picked up a tin of biscuits to examine it, and put it back again. Then he rested a forefinger on the card, without lifting it, and looked at Rozie again.

"The Queen Mother's favorite flower, the white camellia. Did you know that?" There were tears in his eyes, Rozie thought.

"No, I didn't."

"My wife's, too. I told her that once, seven years ago, when Mary died."

"Oh." Rozie did a rapid mental calculation. The Queen Mother had died in 2002—Sandy wasn't referring to a conversation with her.

"Once," he repeated, his finger still resting on the card. "Seven years ago. What a woman."

Rozie coughed. "As I say, we at the office just wanted to . . . We probably shouldn't have . . . but we—"

"Tell her thank you," he interrupted, in his Highlands burr. "Thank you very much."

Rozie found she had a lump in her throat. She nodded, unable to help herself, and said she had better leave.

Her visit to Adam Dorsey-Jones's flat was slightly different. For this, she drove south of the river to a row of converted Georgian houses in Stockwell. There was no card with a white camellia this time, but the man in jeans and green woolen jumper who let her in reacted similarly to her protestations that the Queen was not involved.

"Of course she wasn't," he said. "You did this out of the goodness of your heart."

"You could say that."

"Well, thank you very much, assistant private secretary lady I've never met."

"You're welcome."

"You're very generous."

Rozie fought not to grin.

He put the hamper on the coffee table of his art-filled living room and said, "You obviously don't think that because I have a boyfriend who's been to Saint Petersburg I must be a Russian spy."

"I'm not qualified to say," Rozie told him evenly.

"And yet . . . this hamper."

"It's just . . . from the office."

He sat her down then, and told her about the two years he had spent on the digitization project he'd been put in charge of. He recalled his excitement at finding long-lost papers from George II, the nights he'd worked late to meet the deadlines they had given him, the fact he'd missed his boyfriend's birthday party to go to Windsor Castle to get the final info he needed before giving a progress report to visiting dignitaries a fortnight ago.

"They won't tell me what they think I've done," he said, "but it's obvious from their line of questioning they think I'm KGB or FSB or whatever it is. They seem to think if you like Russian literature you must be a fan of the Kremlin. I wrote my thesis on Solzhenitsyn. If you really want to see how they tortured the human spirit, read *Cancer Ward*. Jamie's gallery specializes in early twentieth-century art, when the Russians were leading the way in abstraction and experimentalism. The revolutionaries hated it. They killed or exiled practically everyone, or just made their lives impossible. Doesn't endear you to the Russian State. But what do I know?"

"This will blow over," Rozie said. She knew she didn't have the right to reassure him. She could see herself as a minor character in a historical analysis twenty years from now: the naïve figure from the palace who took pity on the spy. But she felt his bitterness at the way he had been summarily cast aside, and thought that could possibly be the greater danger. "I'm sorry."

He looked across the coffee table at her. "Yeah. I do believe you are."

On the way home, she listened to Radio 4 as she negotiated her way back through heavy traffic on Cromwell Road. The *World at One* was full of the latest sightings of the Cambridges on tour in India. Rozie couldn't quite believe that in a couple of weeks she'd be seeing them in person at the castle, and probably hearing some of their adventures firsthand.

Among other news stories was a report about two City analysts found dead from cocaine overdoses. The journalist, her voice brimming with urgency, wondered, "Is recreational drug use in the Square Mile reaching a dangerous level? And how far are middle-class drug takers responsible for fueling the deadly trade that decimates communities in South America?"

But by now Rozie wasn't listening. The reporter had named the two analysts: a thirty-seven-year-old man called Javier something who worked at Citibank, and a twenty-seven-year-old woman called Rachel Stiles, who worked for a small boutique investment firm called Golden Futures.

"Rachel Stiles" and "Golden Futures" were familiar names to Rozie: she had seen them on the spreadsheet listing all the visitors given rooms in the castle the night of the dine and sleep. The one the master of the Household had pulled together for the police and that the Queen had asked for. "Golden Futures" had stood out to Rozie because it seemed to hold so much promise.

And now, at the age of twenty-seven, the girl was dead.

PART 3

Belt and Road

15

I T'S NOTHING TO DO with the Russian," Sir Simon assured the
Queen that evening, after Rozie had mentioned the coincidence. "Chief Inspector Strong checked with the local CID team
in Shepherd's Bush, where Dr. Stiles died. She had a bit of an
alcohol problem."

"Goodness. Did she?"

"The City takes its toll, I suppose. She took a lot of pills, then
the cocaine on top. Almost certainly accidental. Tragic, of course."

He meant it. Sir Simon and his wife did not have children, but
his niece was twenty-seven. She, too, had worked in the City, before
setting up a company that seemed to mean she worked day and
night from her laptop at home. She was a beautiful young woman,
an only child with a shining future ahead of her. Sir Simon knew his

brother and sister-in-law would never recover if anything happened to her.

"What was this young woman doing at the castle, precisely?" the Queen wondered. "Remind me."

"She was a guest of the governor," Sir Simon said. "He was hosting a little meeting about foreign intelligence for the Foreign Office."

"Ah, yes. The young man from Djibouti."

"Ma'am?"

"I remember the governor was very impressed with a man who had flown in from East Africa. Though I had rather thought his meeting was more about China. I must ask him about it sometime."

"Yes, ma'am. That would make sense, actually. Dr. Stiles was an expert on the Chinese economy."

"Oh?"

"She had a PhD in Chinese infrastructure funding. Golden Futures has several investments in Asian markets. She was a rising star."

"You're very well-informed, Simon."

"I try to be, ma'am. There is another thing."

"Yes?"

"You asked the commissioner about Mr. Brodsky's family—whether anyone has come to collect the body. Well, they checked with the embassy and, no, nobody has as yet. They think—the embassy does—that his mother is in a mental institution. He had a half brother, who seems to have died on exercise in the army. Their army, not ours. We know about the father. You may recall he died when Brodsky was a child. That seems to be it. I imagine the Russians will repatriate the body eventually."

"Thank you, Simon."

She was looking grim again, he thought. Well, she was a mother of sons. These conversations were never easy.

"CHEER UP, LILIBET," Philip insisted. "Nobody's *died*. Oh."

They were in the car on the way to a private dinner with a trainer they had known since William was a baby. His horses had beaten hers twice last year, but she didn't hold it against him. It would simply be a pleasure to talk nothing but racing for a whole, enchanting evening. And his eldest son ran a large estate up in Northumbria, so Philip could talk livestock yields and advances in organic farming and the vagaries of the shooting season.

She had been looking forward to it all day, and was resplendent in silver lace and a new pink lipstick, of which she had high hopes. Philip, of course, was like something out of a magazine, even at ninety-four. She had never known a man to look as good in uniform or in black tie. He had been the most eligible man in Europe when they'd married. She felt lucky then, and lucky now—even though he was, of course, utterly maddening half the time.

"Nobody has come to collect the body," she said, to explain her expression.

"Well, no doubt somebody will."

"I really don't think so."

"That's hardly your problem, though, is it?"

She sighed. "It feels as if it is."

"Come on, Lilibet. You're not responsible for the whole world, you know. You had one dance with the man. That hardly constitutes a date."

"*Philip*. Really."

She looked out of the window at the cars overtaking the Bentley, which resolutely stuck at sixty-nine miles an hour and was so smooth it hardly seemed to be moving at all. This car was a treat.

They saved the Bentley for special occasions, so it still smelled of fresh leather, rather than old dog and the cleaning fluid they used to disguise the smell of dog—with limited success. It was disconcertingly quiet, though, like speeding along in one of those padded listening booths they used to have in record shops.

"Come on, spit it out. What is it?"

She wasn't sure what it was that bothered her, until she turned back to Philip and saw the gleam of light on his white-blond hair, the curve of his jaw, the confident way he sat, even relaxing in the car, as if poised for action.

"He reminded me of you," she said, before she could stop herself.

"What, the Russian? Did he?"

"When you were younger."

"Pah! Thank you very much!"

Philip was one of the best-looking men she had ever encountered, but not the most sensitive. He knew her inside out, and one of the things she loved most about him was that he didn't kowtow to her as most people did. He saw her as "Lilibet," much as she saw herself. He was straightforward, but hardly tender. So, he was not the best person to explain her feelings about the young Russian to, even though he was responsible for them.

Without her realizing it, Maksim Brodsky had taken her back to the days in Valletta, when she had danced the night away with the other navy wives and rejoiced in her freedom with her glamorous man, safe in the knowledge that her father was king and would be a wise monarch and personal guide for years to come. He was dead a year later. Those months in Malta were preserved in amber.

Now she knew why the image of the young man in that wardrobe was so hard to take. Knowing didn't make it easier, exactly, but at least she understood.

"Feeling better?" Philip asked, without really looking.

"Yes, thank you," she said.

He reached for her hand and gave it a squeeze. The car whisked them on through the Berkshire night.

SIR PETER VENN, asked to drinks before lunch at Windsor on Saturday morning, accepted without question. He and his wife had been planning to see an exhibition at the National Gallery with some old friends from his posting in Rome, but he put them off without a murmur. If the Queen wants you to go to drinks, you go.

There was no obvious indication of why he'd been invited, and with a courtier's discretion, he didn't ask. As governor of the castle he was very familiar with the room—in this case, the Octagon Room in the Brunswick Tower, overlooking the park. He mingled with Lady Caroline Cadwallader, the canon chaplain of St. George's Chapel down the hill, and the few other senior members of the Household scattered about. Her Majesty was in upbeat form, looking forward to the Royal Windsor Horse Show in a month's time, which was always one of her favorite events. She chatted about her hopes for Barbers Shop, which she had entered in the Ridden Show Horse category. Unlike others in the small group that had clustered round, Sir Peter was not a horseman and was not entirely sure what a Ridden Show Horse was (surely all show horses were ridden?), but it was obviously something important if the Queen was excited about the chance of winning.

"I know you've been busy recently, Governor," she said, turning her bright blue gaze on him, and he wondered if he had looked unsuitably bored just now.

"Have I?"

"That meeting you hosted. You introduced me to a painfully shy young man from Djibouti."

She did a rather brilliant imitation of a young man avoiding eye contact and staring at his shoes. The rest of the group, having the finest-honed diplomatic skills in the country, saw that they were not needed for this conversation and melted away. Sir Peter, who had been somewhat disappointed by Kelvin Lo's failure to shine that day, was pleased to have the opportunity to talk about him a little bit more.

"You remembered, ma'am! Yes, Kelvin's rather a genius. He started working for us a few months ago. He's already unearthed untold amounts of information about the Belt and Road."

"The Belt and Road?"

"Yes. That was the real focus of the meeting. China's grand plan to connect Asia, Africa, and Europe. Awfully confusing, really, because 'belt' is for the land bits, which are often roads, and 'road' is for the sea bits, which never are. Except metaphorically. The Chinese are very metaphorical, I find."

"Oh." It rang a bell. "Is that the same as the New Silk Road? We talked about it when President Xi came last year."

"Well, that might be a romantic name for it, ma'am, but it's anything but. I'm not an expert myself, but I was glad to be able to host the meeting here at the castle. It was a classified thing the Foreign Office organized, with help from MI6. Having it here gave everyone the privacy they needed, and it was useful for Kelvin, being so close to Heathrow. He was able to fly in and out quickly on his way to a conference in Virginia, although of course his plane here was delayed by bad weather so he was rather late for everything. We put off the main part of our meeting by a day to include him, because he has such an intriguing insight into what the Chinese are doing in Africa. I'm sorry—is this more detail than you were hoping for, ma'am?"

"No, it's fascinating. Do go on."

"He's created a computer program to map their infrastructure investments across the continent and to neighboring countries, and

they really are much more massive than anyone had anticipated—
or than the Chinese are owning up to."

"Are they?"

"Oh, yes, ma'am. They're building whole ports, and railways
and superhighways, and even courts to settle trading disputes."

"So different from the last century, when they would hardly talk
to anyone."

"Indeed, ma'am. President Xi's making up for lost time. But
there are big questions about how much debt the host nations
are getting into, and whether the infrastructure can be used for
military purposes. I mean, goodness, don't let me bore you with it
all now. You'll see it in the report MI6 are putting together. And
the other one the Foreign Office people are finalizing, with some
of our more strategic concerns. That's the one this meeting was to
discuss, of course."

"And who was at it, exactly? They all seemed so young."

"They were, ma'am. It's rather frightening, isn't it? When people
your grandchildren's age suddenly seem to be running the country.
We had various boffins from the City and academia and GCHQ.
Hardly anyone over thirty-five, I'd say. Kelvin is twenty-six, would
you believe?"

She noticed that behind Sir Peter's shoulder, Lady Caroline was
trying to catch her eye. The drinks were overrunning and the chef
was probably worrying about the fish.

"Yes, well . . . Isn't that interesting?" she said, twisting her wedding ring so Lady Caroline could come in and break up the conversation. It was a shame, because it really *was* interesting, and
she would have liked to have chatted more. She hadn't realized Sir
Peter's meeting had been so secret and strategic. It gave her a lot
to think about.

16

THE REST OF THE WEEKEND was very relaxing. Edward and Sophie came over with their children on Sunday after church, and they all went out for a hack. Back inside the castle they looked through the albums of Barbers Shop winning his races as a gelding, and subsequently triumphing at several Ridden Show Horse events. His trainer was bringing him over from Newmarket for the horse show. At fourteen, he probably only had another year of showing in him. Everyone would miss him. He had been such a star—on the track and in the ring. It was nice to see Louise asking intelligent questions about his bloodline and schooling.

Sir Simon appeared that evening with her schedule for the week, and for the first time in a month it looked busy: the Privy Council, the post office turning five hundred, herself turning ninety, and then, to round it off, the Obamas. Actually, that was the event she was most looking forward to. They had a glamour about them, that couple, reminiscent of the Kennedys and the Reagans. They were intelligent and warm, and had got on with all the family when they visited last time. That had been all the bells and whistles at Buckingham Palace. This would be something quieter and more intimate. She wanted Windsor to be at its best: ideally without the unsolved murder of a foreign national and her own Security Service's hunt for traitors in her Household hanging over it.

SHE WENT TO BED EARLY, but couldn't sleep. Thoughts of the Belt and Road meeting kept bubbling up to bother her. It fitted with *something*. Something that had happened that evening, when she had gone over to the Norman Tower, where the governor was treating his guests to a drinks reception of their own in his private drawing room, and she had agreed to pop in and say hello.

She hadn't stayed long. There were about eight of them in the drawing room, she recalled, most of them ridiculously young, and Sir Peter had made the introductions. They were an unusually incohesive group. She had put it partly down to nerves, but they really didn't seem to know each other on the whole. It was as if they had been plucked from their various organizations and institutions for this particular event, and were still on awkward social terms. So different from the military cocktail parties she had so often attended, where the officers were a tight little band, keen to josh each other and make jokes.

They had dressed for the occasion. Not evening gowns, of course, but black tie and cocktail dresses. All but two were men, including the senior official from the Foreign Office who had arranged the meeting and a couple of spooks from MI6. All the others were analysts and academics, she supposed. One of the girls had been very pretty, with elfin looks and a cropped, blond shingle that reminded one of Twiggy. The other was dark, with curtains of

straight hair that half obscured her face. This was Rachel Stiles—
the young woman who would soon be dead of an overdose. Had
someone in that room caused her to take it? All must have stayed
the night, if the main meeting had been postponed to the following day.

China and Russia.

Could there be some connection? Geopolitically—as Sir Simon
would say—of course there could. Was Maksim Brodsky some sort
of Russian spy? Had he been planted by Peyrovski to get hold of
Chinese secrets? Had Rachel Stiles been helping him? Is that why
they both had to die?

Oh, for goodness' sake, she was getting as bad as the director
general. The very idea was absurd. And yet her mind kept going
back to that little gathering in the Norman Tower. Something was
wrong. She'd noticed it at the time, and then dismissed it, but now
she knew she should have trusted her instincts. If only she could
remember what it was.

She tried to picture the men. One had been unusually tall, she
remembered. One had an Indian-sounding name. One had talked
exceedingly fast about something to do with debt ratio formulas
and then stood waiting for her to say something intelligent. She
had smiled and said, "How very interesting." What else was one
supposed to do?

Meanwhile, if she was going to find the killer by the president's
visit on Friday, she would have to work very fast indeed.

ON MONDAY MORNING Rozie showed up for work wearing borrowed
jodhpurs and an old tweed jacket over a long-sleeved T-shirt. This
was not how an assistant private secretary usually dressed, but she
had been told to meet the Boss at the back entrance of the Royal
Mews, ready for a ride.

The Queen was already there, in a quilted jacket and with a

signature silk scarf knotted into position. Rozie couldn't remember ever having seen her in a hard hat. Queens did not fall off horses, it seemed. And to be fair, the glossy black Fell pony looked the most placid of creatures, waiting patiently with her groom in the immaculate yard, next to a mahogany bay with short, powerful legs and a black silky mane that he tossed flirtatiously in Rozie's direction.

"Ah. Hello!" The Boss greeted her with a grin, indicating the bay. "We thought we'd get Temple tacked up for you. He's about the right size and a nice character, as long as you tell him who's in charge."

Rozie curtsied, which felt odd in riding boots. "Thank you, Your Majesty."

The Queen was in good spirits, but sharp. "One reads one's papers. I gather you learned to ride in Hyde Park. So did I. Come on."

They mounted their rides and two grooms accompanied them, one on a black pony almost identical to the Queen's, and one on a sturdy Windsor Grey. The day was gloomy, with scudding clouds and a distant hint of rain. The Queen glanced up at the sky.

"I checked the weather on the BBC. We've got an hour or so, apparently."

They headed east, over grass and under trees, towards the wide spaces of Home Park, where Temple settled into a steady walk and Rozie flexed her riding muscles, relaxing into the rhythm and realizing how much she needed this.

"You grew up not far from where I did," the Queen observed, meaning her parents' house in Mayfair.

"Yes, ma'am."

"I'm very impressed that you rode in central London. It can't have been easy, getting lessons?"

She was too polite to say exactly what she meant, Rozie thought, but she was right: it had been bloody difficult. Girls who grow up on council estates aren't supposed to ride horses. Yes, it was near Hyde Park, but it's one life if you live in one of the big houses in Holland Park or Mayfair, and quite another if you live in a two-bed flat in Notting Hill and your dad works on the London Underground, putting up with passenger aggro every day, while your mum works as a midwife and a volunteer in the local community to replace the services that somehow kept disappearing. Time and money for horses weren't exactly a priority.

But maybe they had one thing in common apart from Hyde Park, which was being elder daughters, whose parents had high expectations of them.

"I found a way, ma'am."

"Oh? How?"

"I worked at the stables."

Night and day, first thing in the morning, weekends—whenever they would let her, to pay for rides. Rozie often did an hour before school and another couple of hours in the evening, fitting in homework somehow, never quite making top of the class but keeping her head well above water academically, which was the deal with Mum: "If you can't get good grades, say goodbye to the ponies." "Horses, Mum." "Whatever."

"And you rode competitively?"

"Yes, ma'am. For the army."

Rozie did everything competitively. After combining school and the stables, uni seemed like a breeze and she had joined the Officer Training Corps and still got a First. She wasn't the world's best rider, never would be, but she was utterly fearless going round an eventing course. Give her a decent horse and a bit of practice, and she would fly, swim, whatever it took.

She was a good shot, too, with a top 100 badge from the army shooting competition at Bisley Camp. Rozie always felt out of place in those worlds, but beat the boys at it anyway. There was nothing in life as satisfying as beating a posh boy at something he was good at. Early on, she had also learned to look like she didn't care, which made it better. And now here she was, with a good degree, a tour in Afghanistan, and a fast-track job in a posh boys' bank, working for the Queen.

Normally, she put all of this behind her and just got on with the day, but the horse underneath her took her back to those Hyde Park early mornings. How could she ever possibly have imagined she would end up here?

"What do you think of Temple?" the Queen asked.

"He's not happy." Rozie laughed. "I can sense he wants to get going."

"Don't let him."

"He's very taken with himself, isn't he?"

The Queen grinned across at her. "And quite right, too. With looks like that. Yes, Temple, you're gorgeous and you know it."

They ambled along one of the walks, listening to birdsong between the full-throttle roar of the jets overhead. Rozie had never seen the Queen so deeply in her element. She felt as if she had somehow crossed a threshold, and now she, the girl from the council estate, was one of them: a fellow rider, a member of the inner circle. Was this ride a reward for the work she'd done in London? The Queen would never say, and Rozie would never ask, but it felt that way.

They talked about Rozie's recent trip to Lagos, and how big the city had grown now, to contain twenty million people. This was not news to the Queen, who was familiar with the capital cities of all the Commonwealth countries. It had been a big surprise to Rozie, though, the first time she visited. She realized how prejudiced she had been about Nigeria, assuming it was some kind of would-be England in the sun. If anything, it was the opposite—

heading in its own direction with confidence that put this little island in the shade.

"And was it your grandparents who first came to live in London?"

It was. Rozie talked with pride about her father's parents, who had arrived in the sixties. Her grandfather had started out washing bodies in the morgue. It was the only job they would let him have, but he had always worked hard for his community. Everyone in Peckham knew Samuel Oshodi. If there was anything you needed, he worked out how to get it and made it happen somehow.

"He got an MBE," Rozie added. "I was tiny when he received it, but I remember him going to the palace and we all met up afterwards to celebrate. He met you that day and—" She stopped, still smiling at the memory. He had said Her Majesty was "very small, but quite dazzling; even her skin seemed to glitter." It was family folklore now. It was meant to be flattering, but Rozie wasn't sure how the woman herself would take it.

The woman herself was giving Rozie the strangest look. Had she accidentally said the words out loud? She was sure she hadn't. The Queen was staring at her as if she had asked a difficult question. Or as if somebody else had, and Rozie wasn't even there . . .

She had it now, the memory that had been so elusive.

It had come back with Technicolor clarity while Rozie was talking—so strong, in fact, she was amazed she had forgotten it at all.

"Let's go back," she decided, cutting short the ride. "The sky looks threatening."

The Queen was right. Steel-grey clouds had given way to huge columns, the color of Tahitian pearls. The temperature had dropped by a degree. Not for the first time, the BBC weather report had been unduly optimistic. They turned for home and set the horses and ponies to a trot.

All the way she pictured the seraphic look on Rozie's face when she had talked about her grandfather's MBE. That's how it was with medals. She should have thought of it at the investiture last Wednesday, but that had been routine, though pleasant. It took Rozie's memory of childish excitement to bring her own, half-buried memory back to life.

Awards were a special thing, personal and enduring. The odd person turned them down, but anyone who accepted treasured theirs with fierce pride. They remembered the day they got it, and everything they had done to earn it, and so did their families. She had had countless conversations with proud wives and widows, husbands and sons, about decorations won in war and in the community. People could be shy on first meeting, but never when it came to medals. One question, and they opened up. Sometimes they were overcome with emotion, if friends and fellow soldiers had died during a brave campaign, or if they were wearing it on behalf of a relative who had died. But they were never neutral, *ever.*

Rachel Stiles had been wearing a fitted dinner jacket over her cocktail dress. On the lapel was a miniature silver cross, backed by a laurel wreath. She was not the only person in the room to be wearing a decoration. Sir Peter had seven, after an illustrious career, and two of the other men in the room had one each. Dr. Stiles's particularly interested the Queen, though, because it was the Elizabeth Cross, awarded to the next of kin of members of the armed forces killed in action or in a terrorist attack. She had instituted it herself, to recognize their sacrifice, less than ten years ago.

"And who was this for?" she remembered asking.

The girl had looked startled. "My father."

The words had seemed forced, and came out almost as a question. Nevertheless, one persisted. "Where was he?"

Now the girl looked confused. "Er, Buckingham Palace?"

She had been trembling, the Queen noticed, eaten up with

nerves. The Queen had decided not to pursue it, and she had blamed herself a little for being vague with her question. She didn't mean "Where did he get the medal?" of course, because he must have been dead in order for it to be awarded to his family. But that was obvious, surely? She meant "Which attack had he been in? Or which campaign?"

This was a sensitive subject, naturally, but she had learned over the years that families were keen to share their loss. Perhaps it was because one was in some way representative of what they had died for. Perhaps it was because she cared very much, and had met many other families in similar situations, and indeed lost very dear loved ones to war and terrorists herself.

She had been expecting, in brief, the undoubtedly tragic story behind the medal—not a two-word answer for where it had been given to someone else. Although Buckingham Palace was an unusual answer in this case. The Elizabeth Cross was normally presented by lord-lieutenants in ceremonies around the country. She had personally given only a handful of them to relatives, and rarely at the palace. But perhaps this was why it had stood out.

It was a complicated situation, she had told herself at the time, in the brief flash during which she had considered it. The girl was emotional, and shy. That explained the strange answer. Clearly, she was not a great conversationalist. It was this girl she had been briefly reminded of by Kelvin Lo's insistence on staring at his shoes the following day. She who had looked unwell, standing in the group behind him.

Soon after their brief exchange that first evening, the Queen had gone from the Norman Tower to the State Apartments, and then she was focused on the evening *à la russe* with Charles. She had thought no more about it.

But Rachel Stiles had not been emotional. Her confusion was just that. Her answer had been plain wrong—about an event that should have been seared into her very essence. She was not the owner of that medal. She did not know what it meant. She was wearing somebody else's jacket.

Was she even Rachel Stiles at all?

As if on cue, there was a sudden clap of thunder in the skies above the park and the first heavy raindrops began to fall. Emma, the Fell pony, shook her head slightly and carried on at a steady trot, but Temple glanced up as if at a gunshot and rocketed forward without warning, taking Rozie with him.

"Go after them!" the Queen instructed the groom on the Grey. Temple was heading for the trees at a canter. Rozie might get knocked off by a branch if she wasn't careful.

The rain was bucketing down now. Cursing the BBC forecast, the Queen followed as fast as she dared.

17

A N HOUR LATER, they were back at work in the private sitting room. Rozie was aware of sore thighs after such a long time since her last hack, but it was worth it for the exhilaration of the ride. She still felt a glow, thinking about it, and especially that last bit, racing across Home Park at hyper-speed, until Temple finally agreed to submit to her commands and trot for home like a show horse at Olympia. She was very fond of him already. He was a rascal, but she had the measure of him. The Queen had told her she could ride him whenever she was free. Rozie stood in a bubble of happiness.

The Queen, in cashmere and pearls, and looking as if she had spent half a day in a salon, nursed a cup of black tea with honey. The squall had passed quickly, but had drenched them all anyway. She had gone upstairs immediately to spruce up and put her head under the hair dryer. The last thing one needed was a head cold this week.

She brought Rozie up to speed on the incident with the Elizabeth Cross.

"So, you think she stole the jacket?" Rozie asked.

"Possibly." *Or the very identity,* the Queen wanted to add. But she couldn't quite bring herself to say the words out loud. "Can you check, please, whether the Stiles family were awarded the medal? And can I see a picture of her?"

"Yes, ma'am."

"Oh, and, Rozie?"

"Ma'am?"

"There is a gentleman called Billy MacLachlan who lives in Richmond. He was in my protection team a long time ago. You'll find his contact details in the files. Could you ask him, very privately, to double-check with the pathologist that there was nothing unusual about Dr. Stiles's death? I think he still has good links with the police. You might get him to suggest he has a source who thinks it might not have been a simple overdose."

"Yes, ma'am."

"And I needn't say . . ."

"No, ma'am, of course. Now, about Thursday. The Prince of Wales and the Duchess of Cornwall will be arriving from Highgrove at about midday. . . ."

THE AFTERNOON WAS SCHEDULED for a haircut and a long session with Angela, the Queen's dresser. There were several outfit changes to finalize for the coming days, and the weather remained resolutely unpredictable. There was also jewelry to choose, laid out for inspection in a series of open, velvet-lined boxes. It was always good to spend time with someone who, in other circumstances, she would have called a close friend, but today she had a lot on her mind. The Queen tried to concentrate, but it was more difficult than usual. It took tremendous patience to wait for Rozie's evening appearance with the next day's schedule and an update on the morning's activities.

The news was mixed.

"Dr. Stiles's father, Captain James Stiles of the Royal Engineers, was killed by an IED in Kosovo in 1999," Rozie reported. "Rachel was ten. The Elizabeth Cross was presented to her mother, who subsequently died of ovarian cancer, by the Lord-Lieutenant of Essex at Merville Barracks in Colchester in 2010. Rachel had a younger brother, but she seems to have taken on the right to wear the award."

"I see."

"I have a picture of Rachel here, ma'am."

Rozie submitted a printout of the form submitted to the castle security team for vetting, with a passport photograph attached at the top. The image was small and unremarkable, showing a young woman with blue eyes and familiar curtains of thick, dark hair.

"I looked for others, but they're quite hard to get hold of," Rozie admitted. "For a millennial, she kept herself out of social media. There wasn't a photo on LinkedIn—that's the website for professionals, ma'am—and she wasn't on Facebook or dating sites or anything like that." There had been a few group pictures of office parties at Golden Futures, but nothing particularly useful. The news feeds had gone with a fuzzy graduation picture when they had announced her death.

The Queen examined the photograph with a magnifying glass from her desk drawer. From a distance, without the glass, one would have said it was her. But she saw now that was largely because of the hair. The nose on this girl was different to the one she dimly remembered. This one was larger and less attractive. The chin was longer. Or was it? If someone had asked her to swear, right now, that this was a different person (luckily nobody ever did that sort of thing), she couldn't have done it. She *felt* it was, but that was all.

However, Merville Barracks was most definitely not Buckingham Palace. That conversation about the medal ceremony made no sense. It was ironic that the Elizabeth Cross was one of the few decorations *unlikely* to have been presented at the palace. Not many people would instantly think of that, of course—but she happened to be one of the few who did.

Would that convince anyone else? Rachel had not even been the person receiving the award: that had been her mother. So easy to say a girl might not remember, or that she had been confused in the heat of the moment meeting the Queen.

But one knew. One *knew.* One just did, and that was the end of it.

Rozie sensed some of what she was thinking, and looked uncertain. "Wouldn't the security checks have found her out if she wasn't the right person?"

"That *is* their job," the Queen mused.

"And what about afterwards—after the murder, I mean, when the police interviewed everyone who'd been here? Wouldn't they have noticed?"

"You would think so." She sighed and changed the subject. "I don't suppose you've heard back from Billy MacLachlan?" she asked without much hope. Rozie had presumably only contacted him a few hours ago, at most. He could hardly have discovered anything by now.

"No, ma'am. But he said he'll let us know as soon as he hears anything useful."

"Good." The young woman hovered. She looked nervous, the Queen realized, and hesitant: not normal demeanor for her APS. "Was there anything else?"

"Actually there was, ma'am. I think I've made a terrible mistake. I'm sorry."

"Spit it out."

The Queen watched as Rozie screwed up her courage and lifted her chin.

"I rang Rachel's office and asked about her next of kin. I thought you might want me to talk to them later. Anyway, I said I was calling from the housekeeper's office here, and she had left something behind and now we realized it was hers we wanted to return it. And the woman at the office said she had no idea Rachel had been to Windsor Castle. I'd forgotten the meeting was so highly secret, ma'am—or rather, I assumed her office knew, at least. But anyway, they didn't, or not the desk manager I ended up talking to."

"Oh, dear. You didn't mention the nature of the meeting, I assume?" The Queen's voice was even. This was unfortunate, but not a disaster.

"No, ma'am, of course not. But she said, this woman, that she was surprised Rachel had come at all. She'd been sick for several days and they hadn't seen her. I asked for how long, and the woman said for a week before she died, which would take it back to about the time of the dine and sleep."

"Thank you, Rozie." The Queen was thoughtful.

"Do you want me to tell anyone, ma'am?"

"You might find out from Chief Inspector Strong, in passing, whether his team managed to interview everyone on that list of visitors after Mr. Brodsky died. That was my impression, certainly. And tell the superintendent I'm concerned about security and I'd like him to look into the procedures that day and the following one—whether everyone's clearance was double-checked. I imagine he's done so already. He can tell me what he found."

THE QUEEN WAS not superstitious, but she had often noticed that bad news seemed to come in threes. The following day, after what seemed like a promising report, three setbacks arrived within an hour.

She was just preparing for another Privy Council meeting when Rozie popped in.

"I've heard back from Billy MacLachlan, Your Majesty."

"Oh good. Anything interesting?"

"As a matter of fact, yes. There was a slightly strange toxicology report on the body of Rachel Stiles. As well as the cocaine and alcohol, there were traces of a tranquilizer she hadn't been prescribed. But they said she'd been struggling with anxiety for a long time. She lost both her parents young, as we know."

"I see."

However, Rozie's next report put paid to the Queen's emerging theory. DCI Strong's team had indeed interviewed everyone they wanted to in the days after the murder—including Rachel Stiles, who had been at home in her Docklands flat and happy to be interviewed by two of his detectives, despite recovering from flu. So she had been aware of events, at least.

On top of that, the castle superintendent had got the head of security to double-check the procedures, and everything had been done properly. If Stiles had got someone to impersonate her, they had done it very well.

However, the third blow was by far the worst.

Humphreys reported, with some glee, she felt, the discovery by the team in the Round Tower that Sandy Robertson had purchased a pair of lacy knickers online last year that were identical to the ones found near Brodsky's body. They were closing in.

The deadline she had set herself was approaching, and she wondered if she had made any progress at all. She was certain she was onto something, but Strong and his team had unwittingly suggested otherwise. For now, however, it was important to focus on the days ahead, which would be busy enough to keep her fully occupied. History would be made, and the world would be watching. Poor Sandy Robertson would have to wait.

She couldn't bear it, but there was nothing she could do.

18

As a little girl, when asked who she would like to be when she grew up, Princess Elizabeth had said, "A lady in the country, with animals." For the past few weeks she had been just that, but for the next few days it was time to be Queen.

Her birthday was still a day away, but on Wednesday she and Prince Philip celebrated the five-hundredth anniversary of the Royal Mail by visiting the Delivery Office in Windsor. There were crowds and cheers and bunting, and the weather was kind. Angela had done a very good job with a pink coat and hat, which would photograph well in the sunshine. The Delivery Office was to be renamed in one's honor, and there was an exhibition to review, and the inevitable commemorative stamp.

It was all very jolly, and only exceeded in its essential Britishness by what followed straight afterwards, which was a trip to nearby Alexandra Gardens, where there was a new bandstand to open and crowds of schoolchildren who sang, while others performed an extract from *Romeo and Juliet* as part of the Shakespeare Schools Festival.

Back at the castle, somewhat exhausted, she and Philip both had a nap before hosting a private dinner for the family members who had already started arriving for tomorrow. The Private Apartments were filling up with children, grandchildren, and great-grandchildren. She hadn't seen most of them since they had posed for family portraits after Easter, shortly before the dine and sleep.

These pictures, taken by Annie Leibovitz, would be released to the public soon. She was quite happy with them, though she preferred her private snaps, really. She liked people caught off guard, being silly and having fun, and that was hardly the Leibovitz style. But the image of her and Anne had a certain something. Another with the dogs on the castle steps was rather nice. And the public would adore the one with little Louise and James, the great-grandchildren, and the handbag. Yes, all in all, although the American had arrived with her usual retinue and outrageous amounts of equipment, and taken four times as long as one really wanted to spend, it had been a success. She would show the results to the children tonight.

Rozie watched the family from a distance, with the Queen at the heart of it, her face alight with pleasure. She really did dazzle, just like Baba Samuel said. It was something about her skin, which was flawless, and also her eyes, which danced with delight whenever there was something to amuse her. The ready presence of pearls and diamonds did no harm, obviously—but Baba Samuel was right: even in her dressing gown she seemed to glitter. Now, in a silk damask evening gown and antique sparkles, she looked radiant.

So Rozie decided that she wouldn't spoil the moment, today or tomorrow, by mentioning Vadim Borovik, Yuri Peyrovski's valet, who had been discovered, badly beaten, in an alleyway in Soho. Masha Peyrovskaya had called Rozie this afternoon in a paroxysm of panic and despair.

"Yuri know he helped me! He order it! He punish him and it is me soon!"

It had taken some time and all Rozie's skill to calm her down a little. Masha refused to believe the police "story" that it was a typical homophobic attack. "Of course they say that! Because he is gay, everything is possible!"

"Will he be all right?" Rozie had asked.

"Who knows? Perhaps he die in the night."

Russians really were very melodramatic, Rozie thought. But she decided to check on the valet's health tomorrow, to be on the safe side. If she could find a spare moment.

Tomorrow should have been her day off, but the birthday meant all free time was canceled. Various royals were arriving from around Europe to attend the Queen's birthday party at the castle. And meanwhile the president of the United States would be arriving at Stansted Airport, before meeting the Queen the following day. She and Sir Simon would be on their feet from dawn to dusk, liaising, troubleshooting, and overseeing. The whole world would be looking in, to check that everything was done to the highest standard known to man, every second of the day. Queen Victoria had lived to be eighty-one. Ninety was new territory for the monarchy. It was important for the Queen to start the next decade as she meant to go on.

THE NEXT DAY, there was still no news from the Round Tower. But it was the twenty-first of April, and it seemed as if the whole of Windsor was out on the streets. They crowded against the barriers and stood on balconies and at windows, waving a sea of Union flags. The bells from the chapel rang, and there were bugles and the band of the Coldstream Guards.

The Queen put her thoughts about the investigation to one side and focused on the job, which was to be herself in public, and which it took a lifetime to learn. During the walkabout below the castle, it seemed as if everyone had a bouquet to give. There were giant pink balloons, and fellow nonagenarians to meet, an official walk to open (she was very good with velvet curtains and little cords), and a giant purple cake made by the lady who won the baking show on the BBC, featuring an unusual array of flavors, which she did not get the opportunity to try.

Last year the people at Land Rover had created a sort of popemobile out of an open-top Range Rover, and she stood in the back of it with Philip at her side, waving to all the flag-flapping well-wishers. The sun had consented to shine again, appearing decorously through silver clouds. It was chilly, but not unduly cold. She was warmed, anyway, by the cheerful mood of the people, who burst into snatches of "Happy Birthday" along the route.

She thought of her namesake, and her royal progresses round the country. What would the first Queen Elizabeth have made of the queen-mobile, as Philip inevitably called it? She would have been pleased with the crowds, no doubt. One tried not to think of the snipers on rooftops, keeping an eye out for trouble, and to be grateful one could still do this. These days, it was usually all bulletproof glass and safety vehicles. But that was for the prime minister. If the monarch could not be seen, what was the point of her? Hence today's outfit in spring-grass green, in honor of the season, and gratitude for clement weather, and the iron constitution that meant she could still stand up in an open car.

Later, the setting sun tinged the silver sky with oyster pink. Charles made a short and heartfelt speech and invited her to light a beacon. It would be the first of over a thousand around the UK and as far as Gibraltar, starting with a rather splendid chain of flaming torches down the Long Walk, burning bright against the darkening sky. It reminded her very much of the celebrations after the war, and the way the kingdom had spread news since the Armada. Meanwhile, Sir Simon informed her that over a quarter of a million people had sent birthday wishes via Twitter. Thank God they hadn't sent cards.

She had asked for as little fuss as possible today, and this was as little fuss as it was possible for the country to make. It had been tiring but joyful. So very special to spend the day at Windsor. She felt as if she had shared it with the whole town, and they with her. Now it was time for dinner at the castle—done Charles-style, which meant a table for seventy in the Waterloo Chamber, an abundance of flowers, and lots of funny speeches. And, one hoped, everybody still alive by morning.

If Putin *had* wanted to send a message, she thought, he should have chosen tonight.

She went upstairs to change. On her pillow was a packet of handmade Scottish fudge from Philip, with a note. He hadn't forgotten. She ate a piece, to keep her going for the night ahead.

19

FRIDAY MORNING DAWNED clear and grey, after a night of rain. President Obama was in London and due to visit Mr. Cameron in Downing Street, which took the news away from Windsor for a few hours—for which she was grateful.

He and the first lady were due for lunch, and although—thankfully—no one had come to inform her that another visitor had been murdered, the first was still very much under investigation. As the hours ticked by, she had hoped for a nod from Sir Simon, or a request for a meeting from Gavin Humphreys, to tell her about a stunning breakthrough, but there had been nothing.

Later that morning, Sir Simon did arrive with news of a sort, but it only muddied the waters further. Given the similarity in hair type, and the unexpected subsequent death, the police had tested DNA from the hair found on Brodsky's body with that of Rachel Stiles and found it to be a match.

So the girl *had* been here. And yet she couldn't explain her own father's medal.

"You look surprised, ma'am."

"Not really," she said, regaining her composure. "Did they know each other?"

"Not as far as anyone knows. But she did say she had a brief conversation with him in the corridor the night before he died. One of the housekeepers confirms it. Maybe that's how the hair got transferred. DCI Strong is liaising with the divisional CID in the Isle of Dogs, where the body was found. They're going to get someone to look into whether they knew each other before. But it doesn't seem likely, and if she did, it doesn't explain much. She didn't know she'd be sleeping over until late afternoon, so she could hardly have planned to kill anyone."

"I see. Thank you for letting me know."

"Ma'am."

And there it was. The president was about to climb into Marine One to fly down to Windsor, and the whole investigation into Brodsky's death had just taken two steps backwards. Not MI5's investigation, obviously: that still continued down the straight, firmly blinkered. But one's own theory, which was only half formed anyway, and was now back at the starting gate.

So be it. One would simply have to, as Harry reliably informed her was the current lingo, "style it out."

AFTER MUCH TO-ING AND FRO-ING between offices, it had been decided to meet the president and Mrs. Obama in person as they landed at Home Park, just below the East Terrace. It wasn't normal procedure, but then, one didn't normally get to celebrate one's birthday with the president and first lady at one's favorite castle. She would pick them up in a Range Rover. Philip would drive.

There were three helicopters in all, and it was a relief when they managed to navigate their way through Heathrow airspace to land safely on the golf course. The day was breezy, and the Queen protected her hair with a headscarf, while Philip stayed warm in a mac. Emerging from Marine One, with his protection team in place, the president was all smiles.

There was a bit of a question mark about who was going to sit where in the car, but that was soon sorted. The staff seemed to have assumed it would be like a state dinner, where the visiting gentleman accompanies the lady host—but it felt to the Queen more like a shoot, where obviously the men would like to go in front together so they could chat. She sat in the back with Michelle, who was as charming as always once her nerves began to settle.

The first lady was unusually tall. The Queen got a bit of a crick in her neck looking up at her. However, she still radiated that star presence one was rather fond of. It was nice not to be the only woman the press wanted pictures of. Mrs. Obama's every public move was commented on and dissected, and she was used to being both adored and vilified, and never entirely alone. They had quite a lot in common—although of course one had been on the throne for nearly a decade before Michelle Obama's husband was even born.

The castle was crawling with security by now, and TV cameras and crew. There was a quick press call in the Oak Room to keep everyone happy, and then at last they could relax. There was a lot to talk about, what with the upcoming referendum and the elections, and the couple's plans for life after the White House. She would miss them. But the idea of a female president of the United

States was an interesting one. How the world had changed since 1926. Who could possibly have foreseen such an eventuality back then?

It wasn't until after the lunch, walking back towards the cars to say goodbye, that the president leaned down to her and said, "I understand you've been having a little local difficulty. With a young Russian. If there's anything we can do to help—"

The Queen turned to him gravely, before flashing a quick, dismissive smile.

"Thank you. The Security Service seems to have it under control. They seem to think the butler did it."

"That would be in keeping."

"I hope he didn't. I'm rather fond of my butlers."

President Obama thought of his auntie's house in Hawaii, his student digs in New York, and now the diligent team in the White House who catered to his every whim, and nodded sagely, but with a wicked glint in his eye.

"Aren't we all, ma'am? Aren't we all?"

20

ROZIE SAT IN HER BEDROOM with the light on, willing herself to go to bed after the most exhausting day she could remember, but she was still too wired to sleep. It was two in the morning. Almost all the windows in the castle were dark. She wanted to FaceTime Fliss in Frankfurt, but her sister would be asleep like everyone around here—and also like everyone around here, she would be getting up early in the morning.

Less than five hours until the alarm. Rozie knew she should have a quick shower and a warm drink and switch off that bit in her brain that kept going over the day in five-minute intervals, grading every decision and reaction according to how well it had gone. Instead, she went over to the decanter tray (as normal at Windsor as a kettle in Notting Hill) and poured herself a whiskey.

She'd already eaten all the plantain chips she'd brought back from Lagos, so she also helped herself to some little jam sandwiches, cut to the size of old pennies, from a Tupperware pot. These were leftovers from the children's teatime yesterday passed along by the kitchens. What would her grandfather say if he knew she had shared a joke with the Crown Prince of Denmark and was eating Prince George's spare jam pennies?

Her laptop was still open and she checked tomorrow's schedule before cycling through Twitter, the BBC, the *FT,* the *New York Times,* and the *Washington Post.* Then, on her sixth jam penny, the *Daily Mail,* the *Daily Express,* and the other rags that followed the Royal Family, to make sure they hadn't misreported today's events with any greater magnitude than normal. From her playlist she picked Art Blakey, hoping that some Blue Note jazz would compensate for her cortisol crash. She went down several rabbit holes on YouTube: "President Obama Arrives at Windsor Castle: LIVE," "Hillary Clinton Addresses Her Losing Streak Cold Open: *SNL,*" "Top 9 Funniest Julia Louis-Dreyfus Old Navy Commercials." (By now she was hating herself.)

On Facebook, she stalked her sister and various cousins, before randomly searching for people she knew. The clock on her screen told her it was nearly 3 A.M. If she didn't turn off the laptop soon she would . . . She was too tired to think about what might happen tomorrow, but it would be bad. Whatever. She ate another jam penny and typed Meredith Gostelow's name, but the architect did not appear as a Facebook member. How weird. Did the woman not have a life? Then she tried Masha Peyrovskaya, hoping for endless photographs of exotic holidays and high-powered ladies who lunched. But though there was a profile, it was private. *Fair enough,* Rozie thought. On a roll now, prompted by that day in London, she typed in "Vijay Kulandaiswamy"—not an easy name to forget.

This time, it was different.

There was only one entry that matched the search, and the profile photo matched the man she had met in Brodsky's Covent Garden flat. Vijay was a sharer. His feed was full of updates for anyone to see. He liked GIFs and memes from the US elections, which made Rozie feel right at home, and pictures of himself and friends at bars and restaurants around the world. Rozie scrolled up and down, feeling welcome sleepiness finally descend, but when she got back to the top of the feed she was wide awake again.

The most recent photograph, which she had ignored at first, was an old one of Vijay with a group of disheveled friends, looking drunk and happy at the end of a party. "Miss you forever. RIP," the caption began, and as she had Maksim Brodsky on her mind she assumed at first that it was prompted by his death.

But this farewell message wasn't for Brodsky. It was for someone else—a girl. Rozie felt bad for Vijay. What an unfortunate coincidence to lose your roommate and a female friend within two weeks of each other. This girl was twenty-six, the caption said. Her name was Anita Moodie and it wasn't clear how she had died. She had been a talented singer, a linguist who had traveled the world. Vijay also shared a picture of her and his brother, taken on the Peak in Hong Kong a couple of years before. Their smiling faces spoke of hope and promise.

For no obvious reason other than rabbit hole Internet curiosity, Rozie wanted to know what had happened to the girl. It felt as though Vijay was being coy about it. Had it been a terrible accident? A disease?

She clicked on Vijay's brother, Selvan, who was tagged in the photos, and he turned out to be another sharer. His feed was full of pictures of himself as a teenager with Anita and friends. In a couple of them, Maksim Brodsky was stretched out on the floor, his limbs languidly arranged for the camera, or sitting, laughing, with one of the girls on his knee.

Rozie checked out Selvan and Vijay's bios: they had gone to Allingham School. She remembered Vijay telling her that day in the flat that he and Maksim were old school friends. Rozie clicked the link to Anita Moodie's page. She had gone there, too. According to their birth dates, she must have been in the same year as Selvan, which would be the year between Maksim and Vijay. Judging from the old photographs, they had all hung out together at least a few times.

Back on Selvan's page, buried in the recent comments were references to Anita's life "cut short." "I had no idea about her mental health," somebody said. Selvan had answered with a crying emoji and a "Me neither. Shock to us all."

Rozie took a sip of whiskey and felt a tingle travel up her spine. Three people in their midtwenties had died in the past eighteen days, and two of them went to school together. She couldn't begin to put together how Anita Moodie's death could be connected to Maksim Brodsky's, never mind Rachel Stiles's, but it couldn't be pure coincidence, could it? Well, it could—but was it?

Behind her and up the hill was the Round Tower, housing DCI Strong's office. *I should go there in the morning,* she thought. But she knew she wouldn't. Sir Simon had told her how uninterested the police were in the detail of Rachel Stiles's hair on Brodsky's body. Yes, it was part of their inquiry, but they were much more excited by the knickers. Rozie had studied enough statistical theory at the bank to know how easy it would be to argue for coincidence in the school connection. Young people died. They took drugs and committed suicide. It was tragic, but they did. And, anyway, how would she explain her late-night, online stalking of Vijay Kulandaiswamy— a man she was supposed never to have met?

She felt strangely calm, though. Knocking back the last of her whiskey, she left Art Blakey playing on the laptop, crawled into bed in her clothes, and turned out the light.

IT WAS 9 A.M. when she woke up, with a blinding headache, having somehow failed to set the alarm. Her first thought was to thank heaven it was Sir Simon's day to deliver the boxes. Rozie knew they would be fuller than usual after the relative ease—from paperwork at least—of the last two days. Yesterday she had personally put together a small selection of letters and cards written to the Queen by members of the public, which she would also want to see. Yes of course the nonagenarian monarch would be working over the weekend to make up for lost time. Sir Simon said she had looked startled and offended when he had gently suggested otherwise.

He would be taking the boxes through in an hour or so. He, and not Rozie. She hadn't thought about that last night. She wasn't scheduled to see the Queen at all today, or tomorrow, which was Sunday. She wondered for a minute whether she could wait until Monday to share her discovery. It might not mean anything, after all.

But a man was dead. The Queen cared deeply. So did Rozie.

She made herself a cup of tea and finished off the last of the jam pennies. The headache abated slightly and she felt better after a shower. Ten minutes later she was dressed in a body-hugging pencil skirt, white shirt, and a tailored jacket that had cost her first month's wages, her hair and minimal makeup done, her feet shod in her signature heels. She had thought of a plan and it just needed a couple of carefully timed phone calls to make it work.

Sir Simon was talking to the master of the Household when she walked past his open office door. He merely tapped his wristwatch and gave her a quizzical look as she went to her own office next door. Timekeeping was not quite so essential at weekends when one was not "on" with the Boss.

Rozie brought up the Queen's updated schedule for the day on her desktop monitor, paying close attention to the hour before lunch. She made a quick call to the prime minister's office to talk to Emily, the PM's private secretary, who had become a friend in the last couple of months.

"We've had some thoughts about presents the Cabinet might like to get for the Queen," Rozie said. "Sir Simon has a list."

"Oh, *does* he? Because David's desperate. He keeps coming up with all these ideas but she's either got one already, or got it in gold, or Samantha thinks it would be silly, or one of the ministers makes a face and David changes his mind."

"Simon thought of some brilliant ones yesterday."

"Fabulous. Because we've only got till June and it doesn't feel like very long if it's bespoke. Plus of course David's got a lot on his mind. Thank God she didn't want anything for her *actual* birthday. Did the president get her anything?"

"I don't know."

Rozie had been manning the office phones during the visit. Sir Simon would have been the one to see. For a second, the surrealness of her job hit her again. If she wanted to know what Barack Obama gave the Queen for her birthday, in private . . . she could just ask.

"Can I talk to him now?" Emily asked. "Simon, I mean."

"He's away from his desk. Try him at around eleven."

"No worries. Thanks, babe."

Rozie put the phone in its cradle with a satisfying click. Emily was diligent, persistent, and obsessed with the prime minister's to-do list. The present from the government for the Queen's official birthday had been high on that list for a long time and she would do anything to tick it off. Rozie then made a couple of other calls.

At eleven, she made sure she was discussing the debrief from yesterday with Sir Simon and the head of castle security. At eleven fifteen, as instructed by Rozie, a clerk from St. Paul's Cathedral rang him to talk about details of the official birthday Thanksgiving Service. As the minutes ticked by, Sir Simon kept glancing at his watch. The Queen would be finished with the boxes soon. But at eleven thirty his secretary came over to say the prime minister's office was on the phone for the third time and wanted to talk to him directly, about something quite urgent.

With a sigh and an eye roll, he nodded to her. "I'll take it." He gestured to Rozie. "Go and get the boxes. Do you mind?"

Rozie didn't. When the call came, she walked smartly out of the office, making him marvel once again at how she managed such rapid strides in those skirts and heels.

"AH, GOOD, IT'S YOU," the Queen said without surprise, putting the last of the papers back in its box and making sure she hadn't missed anything.

"Yes, Your Majesty." Rozie curtsied. Mastering *that* in a tight skirt had been an interesting learning curve.

The Queen put her teacup in its saucer. "Thank you."

The coffee maid, who had been hovering in the background, picked up a tray and left the room. The Queen turned back to Rozie.

"Is there any news?"

"Yes, ma'am."

Rozie had practiced several times what she would say, and how to do it without wasting precious time. She told the Queen about Vadim Borovik being beaten up in Soho, reassured her that he was discharged from hospital, and mentioned how Masha Peyrovskaya was worried her husband was the cause. She then explained about last night's Internet session and the curious coincidence of Anita Moodie's death.

The Queen was intrigued.

"This girl was good friends with him, you think?"

"Well, they knew each other, definitely. Also, there might be a link with the music department at Allingham. Maksim played piano, of course, and I looked up Anita this morning. She studied music at uni. In fact, she got a diploma in singing."

"And that's what she did afterwards? Sing?"

"From what I could tell. She didn't post much on Facebook, but friends referred to her performing."

This didn't entirely fit. The Queen absorbed the information without really knowing what to do with it. "Is it certain it was suicide?" she asked.

"That's what her friends seem to think. They were all surprised, though."

"Do you have a picture of her?"

"Yes, ma'am."

Rozie had used her phone to screenshot various pictures from Selvan's timeline and Anita's own Facebook page. She leaned down and scrolled through them now, as the Queen peered through her bifocals. They showed a pretty young woman with serious, dark brown eyes and a glossy, reddish bob that swept sharply below her jawline. In each picture she looked nicely presented, in feminine, well-cut clothes. The Queen's mind was whirring.

"Thank you, Rozie. Very much. You might ask Mr. MacLachlan to look into Anita Moodie for us, would you? It would be interesting to find out a little bit more about her life. Would you mind asking him to find out if she spoke Mandarin Chinese? Also, I wanted to ask, could you possibly discover what sort of underwear Sandy Robertson is supposed to have bought online?"

"Actually, I already did, ma'am. Yesterday," Rozie said. She regularly popped up to DCI Strong's little incident room in the Round Tower for a word. Often bearing jam pennies or spare slices of Dundee cake, which went down well.

The Queen looked surprised. "Really?"

"I thought you might be concerned about the purchase." Which was the polite way of saying they both thought the knickers theory was ridiculous. "They were bought from Marks and Spencer last summer. They were the own-brand's third most popular line and they sold over a hundred thousand of them. Mr. Robertson maintains he bought them for his daughter, Isla, who lives at home with him. She's sixteen. He regularly shops for things for her and she has various pairs like it. Of course, that doesn't prove he didn't buy others for a different purpose."

"No. Is DCI Strong *very* excited about the link?"

"I would say he's *quite* excited, ma'am. A hundred thousand is a lot of knickers."

"Thank you."

Rozie picked up the boxes and took them back to Sir Simon's office. He was still on the phone, talking to Emily about engraved silver gilt champagne coasters. He rolled his eyes dramatically, tapped his watch again, and rolled his eyes some more. Rozie laughed. She was really very fond of him.

It was bad to lie to a man like that, but, damn, it was exciting.

21

THE QUICK TALK INTERNET CAFÉ in Clapham Junction contained three tables, a bar selling stodgy cakes and fizzy drinks, and a counter along the left-hand wall lined with eight computer monitors, six of which worked. It was fairly full for a Sunday morning, with five customers typing away at the keyboards and nursing their drinks. Two women in hijabs chatted quietly to each other, keeping an eye on a sleeping baby in a pram by the door. In the middle, a young man in a T-shirt hunched over his screen, lost in concentration, while the elderly man beside him muttered to himself, scattering his keyboard with cake crumbs as he hit each new key with his middle finger and waited for the result.

The neatly dressed, slightly balding man in an open pea coat nearest the counter had not come here to chat or eat cake. He was on a diet and none of the food suited him. The tea was stewed and crappy. He sipped from a chipped glass of tap water and wished he was at home in his flat in Richmond, with all mod cons and a decent kettle, and a computer he knew his way around better than this one.

But his home computer had its own IP address. He was aware of private browsing protocols, but equally aware that if anything went wrong, the best hackers in the country, working for the government, would be on his case in a heartbeat. Better to be here, in this anonymous little café, a ten-minute train ride away.

Billy MacLachlan had been researching Anita Moodie for twenty minutes, and as far as he was concerned, he had already struck oil with her Instagram feed. The girl was addicted to selfies, and she'd been posting for years. There were over two thousand pictures and he was going through every one of them. This part of the job was no hardship (though that tap water tasted foul; even the tea had been better). The girl liked to travel. She'd lived the high life. She enjoyed beautiful things and beautiful places. He enjoyed looking at them, through carefully chosen filters, pausing to make notes for follow-up research.

There was a pattern to the singing gigs she had done since leaving the School of Oriental and African Studies, where she'd got her first degree. A very interesting pattern. MacLachlan sketched it out in the cheap spiral-bound book beside the keyboard. He took a sip of water, followed it with tea (no, the tea was still worse), and scrolled down some more.

THE QUEEN WAS not the only person chagrined by the thought that Obama had arrived, with all the intelligence power the CIA could provide, and meanwhile the best brains in the police and MI5 hadn't been able to solve a little local murder. It wasn't for lack of trying.

DCI Strong looked up at the board attached to the partition wall in his Round Tower room, displaying an alarming array of suspects and question marks. A lot of people had access to Maksim Brodsky's room that night, assuming he let them in, or they knew their way around a basic Yale lock. Once there, all it took to actually kill him and stage the scene was a strong pair of hands, a bit of training, and some preparation. But who would want to? That was the problem David Strong kept coming up against.

The director general was still convinced about the sleeper spy theory, and he could be very persuasive. He was known in the intelligence world for a couple of fascinating insights into new and alarming strategies of supposedly friendly nations, based on painstaking backroom research. Patience and attention to detail were Humphreys's watchwords. Patience, he assumed, had been the key characteristic of the palace sleeper, and if he was right, it had served the man well. The murder had been committed, the crime remained unsolved—from the sleeper's point of view, it must be seen as a great success.

Although . . .

Strong was too polite to bring this up directly with Humphreys when they met with top brass, which was two or three times a week—but the Russian intelligence community was not gleefully celebrating the brilliant assassination of a dissident under the very nose of Her Majesty the Queen. Or, if they were, they were doing it so quietly that not a whisper of it had made it through to MI6's ears in the Kremlin and various Russian outposts.

If you're going to go to all that trouble to kill someone, and kill them in such a way, and after so much time inserting your killer into position, why keep it so firmly under your furry hat? After the killings of Markov in 1978 and Litvinenko in 2006, and the attempt on Gorbuntsov four years ago, the intelligence community had been alight with gossip and speculation, triumphalism and bravado, typical of Putin and his lot. Strong knew this, because he had asked. He wanted to understand Humphreys's world, and when you work out of Windsor Castle, people tell you things.

This wasn't the only reason Strong kept the field of suspects open. His natural due diligence was part of it. His team had investigated the ballet dancers exhaustively, and the boyfriend one of them was supposedly FaceTiming. (She was.) They had looked into Peyrovskaya's maid, even though she was tiny. There was no DNA match with anything in Brodsky's room. Not conclusive proof she wasn't involved, but hardly proof she *was*.

Then there was the girl from the intelligence meeting. She had bumped into Brodsky in the corridor outside his room, after he got back from playing the piano in the Crimson Drawing Room. They had been seen together at the time by a passing housekeeper. She said she had dropped a contact lens and he had helped her find it, and the housekeeper had confirmed her story. For a time, Strong thought she was the last person to see him alive. But why would she attack him? It couldn't have been planned. She didn't know she'd even be staying till a few hours before.

Had they had a mad sexual tryst? Had he abused her in some way? Had it gone wrong?

Strong had wondered about this, but then he had made the bombshell discovery about the Russian valet. It was prompted by something the commissioner had said, relating a story he had heard (he said from the Queen herself, although he might have been embellishing) about shenanigans between visitors and servants, and bets about getting people past security and into the guest suites.

This had got Strong thinking one evening last week, as he ran through every possibility once again with his little on-site team of three. Of course, the main security at Windsor Castle was designed to keep out outsiders and, above all, to protect the Royal

Family. It wasn't particularly designed to protect visiting princi-
pals, as they were called, from their own servants. Yes, staff were
not permitted to head down to the guest suites without an explicit
invitation—but if a guest wanted to conspire to play musical beds
with their maids and footmen, was there anything specifically to
stop him? Or her?

Anyway, it had kicked off an interesting line of inquiry. The
footmen and policemen on duty that night had been questioned
again, a little more rigorously, and Strong had discovered that
Vadim the valet had gone up twice, to visit first the beautiful Masha Peyrovskaya, then his master.

The first time the master had been drinking downstairs with
his hedge fund friend so it all made sense. But one of the DIs on
the team had noticed a couple of strange details in the footmen's
accounts. The first time, the valet had kept his head turned away
from the men in the corridors, talking to his companion, and his
suit was grey. The second time, he had looked them square in the
face, and his suit was black.

Bit odd. So the team had questioned the valet pretty hard, and
in the end he'd cracked. Turned out, he hadn't been having it off
with the gorgeous mistress at all. He was gay, as he'd said, with a
steady boyfriend. He had gone along with the story to please her,
but the very last thing he wanted was any suggestion that they had
done anything together.

It had *not* been he, Vadim, the first time, who went upstairs
with her. Nor any other man with the intention to make love to
her—Vadim was sure of that. Masha Peyrovskaya was a precious
jewel. She was loyal to her husband, and so excited to be at the castle that night. She would have done nothing to spoil the evening,
she was not that kind of woman. In fact, it was Mr. Brodsky who
had gone up with her, and they were friends, just friends. They
both loved music. Perhaps he had gone to discuss Rachmaninoff?

When they'd talked to Masha, she had sold out Meredith Gostelow instantly. The architect was in Saint Petersburg at the moment for work, so they couldn't talk to her in person yet, but she hadn't denied Masha's claim that *she* was the object of the young man's attentions. So, Brodsky had had it off with the old lady, not the young one. Who'd have thought?

Which meant he'd been away from his room for a couple of hours that they'd had no idea about. Strong was ashamed of himself for that. It didn't explain what happened next, though. The same security staff were certain the man they now knew to be Brodsky had gone back upstairs to the attic corridor alone. Meredith Gostelow had not accompanied him on that last journey. This put paid to Humphreys's conjecture that, because she was working on a project in Saint Petersburg, the woman was somehow a Putinesque, middle-aged Mata Hari, sent in to seduce and murder Brodsky after chicken and petits fours. Shame, though. Strong had rather liked that idea.

Vadim could have killed Brodsky himself, when he got back from putting Peyrovski to bed, Strong considered. Again, why? Because Brodsky had impersonated him? Murder seemed a bit of an overreaction.

The person who seemed most terrified about the whole thing was Meredith Gostelow. From her hotel room in Saint Petersburg she kept begging them not to say anything, because of her reputation as an international architect. (Strong had never heard of her. That didn't prove much, though, in the world of international architecture.)

Anyway, luckily for her, there was little danger of this nugget of information leaking out, because absolute paranoia about headlines in the press meant that this was the tightest, most-locked-down murder investigation Strong had ever conducted, or was likely to. His micro team were the most loyal men and women he could hope to work with. No documents were left lying around, ever. No stray messages made their way onto WhatsApp groups. Other officers at the Met, helping with research and interviews, were given strictly limited background details. All questions, even from close friends in the force, were met with bland replies. Even so, various very senior government officials and Humphreys's underlings would get in touch at regular intervals to make dire and unnecessary threats about what would happen if they were ever careless.

Only Singh trusted them to get on with their job and do it properly, the way they'd been trained. Strong liked the Met commissioner. He took a lot of crap and didn't pass it down the chain.

Meanwhile, Vadim Borovik had been the victim of this so-called homophobic attack in an alley off Dean Street in Soho. Strong was pretty sure that was a private matter to do with Peyrovski and his wife. He looked at his board again. Should he get the commissioner to tell Her Majesty about that, and about Brodsky being out and about after lights-out? She probably had better things to think about. It was up to men like him to deal with the nasty details.

An email alert arrived on his laptop with a ping. He opened it and swore loudly. This was something the Queen *would* want to know about. He was just glad he wasn't the one who would have to break the news.

22

I T WAS THE LAST QUIET WEEK at Windsor, before a return to town. Although "quiet" was always a relative word for the castle, and especially so with the horse show coming up in just over a fortnight, and over a thousand horses to accommodate. Philip was in his element.

"I'm off to Home Park to see how the obstacles are coming on for the driving."

He was standing by the door, jacket on, car keys in hand. The Queen looked at her watch. In less than ninety minutes she had a meeting with the master of the fabric of St. George's Chapel, to look at a proposal for more attractive nighttime illumination. You wouldn't think that lighting an ancient building from the outside would be a major issue, but for the denizens of Windsor, the furore over white light versus slightly blue overshadowed the whole debate about Brexit. She needed a clear head for it.

"I might come with you."

It was a five-minute run in a Range Rover down to the arenas in Home Park, within sight of Castle Hill, which rose majestically behind them now, above the trees. Philip, as ranger of Windsor Great Park, took his role very seriously and liked to inspect any important goings-on—and nothing was as important as the latest Royal Windsor Horse Show, which was about to play host to a record number of horses, several thousand visitors, and a television team from ITV.

At the moment, the land in question was a quagmire, lined with flatbed trucks and metal tracks and endless stacks of portable barriers. The foreman of works, anxious in steel-toed boots and a construction hat, pointed out areas of grass where the horse boxes would be parked, water and food provided, and where the shopping tents would go.

Further along, work was being done to improve the grandstands.

"The Queen's been coming since forty-three," Philip was telling the foreman. "Since the first one. They had dogs in the show then, too. Until a Labrador snaffled the King's chicken sandwich and they were banned forever." His barking laugh caused the foreman to take a step backwards.

"Actually, it was a lurcher," she corrected him, coming over. "And they raised over three hundred thousand pounds. Enough for seventy-eight Typhoons."

"The tea, ma'am?" the foreman asked, crinkling his brow in puzzlement.

"The *aircraft*. We used them to help win the war."

"My granddad was at Dunkirk, ma'am," the foreman ventured more confidently, since they were being conversational.

"Oh was he? How interesting. Did he survive the war?"

"Yes, ma'am. He played football for Sheffield Wednesday. He passed away five years ago. Fit as a flea till near the end."

"Good for him," she said. Though she was thinking the gentleman would have been not much older than she was. A generation hanging on by its fingernails.

Back in the castle, she felt grateful for that little burst of fresh air. Now she was plunged into a thousand details to consider. The whole family would be descending again, along with the King of Bahrain and his entourage. There was the question of the bedding for room 225, the preferred suite for special guests. A housekeeper had noticed that the favored linen was slightly frayed. Obviously they couldn't use it, but should they recommission the Edwardian embroidery, and what to replace it with in the meantime? And would Margaret's children mind not sleeping in their usual rooms, because they were needed for someone else? And then it was time to visit the master of the fabric in his den near the chapel, and oversee the fateful decision about the lights.

That done, there was a message from the trainer to say that Barbers Shop had pulled a muscle during a workout and was less than 100 percent certain for the show. It would be a tragedy if he couldn't make it. He had a real chance for the Ridden Show Horse and thoroughly deserved it, and anyway, she hadn't seen him for months and was looking forward to his arrival from Newmarket with his trainer. When Sir Simon approached her in the Grand Corridor, looking dour, she said, "No bad news, thank you. I've had quite enough for today."

But he didn't give his little sardonic smile. Instead his face hardened. "It *could* be worse, Your Majesty."

Which was hardly cheering.

"Come in. Tell me."

They went to the Oak Room, overlooking the quadrangle,

where she sat down and he explained that Sandy Robertson, her favorite page, had taken an overdose of pills and was recovering at St. Thomas's Hospital, having been discovered at home in Pimlico by his daughter.

"Thank you, Simon."

She looked utterly bereft, he thought. Bleak and defeated. He backed out of the room quickly to give her time to wipe away a tear if she needed to.

Alone, she took a breath.

"Bastard," she muttered, and she didn't mean poor Sandy.

DAYS PASSED without noticeable progress. In the kitchens, the laundry rooms, and the master of the Household's offices, nerves crackled and tempers frayed as everyone got by on too much coffee and too little sleep. In one of the cold rooms, the pastry chef was pouring a third batch of chocolate into molds for a new type of truffle to be served at one of the big receptions in a fortnight. He had been trying to get the ganache finish right for two days now, and it refused to work. He only had a few hours left in this room, with these molds, before he had to pack up his section's equipment to take back to Buckingham Palace. They only took the essential, personal implements they liked to work with every day, but even so, it added up. Then he'd be straight into garden party preparation before heading back here for the horse show, with only three days on-site to get ready.

The underbutler, who had speculated so accurately about the initial police investigation into Mr. Brodsky's sex life at the castle, was busy wondering if she was in the right place. For years, the idea of working for the Queen had been a dream. Then, after her top-class training, she was thrilled out of her mind when she passed the final interview. But for the last few days she hadn't got to bed before one in the morning. Each shift seemed to bleed into the next. And this morning she got shouted at by Prince Andrew for accidentally blocking a doorway while carrying two heavy chairs. She wouldn't mind, but what was it for? When loyal servants like lovely Sandy Robertson got suddenly sent home, and everyone told not to contact him, and now there was a rumor the poor man was in hospital. Is that what it came to? Is that all you got? There were websites offering six-figure salaries in big houses in warm countries for people with her background. Tonight, she might have another look at them.

In his study in the Norman Tower, overlooking his private garden in the old moat, Sir Peter Venn went over his list of meetings for the following week, ready to take over as titular head of the castle while the Queen was away. He sensed the unrest in the kitchens and corridors. Normally, that would calm down once a big event was over, but at the same time, he was acutely aware of the police team in the Round Tower next door, still busy with their investigation. Yesterday, out of the blue, he had been contacted by a journalist asking awkward questions about the Russian and why the autopsy report was not available. It was only a matter of time before idle curiosity turned into something more serious and somebody really started digging. Then all hell would be let loose.

Meanwhile, the head housekeeper had given him the updated plans for guest accommodation during the horse show. His wife, who was normally a paragon of unflappability, was in a bit of a panic. Over the years she had hosted ambassadors, field marshals, two astronauts, and several duchesses, but even she wasn't sure how to impress the likes of Ant and Dec and Kylie Minogue.

Rozie felt the rumblings in the air, like summer thunder. She tried not to worry, but she saw how hard everyone was working and sensed that something fragile was holding the castle family together. It was the same thing that made her not mind *too* much when cousin Fran had to schedule the wedding around her. And made her want to work on her days off, and put up with a damp outside wall in her bedroom, and accept she wouldn't be around for family Christmases and birthdays.

It was something about duty and trust and affection, but it worked both ways. What was happening to Sandy Robertson felt as if it was shaking the foundations of the castle. And what would happen then? What would all these people do who were giving up their lives—giving them willingly—to make one person happy? If the trust was gone, if the affection soured? It would be an earthquake, and the whole edifice could come tumbling down.

Rozie did what she always tried to do when she sensed the stress was getting to her: she got changed and went for a lunchtime run. Putting the miles behind her round the Great Park, she tried to make sense of what she knew. It was Rachel Stiles the police should be focusing on, surely? The girl drank; she took drugs; her DNA was found in Brodsky's room. Did she kill him and commit suicide? But what about the new girl—Anita Moodie? Did Stiles kill her, too?

After forty minutes of lung-punishing exertion, Rozie knew she hadn't made much progress in fixing the problem—but she felt better anyway.

"You're looking chipper," Sir Simon observed when she got back to the office. "Good news about your mother?"

Lying shamelessly, she gave a detailed health update on the hip. The endorphin high got her through the afternoon.

THE WEEK WAS coming to an end. Billy MacLachlan sat at the wheel of his four-year-old Honda Civic on Saturday lunchtime and marveled, not for the first time, at how bloody far away Suffolk was from . . . anywhere. Very nice when you got there, but for God's sake. Bloody miles.

His car radio lost the signal for the classical station he'd been listening to and he used the silence to mull over the conversation he'd had with a young woman in Edgware yesterday. She was a teacher at a posh girls' school in North London. Music, with a sideline in netball coaching. He'd caught her between lunchtime choir practice and a warm-up session for the Fourth Form B team, huddled at the back of an empty classroom cradling staff room coffees in thick, ceramic mugs.

Escort.

She had definitely said the word "escort." After about half an hour of talking, when she'd warmed up and the coffee had gone cold. He'd check his phone recording later, but he was sure of it. As in, "I know she was doing well, but even so, she liked nice clothes and, like, once I saw her in this amazing coat and then I realized it was this-season Gucci. And she had an Anya Hindmarch cross-body bag I'd wanted for ages and when I asked if she found it on Vinted she said no, it was new. And her main bag was Mulberry, and that looked new, too. Not being funny or anything, but I did even wonder a couple of times . . . I shouldn't say this."

"Go on."

"OK, so . . . Not being mean, but I wondered whether she was an escort. I know, it's silly. Anita wasn't that kind of girl. I mean, she was quite private mostly, with men. But she had a lot of nice things, and she wasn't the best singer in our year. She was good but . . . She was just lucky, I suppose."

Lucky, possibly. Talented, certainly. Anita Moodie had been at college with this girl, studying for a diploma in vocal performance. MacLachlan was building up a picture of her through conversations with old friends. To some, he was an old teacher, devastated to hear of her death and keen to find out about her later life. To others, he was a reporter, doing a piece on suicide. The police might pass this way later, and if they did, he didn't want them to notice who exactly had gone before. In a couple of hours, when he eventually got all the way to Woodbridge, he would be an old family friend, gathering reminiscences to pass on to her relatives in Hong Kong.

The Anita he was getting to know was a fiercely ambitious girl. After boarding school in Hampshire she had studied music at the School of Oriental and African Studies in London, focusing on the musical traditions of Africa, Asia, and the Middle East. She had followed it with the diploma at the Royal College of Music, where she was known as a steady if not stellar performer.

It was in her final year at SOAS that friends started noticing her improved lifestyle. She rented the same kind of flats as them in grotty parts of London, but she went on more holidays; wore better clothes; and drove her own car, a bubblegum-pink Fiat 500—all captured to perfection in her stylized Instagram posts.

With the exception of that teacher friend, they put the new bling down to Anita's success finding work on cruises and at elaborate parties in foreign locations. There were several images of her in grand hotels in hot locations: the kind of places that had fountains in the courtyard and McLaren supercars parked under palm trees. Anita looked increasingly at home in ball gowns, under glittering chandeliers. She eventually put a deposit down on a nice flat in Greenwich with a river view, not far from the O2.

What girl in her twenties could afford her own flat in London? Some friends assumed it was family money, but those who knew her well said her parents lived modestly in Hong Kong, running a language school, and it had been a struggle to cover her boarding school fees.

So. Who paid for the rent and the fancy handbags? Did she have some sort of sugar daddy? One of her school friends said that she had remained very close to her A-level music teacher. Maybe a thing for older men? The guy had retired to Suffolk and had agreed to a meeting. MacLachlan kept his mind open.

Maybe Mr. de Vekey had been . . . paternalistic. Or maybe he hadn't been in touch for ten years and would have nothing to say.

But it hadn't sounded like that when MacLachlan had called to arrange a meeting. De Vekey had seemed shocked and shaky and unsettled. A man with a lot on his mind.

As the A12 gradually unfurled its way through Essex towards the coast, MacLachlan wondered what exactly that might be.

23

AFTER TEA, the Queen made her way to her private chapel. Following the fire in '92, the old one had been made into the Lantern Lobby and used as a hall for welcoming guests. As it was where the blaze had started, the thought of worshipping there had been simply beyond her.

She would have come round in time, she saw now. Time heals almost everything. But she still didn't regret the decision.

The new chapel, created out of a converted passageway, had a glorious faux-Gothic ceiling made of green oak lined with cerulean blue. It was a family affair: her most personal contribution to the fabric of the place. Charles had been on the architectural committee, David Linley had made the altar, which was quite plain, as she liked them, and Philip had worked with a master craftsman to design the stained-glass window, which she passed on her way in.

The window was a work of art threaded with memories. The top trio of images depicted the Trinity, raised serenely above a grey-green vista of the castle and the park. God was looking down on them, holding the Household in his loving care. The bottom three encapsulated the day of the fire itself. In the middle, Saint George stood over a red-eyed dragon; to the left, a volunteer held a rescued portrait; to the right, a firefighter battled the flames, with the Brunswick Tower lit like a torch behind him. Philip's original idea for this last had been a phoenix, rising, which she had liked very much, but she preferred the final version. The castle did not rebuild itself: a tight-knit team did that, brilliantly, after the firemen battled night and day to contain the damage.

They were all part of her wider family and she still felt indebted to them, as one would. Though '92 remained her annus horribilis, she felt grateful each time she came in here, for what had followed. "Fear not, for I am with you." "I am your strength and shield." As a little girl she had been taught that if one was steadfast, one would see good triumph in the end. During the war, it was at Windsor that she had sheltered. It took a long time, sometimes, but it was true.

She sat in her usual seat, a crimson chair near the altar. Turning her thoughts to the present, she prayed for the Russian and the City girl and also the singer, whose role she was yet to fully understand. She prayed for her family, small and large, and gave thanks for the future generations who were starting out so well. Now, if only Harry could find a decent girl, that would be something. She prayed for insight, and the power to use what she had already learned to bring light into the current darkness before any more young lives were lost.

She was tempted to pray for insight into the three fifteen at Wincanton tomorrow, but God did not answer betting prayers.

The race required luck and judgment, born of years of experience and application, much like life.

IT WAS AT ABOUT THIS TIME, as he joined the North Circular from the A13 on his way back from East Anglia, that MacLachlan noticed the black BMW M6 three cars behind. He'd happened to spot one just like it on the way up. It had caught his eye because it was sleek and fast, and a model he wouldn't mind upgrading to—if ever they decided to double his pension. And because he was that way inclined, he'd noticed the diplomatic plates. He braked gently and pulled into the inside lane. The M6 coupe slid by a few moments later. Same plates. The driver even turned his head to look.

Numpties, he'd thought to himself. *If you're going to do it, at least find some nondescript car and do it properly.* All the same, he'd felt his heart rate go up as he put his foot back on the accelerator.

Now that he was fully concentrating, he noticed the white Prius, too, about twenty minutes later. This one was older and had standard license plates, just like a thousand Ubers. But it had started to sit about six cars behind soon after he reached Tower Bridge. He saw it drift in and out of view, never more than a couple of minutes out of sight, until he turned off the A4 at Chiswick, the other side of London, not far from home. Which could have been pure coincidence, except he'd added half an hour to his journey by going a convoluted route via Battersea, crossing the river north to south at Chelsea Bridge and south to north again at Putney: a journey that no satnav, however bonkers, would take. They were definitely following him, until they were sure where he was going. Good enough to use two cars. Amateur enough to use both of them badly, thank God.

So it was later than he'd anticipated by the time he got home, and too late to put in a call to Windsor Castle tonight. He'd have called the APS, but on a weekend he judged it would be just as efficient to call Her Majesty direct, if he timed it right. Around sevenish, between drinks and dinner, usually did the trick. It used to surprise him, how quickly she took his calls, if she was free to talk privately. Now he just accepted it as one of the things the gutter press would kill their grannies to know—but would never find out. He'd have to wait till tomorrow, but he was a patient man.

THE QUEEN WAS about to dress for dinner on Sunday evening when her assistant dresser brought in a telephone: the old-fashioned kind, anything but "smart," with a base and a receiver.

"Call for you, ma'am. Mr. MacLachlan."

"Thank you."

The dresser retired. The Queen glanced at herself in the dressing table mirror (tired, a little puffy) and lifted the receiver.

"Billy, how nice of you to call."

"Pleasure, Your Majesty. I think I've got what you were looking for. That Moodie girl didn't take her own life—not if all my sources are correct. Also, you asked if she spoke Chinese and she did. She studied Mandarin at school and spoke Cantonese at home in Hong Kong. I had a nose around to see if she spoke Russian, too, just in case, but I don't think so. She led an interesting life, you might say. Definitely something not quite right about it."

"Tell me as much as you can. I have about seven minutes."

"That'll be ample, ma'am."

He proceeded to fill her in on his investigations into the Instagram account and conversations with Anita Moodie's friends. "Then, yesterday, I visited her old teacher," he added. "She was in a bad way when she went to see him, a couple of days before she died. He assumed it was boy trouble, put it down to her artistic temperament et cetera, but she hadn't ever been like that before.

And she was *really* bad, you know what I mean, not just sad and weepy but really losing it. She was sitting in a spot on his lawn, he said, and rocking backwards and forwards, mumbling things he mostly couldn't understand. She'd seemed beside herself. Despairing."

"Doesn't that suggest suicide?" the Queen wondered. That was what the girl's friends thought, though it had come out of the blue.

"You might think," MacLachlan said, "but once Mr. de Vekey got talking, he changed his mind about how she'd come across— her mood, you know what I mean. She thought she was going to die. He couldn't calm her, he couldn't console her. And he said now he came to think about it she hadn't been upset so much as terrified. Scared out of her wits."

The Queen didn't like the sound of this teacher. "Didn't he think to warn anyone? Her parents? If she was in such a bad way."

"He said she told him not to."

The Queen didn't bother to ask the chief inspector how he had got the information out of the man in that case, because MacLachlan's talents in that direction were the reason she relied on him.

"What would you like me to do now, ma'am? I ought to warn you, though, they're on to me."

"Who?"

He told her about the black and white cars. "The diplomatic plates come from an Arabian embassy. Small country. Friendly. Hard to imagine them arranging an assassination." He named the country in question, and she agreed.

She thought about it.

"Don't do anything more for now. Thank you, but I think that's enough excitement for the time being. Will you be all right?"

"Yes, ma'am," he assured her. He'd like to see them try something. "Just let me know."

But already her mind was elsewhere. The pieces of the puzzle

were all there. She just needed to connect them. The basic shape
of it was clear, and had been for a while, but some stubborn details
refused to fit.

She could perhaps have solved it that evening, but as soon as
she ended the call, her dresser was back with fresh stockings to put
on, and then it was time for the last dinner at Windsor for a week,
which was full of friends and family.

THAT NIGHT, as she picked up her diary, she briefly thought about
the police interview with Rachel Stiles in her flat in the Isle of
Dogs (near the Millennium Dome, where one had spent what was
truly one of the most ghastly nights of one's life, which put a certain slant on things), and the eyes, and that single strand of hair.
And those knickers. Why the knickers? She could not make sense
of that at all.

As she often did when a problem seemed intractable, she decided to sleep on it. But the clock was ticking. If she *was* right,
that meant the hideous Humphreys was partly right, too, and that
meant the country was in danger until it was sorted out.

PART 4

A Brief Encounter

PHILIP HAD AN EVENT in town on Monday and was up and out, with his valet and his equerry, before she went for her last ride. She had hoped that the fresh air, the verdant parkland, and the comforting smell of pony would unleash a revelation, but in the end she was too nervous about the horse show, too sad to be leaving, and too busy with last-minute mental preparations for the week ahead to make any progress at all.

Rozie arrived with the boxes for her to look at before leaving. Rozie was available to travel with her, too, but the Queen wanted time to think.

"I'll see you at the palace."

"Yes, ma'am."

"There are a few things we need to talk about."

"Of course, ma'am."

"Come and find me after lunch."

An hour later, the Range Rover pulled discreetly out of the castle precincts and wound its familiar way towards the M4. Today was Princess Charlotte's birthday. The Queen put in a quick call to Anmer Hall to mark the occasion. They were busy preparing for a little party. She would see them soon, at the horse show. For now, all she got was a shy little "Hello, Gan-Gan" from Prince George. He was not a child who was normally backward in coming forward, but he was still nervous of technology. Perhaps one should be grateful. In a decade or so it would probably be impossible to prize him away from it.

She thought of the tight little Cambridge family, safe and secure and out of the spotlight in their Norfolk home. That was just as it should be. It had been like that for her, too, growing up in Mayfair with the reasonable expectation, then, of a lifetime of privacy. Now it was hard to remember what it had been like: to trust more than a close few friends, to take risks, and make mistakes in the happy certainty that it didn't really matter. Now everything mattered. Almost everyone talked.

The car picked up speed as it joined the motorway. She saw the double takes in several cars that passed them: drivers and passengers seeing the car with its matching escort, and squinting to see if they could spot her in the back seat.

It was a miracle that grubby little murder hadn't made the headlines by now. Only the maximum discretion by all concerned had made that possible. It couldn't have made Chief Inspector Strong's life very easy, keeping the investigation under the radar. Imagine if the tabloid papers had got hold of the story of the knickers and the lipstick. . . .

And then, suddenly, the piece of the puzzle containing the dressing gown and the cord fell into place. *Of course.* Chief Inspector Strong had done exactly what he was supposed to do.

In the miles that followed, the other pieces arranged themselves around it until everything about that night was clear, everything made sense.

It was the hair that had caused the biggest problem, but now that she understood the chain of events, the solution to the issue of DNA was obvious. In fact, it should have been the first thing she noticed.

She was clear in her mind now how the murder scene had been set up, and why. The worst of it was, she realized with desperate clarity, that she was the cause. The jokes she had made with Philip, those minor frustrations, they were not incidental detail—they were at the very heart of the poor man's humiliation. One was responsible for the wardrobe, the purple dressing gown, all of it.

Traffic on the motorway made the journey slow. The Queen looked out of the window to see a queue of planes in the distance, lining up in the sky to land. She forced herself to breathe calmly, and think.

But then, there was the question of what happened next. How could the girl be in two places at once? Or rather, how had two girls been in one place? How had nobody noticed?

It took a while to picture it properly. When she worked out what must have happened, she gasped out loud. Her protection officer turned from his place in the front passenger seat to check she was all right and she nodded to reassure him.

But she wasn't.

She saw what they must have done, and it was awful. Cold and calculating, and chilling, and such a dreadful waste. And even that had not been enough.

She went back over every detail, checking that it fitted with what MacLachlan had said, what Chief Inspector Strong's team knew, and what she herself and Rozie had discovered. Yes, it all connected. MacLachlan's latest findings gave her the courage to believe it was true.

It was patchy, but that could be fixed. If people knew what they were looking for, they would find it, and probably much more. She realized that there was one person above all who could start the process. If only she was still at Windsor! Damn and blast it! She would have to find an excuse to talk.

By the time the Range Rover sailed past Harrods in the mid-morning traffic, she had worked out what was needed and how to make it happen. She felt slightly better, but contemplating so much death and treachery had made her weary. She needed very much to see little George and Charlotte, and celebrate the joy of life. Ten days seemed a long time to wait.

"CAN YOU GET ME the governor of Windsor Castle on the phone? I need to ask him something."

"Yes, ma'am."

The Queen sat at her desk in her private study in Buckingham Palace, the phone nestled among a collection of photographs and flowers. The room's familiar furnishings and family portraits soothed her, but above all she loved its view of the plane trees planted by Victoria and Albert, whose branches now intertwined. She had taken the dogs for a long walk in the garden on arrival, which wasn't in the schedule, but her staff had responded with admirable calm. She felt better now. She could get on.

The switchboard had Sir Peter on the line within a couple of minutes.

"Ah, Governor, I meant to ask before I left, have they sorted out where they're going to park their monstrous television trucks? Because I simply will not have them tearing up the lawn."

For a few minutes she and Sir Peter discussed the niceties of the final horse show arrangements. They were a little less urgent, in his view, than Her Majesty made them seem, but far be it from him to criticize what mattered to her in her own home.

"Oh, and I was just thinking," she said in passing, "about the awful business with the girl who died in London. Yes, the cocaine girl. I suppose it was coming back to town that reminded me. I suddenly thought . . . You must have been one of the last people to see her. Yes, I know, but I wondered if she was taking drugs at the castle. It's the last thing we need. Do you know if Chief Inspector Strong's team next door to you looked into it? I remember meeting her. Quiet girl. Anyway, tell ITV what I said about the TV trucks. That should put the fear of God into them if nothing else will."

Afterwards, she made a quick call to Billy MacLachlan.

"I think it's time for you to do as you suggested. But very gently. Keep an eye on de Vekey afterwards. I'd like to think he'll be safe. And do you think someone should tip off MI5 about the payments? Thank you, Billy."

Rozie was standing nearby, ready to take notes. The conversations didn't fully make sense to her. Especially the one wondering whether Rachel Stiles had taken drugs at the castle. When did that become an issue? She was desperate to ask how things were going, but there seemed to be an unspoken agreement between her and the Boss that they never talked outright about what they were up to.

"Is there anything I can do, ma'am?" she asked.

"Could you find out if Rachel Stiles wore contact lenses? And you might have a word with the director general of MI5. Tell him I'd like to see him on Wednesday. I could do with a progress report."

BACK AT THE CASTLE, Sir Peter pocketed his phone thoughtfully. He was fairly certain that the director of the horse show had already addressed the issue of the TV trucks, but he would make doubly sure before reassuring Her Majesty. Meanwhile, there was that little question of the cocaine girl. Rachel something, was it? Stiller? Snipes?

He doubted she would have dared take drugs at the castle. Not during a top secret conference, surely? But it was true that while she had seemed on good form the first day he had met her, she had been less so on the second. He couldn't see how it would affect the police investigation into Brodsky even if she had been high as a kite, but with ultra-conscientiousness, he felt he should do his bit and check. If they *had* discovered drug taking at the castle, and the press ever got hold of it, that was the *Daily Mail* headline for the next few weeks. He would need to warn the communications team.

Sir Peter had a few people to see in the offices in the Lower Ward, but when his rounds were done and he was heading back to the Norman Tower for lunch with his wife, he popped into the Round Tower next door and trudged up the stairs to the little room on the third floor. DCI Strong was away from his desk, but his sergeant, Andrew Highgate, was there.

Now that he was actually standing in the presence of the police, Sir Peter felt faintly ridiculous about his mission. His conscientiousness began to seem to him more like unnecessary interference. Surely murder was of far greater concern to them than any possible drug taking? (And given what Sir Peter knew about various visitors over the years, it wouldn't exactly be the first time.) Nevertheless, DS Highgate, in the presence of a general, a knight of the realm, and the—to give him his full official title—constable and governor of Windsor Castle, was keen to do a thorough job.

"No, you did the right thing, sir. Thanks for popping in. Let me just pull up what we have on her. . . . Yes, this is Rachel Stiles. Expert on the Chinese economy. Not such a golden future, sadly.

Um . . . yes, sir, let me check. . . . No, this is definitely the right picture. We got it from her office. The original one we had from her security application was a bit small. I don't think we could have made a mistake. I can check again if you like. I'll give you a call in five minutes, unless you'd rather wait while I . . ."

Somewhat alarmed by now, Sir Peter said he would wait.

IN HIS GARDEN in Woodbridge some hours later, Guy de Vekey sipped from a glass of chilled pinot grigio while newly arrived swifts soared high overhead, a quiver of arrows. He loved this witching hour, as day turned to dusk and the sky shifted from peach to purple while shadows gathered on the lawn. Behind him, Elgar poured, bewitching and scratchy, from thick, black vinyl into the evening air.

He had vowed to keep a secret. Already he had told it once, to that man on Saturday, and now he was being asked to tell it again. His first instinct was to be true to his word. Anita was dead; how could he let her down now? And yet, wasn't it true that he felt . . . what was the word . . . released . . . by telling it the first time?

He had taught two generations of schoolchildren how to sing. Several had stayed in contact, some had invited him to their weddings or first concerts, but only a few had become real friends. Usually they were the ones with exceptional talent, but actually Anita hadn't been one of those. She was good, of course, but what really marked her out was how hungry she was—for life, for success, for the best she could possibly get—and how much she was willing to give for it. That was a talent in itself, in the cutthroat classical music industry. Anyway, despite the age gap she trusted him. She valued his advice. He'd seen her once every couple of years—always bubbly and cheerful, keen to show him photos of her travels and share her news. But the way she had been that last time, three weeks ago, when she came to visit . . . He cringed to think of it even now. It was desperate. *She* was desperate, a sniveling, snotty wreck.

And then that family friend had come to ask about her. Mister . . . what was it? He couldn't recall. . . . Anyway, for her parents' sake he'd wanted to understand Anita's state of mind before she . . . did that to herself. Who could know? Who could possibly know?

At the time Guy had thought it made sense for a young woman to have a bad day and be upset. But when the friend had asked about it, he'd been surprised by how bad it sounded. Somehow, in explaining, Guy had let it all come gushing out. Some secret keeper, he.

Talking about it on Saturday, the change in Anita seemed odd. Sudden. Unexplained. Guy saw now it hadn't been sadness he'd felt coming off her in juddering waves—it had been abject terror. She'd even foretold her death. He'd told her, begged her, not to do anything—but perhaps she hadn't been talking about a broken heart.

Perhaps the man was right, when he'd called again just now, concerned. Perhaps Guy should say something to the police. They might think he was a fool, but what if he wasn't?

Looking at it in a new light, had she been trying to tell him something all along? Anita had been secretive and scared, and two days later she was dead. Guy drained his wineglass. He prayed he was wrong.

"Have you decided?"

His partner came out to join him and put a hand on his shoulder. He reached over and put his arm around her.

"I'll call them first thing in the morning."

25

O N TUESDAY MORNING there was a Thanksgiving Service in Westminster Abbey for Sir Geoffrey Howe, who had been very entertaining in the days of Margaret Thatcher, and was another child of '26. The Queen didn't go, because if she went to one, she would have to go to the lot of them, but she would have liked to have attended this time. He was a kind and decent man, an honorable politician—which, God knew, wasn't always the case—and sound on cricket. Another loss.

At her age, and Philip's, they were constantly getting news of death. It was almost daily these days, and always grim. In fact, Philip said last winter, "If they invite me to one more bloody memorial service I shall boil the lot of them." But he didn't mean it. And at least most of their dear friends had lived full lives.

She peered at herself dispassionately in the glass. During the Royal Mail visit someone had reminded her (often, people proudly told one things about oneself that were not entirely news) that hers was the most reproduced image in the history of the world. She had willingly forgotten it the first time: it was information no human being should be forced to bear. One would have thought it would be Diana. A friend in the nineties told her that he had just come back from the higher reaches of Nepal, far from all cars, phones, and even radio. There, in the foothills of Annapurna, he had seen a farmer brandishing a medieval-looking scythe for harvesting, and wearing a T-shirt with her late daughter-in-law's face emblazoned on it. Wherever you went, there she was.

But outdoing all newspapers, magazines, and souvenir shops there were banknotes and postage stamps. So simple, when you thought about it. At home and across the Commonwealth, when in doubt, they used one's profile on the currency or the post. Fortunately from when she was rather younger and had not so many chins. And she had lived an awfully long time. . . .

Leaning forward, she adjusted her spectacles and inspected the royal nostrils for hairs. Aging was such an undignified process. She had never thought of herself as a beauty, but looking back from a great distance, she realized now that perhaps she had been. Fortunate, if they would insist on printing one's face a billion times on everyday objects. Now it was mainly a question of keeping advancing hair follicles at bay.

Billy MacLachlan was lucky to catch her at her dressing table again, at this time in the morning. The conversation was very brief.

"I spoke to Mr. de Vekey, Your Majesty."

"Did you manage to persuade him?"

"I think so."

"Excellent. And you made the other call?"

"Yes. It was an online form, but same effect."

"Thank you."

"No problem, ma'am. Have a good day."

LATER, she was coming to the end of her boxes when there was an almighty commotion in the corridor. Feet stomped, doors were slammed, and voices were raised.

Sir Simon had already come in to collect the papers. He remained impassive, but the Queen looked annoyed.

"See what it is, would you?"

But before he could do anything, the door was flung open and the Duke of Edinburgh strode through it, dark pink in the face and fuming.

"Did you hear what that bastard Humphreys did yesterday?"

"Thank you, Simon."

Sir Simon let himself out without a whisper. She turned to Philip.

"No."

"Interviewed my valet. My bloody valet. For *six hours,* in the middle of the night. Without asking me, or even telling me, by God. I only found out this morning."

"Goodness. Why?"

"Because they think he's a bloody Soviet agent. God knows why. The man's never been further east than Norwich. And you heard about Robertson? Discovered by his own daughter and rushed to hospital. Hounded, is what they're being. I've had enough of Humphreys stomping all over our Household like some tin-pot dictator."

"I know what you mean."

"Do you? He's been farting about Windsor Castle with impunity for weeks, and now he's farting about here. You need to put a stop to it before there's a crisis."

She raised an eyebrow. "Would you like me to sack the head of MI5?"

"Yes, I bloody well would."

"I'm sure that would go down well with the prime minister."

"Stuff the prime minister."

"I'm seeing him this evening," she said. "I'll tell him you said that."

"With bells on. Look, Lilibet, I'm serious." He was calming down a bit. Not many people would have noticed from his demeanor, but he was. He came over to her desk and rested his hand on it. "Humphreys can't go on upsetting our people for no good reason. He doesn't have a shred of evidence for his tin-pot theory."

"I know. And I'm seeing him soon, actually."

"Are you?" He stood up straight again. "And you'll call him off?"

"I'll do what I can," she offered.

Though genuinely furious on behalf of his staff, the Duke knew he was asking unreasonable things from his wife. He was wrong-footed by how placid and accommodating she was being.

"Really?"

"Yes, really."

"I see. That's very good news. When?"

"I'm not sure exactly," she said. "Sometime tomorrow, I think. If we can fit him in around"—she adjusted her bifocals and looked down—"the Commonwealth secretary general, the Bishop of Leicester, and Michael Gove."

"Ha! You're making that up." He was back in good humor now. His outbursts rarely lasted long.

"No."

"The things you do for your country."

She twinkled at him.

"And you'll read Humphreys the riot act when you see him?" he checked.

Her expression was enigmatic, but she smiled. "Something like that."

26

B Y WEDNESDAY, life at Buckingham Palace had slipped into its old routine. It was as if they had hardly been away. Rozie was busy liaising with the Japanese about their prime minister's imminent visit, and the Cabinet Office with arrangements for the Queen's official birthday in June.

Rozie had been able to report to the Boss that Rachel Stiles, the cocaine girl from Docklands, was long-sighted and had worn glasses sometimes but not contact lenses, as far as she could ascertain. The Queen had accepted the news with little more than a noncommittal "mmmm." Rozie was burning to ask more, but didn't. She knew the Queen still didn't believe MI5's theory about the Russians. From all the work Rozie herself had done, and what she knew about Billy MacLachlan's activities, it was clear that Brodsky, Rachel Stiles, and Anita Moodie were connected somehow. She suspected that Anita had impersonated Rachel, but couldn't see where the link was. Had Brodsky made it happen in some way? He knew Anita, after all. Was *he* a spy? Was that what MacLachlan needed to talk to MI5 about?

Rozie felt left out, but not abandoned. This surprised her. She thought she'd be more resentful of the Queen for not explaining herself more clearly—but that was simply how the Boss worked. She was not your friend, and you were not her confidante. For someone who was constantly entertaining, she led a very lonely life and after so many leaks and stories over so many decades, starting with her own governess, who had misunderstood what could and couldn't be shared about the little princesses, it probably took years to earn her trust. Her dresser had it, Rozie thought—but she'd been with the Household since 1994. Rozie had been here for six months.

GAVIN HUMPHREYS WAS a methodical man who lived by an old adage, beloved of his military father, known as the Seven *P*s: *Proper Planning and Preparation Prevents Piss-Poor Performance.* The director general of MI5 planned, he was prepared, and he never expected to underperform.

So, a call to Buckingham Palace to update the Queen on progress in the spy hunt was nothing to be unnerved about. It was only as he was leaving his office on Millbank that he felt a quick flutter of nerves. It would be nice if all the planning and preparation had actually produced an eighth *P* by now: Progress. These things were not to be rushed, of course; Her Majesty would understand that. She was very understanding all round, from what Singh had told him.

However, the Duke of Edinburgh had taken things badly yesterday, apparently. And the valet theory had proved to be a bit of a blind alley, which was awkward. It had looked promising to start with: the man's ex-girlfriend had worked for not one but two hotel chains run by known Putin sympathizers in Turkey. It would have been easy for the FSB to get to him through her, but it turned out he had a new girlfriend—a clerk of some sort in the Royal Household—and he'd been in her bed the night of the dine and sleep. She was the daughter of the deputy head of GCHQ, and as witnesses went, about as unimpeachable as one could hope for, dammit. They were also not significantly further along with the royal page or the archivist. Humphreys was beginning to suspect the agent was planted even more deeply than they'd anticipated.

Vladimir Putin had played his cards brilliantly, not for the first time. He was an unprincipled twenty-first-century dictator, but you had to admire the man.

An equerry accompanied him to the door of the Queen's Audience Room, where the meeting would be. He took a deep breath, and prayed there wouldn't be corgis.

There weren't. The room was surprisingly normal, after all the marble and statues leading to it. It was painted blue, with the usual art and antique mirrors, but it had a light, feminine touch. The high-heeled assistant was there, and the Queen asked if he minded her staying to listen, which he didn't. Even better, there was no sign of a furious Prince Philip. Her Majesty was, as Singh had said, all polite encouragement and sympathy. She knew how difficult, and how essential, the job of protecting the nation was.

They sat on silk-covered chairs. He did a reasonable job, he thought, of explaining the difficulties of exposing Putin's cunning infiltration, but asserted that with time they would most certainly get to the bottom of it. He sensed Her Majesty's continued displeasure at the disruption to life at Windsor Castle. She was too invested in her servants. Humphreys wouldn't know about that—he and his wife had a cleaning lady who came twice a week, and whose surname they still didn't know. It paid not to get sentimental, but of course you couldn't tell the sovereign that, especially at her age. He courteously assured her they were going as fast as they could.

"There's one interesting detail," he mentioned, by way of encouragement. "We've established that a visitor to the castle that night was an impostor. It was the governor who spotted it."

"Oh?"

"She had a minor role, ma'am. No serious threat to national security, but of course we're looking into that, too, and we've already had a lucky break with that investigation. It's very unlikely that it's connected to the Brodsky case. She wasn't even supposed to be staying there. One of those strange coincidences."

He smiled and shrugged. The Queen smiled, too, and it was time to wind up the visit.

"I'll see you out," she said, which seemed to him unusual, but it was her palace, and she said she was going that way anyway.

As they walked down the thick-carpeted corridors, with the equerry and the high-heeled assistant three paces behind them, the Queen mentioned conversationally how busy she was going to be now that the summer schedule was underway.

"Lots of visits to schools and universities, as one does."

She mentioned a few. For someone her age, her memory was pretty sharp. One of them was the school where Brodsky told her he'd learned piano, apparently, which brought the mood down a bit. A place called Allingham. She remarked that the Russian had been an excellent pianist and she was looking forward to seeing the music department. And then they were at the stairs and the visit was over. Humphreys was grateful she hadn't mentioned the valet. More than that, she'd been positively chatty.

As he left through a side door to search for his driver, he sighed with relief.

As soon as he got back to his desk, a call from the Met commissioner came through.

"How was she?"

"Perfectly fine. Any news your end?"

"Actually, something's happened. We've got some interesting CCTV footage. It'll come through your channels anyway, but I thought you'd like to know."

27

ON THURSDAY, the Japanese prime minister came to visit. Standing at a podium next to David Cameron, like President Obama before him, Shinzo Abe warned of the dangers of voting for Brexit in the upcoming referendum. Even the Japanese were concerned. Rozie hated all the doom and gloom, but she wasn't too worried. After all, the Scottish referendum had turned out well in the end. Besides, Japan wasn't her problem today. The audience with the Queen would be a short one and Sir Simon ate that kind of diplomacy for breakfast.

It was Rozie's day off and, as next week would be crazy busy, Sir Simon had told her to take it. So she was meeting a billionaire in a suite in Claridge's for the afternoon. Masha Peyrovskaya had asked to talk to her again.

What surprised Rozie, walking into the gleaming, butterscotch lobby of the smartest hotel in London, was not how overwhelming all the low-key luxury was, but rather how at ease she felt. The job was rubbing off on her. This one, and the one before at the bank, where team-building weekends were routinely held in spa hotels in the country and client dinners in the private rooms of restaurants lit by Venetian chandeliers and fueled by vintage wines. She liked vintage wine now, and knew a bit about it. She liked the click of her Francesco Russo heels on the lobby's black-and-white marble floor. She liked the momentary flash freeze on the concierge's face when she mentioned the Peyrovski name, before she was smoothly directed to the Grand Piano Suite. Her own face did that, too, when meeting a king or president. But she was getting just as good at the smooth part afterwards.

Upstairs in the suite, Masha was seated at the piano, playing something bold and dramatic, her body swaying as her arms reached for distant keys. Rozie stood watching for a while without saying anything. The personal maid who had opened the door to her disappeared into another room.

Eventually, the piece drew to an end. Masha took a deep breath and closed her eyes.

"Tchaikovsky," she said, without turning. "It suits my mood."

"You play really beautifully."

"I know." Masha glanced towards the window to her left, where the net curtains had been pulled back to reveal the Mayfair roofscape. "I should have been a professional." She shrugged and gave Rozie a faint smile. "You came. And how is Her Majesty?"

"Very well, thank you."

"You send her my kind regards?"

"Of course."

"If she ever . . . want to listen to more Russian piano playing . . ." Masha looked wistful.

Rozie wondered at first if she was angling for some kind of job.

Then she realized, the poor woman just wanted to see the Queen again, to be close to her. The Boss had that effect on some people. Actually, on most people, in Rozie's experience.

"It's a shame she can't hear Mr. Brodsky," Rozie said, changing the subject slightly. She was still not entirely sure why she'd been summoned.

"You like a drink?" Masha asked. She got up and walked over to a velvet sofa, throwing herself down on it at a rakish angle. Rozie sat more decorously on one of the armchairs opposite. Masha was wearing skinny jeans and no shoes, a loose T-shirt, and several necklaces. Her hair looked unwashed and unbrushed, and there was not a trace of makeup on her. She was, if anything, more beautiful than before.

Rozie was about to suggest a cup of tea when a butler emerged bearing a tray with tea, coffee, still and fizzy water, two kinds of smoothie, and a crystal bowl of fruit.

"Please, be comfortable," Masha insisted, with a grand gesture to Rozie that dismissed the butler at the same time. He withdrew. Rozie grabbed a pink smoothie, kicked off her shoes, and tucked her feet underneath her. She still had no idea what was going on, but she might as well enjoy it.

"How can I help?"

What followed was a very strange hour, where Masha poured out her marital woes to Rozie in unsparing detail.

"He treats me like a snail under his shoe. He thinks all I care about is art, but how can he know what I think when he never talk to me? We have not made love since seven weeks. He used to be a wonderful lover but now . . . he do it like he hate me." Masha stared up at the ceiling. "His last present to me was a little bichon frise. He say a bitch deserve a bitch. Can you imagine? To his *wife*? I give the dog to the cook. He sack the cook. And she was a good cook." Now she played with her ring, spinning the gull's-egg diamond around her finger, watching it catch the light. "Every day, he question me about Vadim. Is he really gay? Was it a game? Did we have threesome? He is disgusting. He deny ordering the beat-up, but I know it is true. He is mad with me for helping Maks. I said I would leave him and he said go. So I go—here—to the most expensive hotel room I can find. He have me watched but I don't care."

"It sounds . . . difficult," Rozie said, aware of the understatement. She could never stay with a man who used a dog as an insult, let alone the rest. But then, she would never have accepted the gull's-egg ring in the first place. They tended to come with conditions, she thought.

"Do I leave him?"

"I'm no expert—"

"You work for the Queen! You give expertise at highest level, all the time."

"Not in matters like this."

"She has four children, all divorced!"

"Only three of them. The Earl of Wessex—"

"She understands the pain. She asks for your advice, no?"

"She really doesn't."

"I think she does," Masha said with finality, spinning round on the sofa and rearranging her languid limbs so her legs were tucked underneath her, like Rozie's. "I think she trusts you. *I* trust you. You have something. You are the *only* person I trust. That is why you are here."

"I don't think—"

"You don't yap, yap, yap like all the others do, giving me advice, telling me to leave him, like my mother, or stay until I earn a billion in divorce, like my sister, or stay forever, like my baba. What should I do?"

Rozie frowned. "You're really asking me?"

"Of course. Tell me. Now you are smiling. Why are you smiling?"

Rozie refused to be drawn in. "You said it yourself, Masha. You don't want people telling you what to do. You know all your options. What do *you* want?"

"Hmmm." Masha looked genuinely thoughtful. "Nobody ask me that before. Ha! You are clever! You see."

"My sister's a counselor," Rozie admitted. "It's her you should be talking to."

Masha raised an eyebrow. "Oh? OK."

"I was joking. She's in Frankfurt."

"That is where? In Surrey?"

"No—*Frankfurt*. In Germany."

Masha gazed at the ceiling for a moment, thinking. "OK."

"What do you mean, 'OK'?"

"I mean, I fly her back to London for sessions. She can come here, talk to me in Claridge's. *She* can tell me what to do."

A vivid image spooled through Rozie's head: Fliss, getting on a regular flight to Heathrow; Fliss, here, in this suite, sipping a smoothie and talking to a beautiful, sad Russian. She would absolutely love it. And she'd get the chance to catch up with family before going home.

Masha was quite serious about the offer. Pleading, even.

"I'll ask her," Rozie said. But she knew that, though she'd tell Fliss all about it, she'd never present it as a serious proposition. The last thing she wanted was her sister getting caught up in the world of Yuri Peyrovski. She believed Masha's story about how Vadim got beaten up. This stunning woman in the Grand Piano Suite was more at risk, she thought, than most of the people she knew, and she knew plenty of people whose lives were precarious.

Suddenly the sense of threat, which had receded as the Queen looked into the Belt and Road girl, felt very real again.

AFTER THE VISIT, she took the opportunity to do some shopping in nearby Oxford Street. Half an hour later her feet were hurting in their heels and she was shocked and upset by some idiot practically pushing her into the path of a bus. If it wasn't for her quick reactions it could have been nasty. She decided to take the tube from Oxford Circus back to Green Park.

It was at the top of the escalator going down to the platform that she felt the first prickle of alarm. Perhaps the bus incident had done it. But when she got jostled hard and almost flung down the right-hand side, she could have sworn she saw a smirk on the face of the tall, blond guy on the step behind her as she flailed to catch her balance. This time, it was the man in front of her who saved her, reaching out a hand to grab her arm.

"Wear trainers next time, mate. Idiot," he muttered.

"Yes. Thank you," she said, too distracted by the vanishing smirk to take the other guy on.

She glanced behind her as she threaded her way through the lunchtime crowd towards the Victoria Line. She was looking for the shock of blond hair, but it was gone. All the time she wondered if it was just coincidence, if she was being paranoid. But when she reached the platform, she took care to stay well back from the edge,

A train came a minute later and she got into one of the middle carriages. It was comfortingly full of people—so busy, in fact, that she had to stand. A group of rowdy students got in behind her. Only one stop. She'd be glad to get home.

But as soon as the train moved off, she felt movement in the group of students. Her pricked senses caused her to look round and glimpse a flash of blond underneath a dark grey hood. He was three feet away, moving closer, with no expression, but when he briefly caught her eye he flashed the smirk again. The students parted to let him through. A vestige of her military training told her there was something odd about the way he was moving his arms and shoulders. She looked down to see his left hand folded into a fist, at once gripping and hiding something small and dark.

Looking up, she made sure not to catch his eye again. He was calm and steady, the smirk fixed in place. Whatever he had come to do, his body language said he was prepared and unstoppable.

He was a foot away. She guessed his height at six foot two—three inches taller than her—and his weight at about twelve stone. He was slim but muscular, with the neck of a weight lifter and the even tan of a man who exercised a lot outdoors. Some people might think him good-looking, but there was a wolfishness about his expression. She wouldn't have liked him, even if she didn't think he was carrying a knife.

The train was at maximum speed now, plunging noisily through the tunnel. She shifted her own weight onto the balls of her feet and looked around at the nearby passengers, assessing the risk to each one. There was more space near the farther door of the carriage so she pushed her way towards it, apologizing gently as she went. He went at a similar speed, smiling his apologies, too.

Reaching the doors, she stopped. She didn't look round, but she could sense him behind her. Soon his reflection came into view, distorted in the glass. He wouldn't do anything yet. He would want to wait until the train was at the station so he could do what he had come for and make a quick getaway. She guessed a jab to the body—something low and hard to spot. But maybe he wouldn't do anything now anyway, if he thought she'd spotted him.

The train plunged through the tunnel for another thirty seconds, then juddered and began to brake. He was right up close. She took a breath and tried to relax her shoulders. Metal squealed on metal and they were both thrown sideways a little as the train slowed rapidly.

The punch came from nowhere, and the pain was blinding. He staggered back into another passenger, putting his right hand up to his nose. He still couldn't see, and he felt cartilage where it shouldn't be. She'd broken it. The bitch.

He lashed out at her with his other hand, the one grasping the knife, but before he could make contact the handle was knocked from his grip. Instinctively bending to get it, he felt another flash of almost paralyzing pain. She had nutted him in the face this time, knocking his jaw back with the top of her head. Ignoring the terrified shouts coming from behind him, he growled his fury and lunged at her, receiving a sharp knee to the balls. All the breath left his body.

She was just a secretary in fuck-me shoes! Fuck her! He was on his knees and as his vision started to come back fully he saw the knife on the floor, an arm's length away, as the train pulled into Green Park station. Everyone around was drawing back. He made a lunge for the knife; she shouted at him to stop but he didn't listen. Next thing he knew, he was lying prone with her weight on his spine and his right arm bent tight behind him.

"Make a move and I'll break your fingers," she grunted into his ear, so he could hear her over the panic and shouting.

He told her where to go. To his astonishment, she was as good as her word. The pain was excruciating as he felt his little finger snap, and the next two were pulled apart so hard he wondered if he'd have the use of his hand again.

He screamed and swore, and as soon as the train doors opened he threw her off with every ounce of strength in his body and hurtled through the waiting crowd on the platform.

She didn't follow him. The adrenaline rush was already making her dizzy. She was exhausted and, now that it was over, slightly scared. She heard a sound like raindrops and realized that the people in the carriage were applauding.

"Did he hurt you, love?" a woman asked, crouching beside her.

"Shit, the knife! Watch out!"

Someone asked if they should pull the emergency cord, but Rozie said no. The fight had lasted seconds: not long enough for anyone to take a decent video. The last thing she needed was a crowd snapping pictures to paste on Twitter. While she dragged herself outside, they held the doors open, glad to get on with their journeys.

Rozie sat against the platform wall with her head between her knees, catching her breath. Soon London closed around her, and it was almost as if he had never been there at all.

28

Friday involved a trip to Berkhamsted School (not Alling-ham) in the state limousine. The Queen's equerry, her lady-in-waiting, and Sir Simon were waiting for her beside the car. It should have been Rozie, who had organized the day, but she was indisposed. Which was something that never happened. Rozie was not an "indisposed" sort of person.

"Oh dear," the Queen said. "Nothing serious, I hope?"

"She got attacked on the tube. Poor bastard who did it obviously didn't realize he was going for a decorated war veteran. Rozie thinks he was trying to steal her handbag. But he—" Sir Simon stopped.

"What, Simon? He what?"

"He had a knife, ma'am," he admitted. And regretted it. The Queen looked really shocked, which was rare.

"Is she all right?"

"Absolutely. Just a bit shaken. He isn't, though. She thinks she broke three of his fingers."

"Good girl." The Queen had a clear idea about goodies and baddies, and what should happen to each. All her children had had self-defense training and Anne had needed it, when she was nearly kidnapped all those years ago. The papers had gleefully reported her retort, when ordered to get out of the car by a man wielding not one gun but two. "Not bloody likely!"

That was her girl. It was a tremendous relief, to know her APS was made of similar stuff.

When Rozie appeared again on Saturday, the Queen was contrite. She didn't say so, of course, because one didn't, but she was.

"How are you, Rozie? Better, I hope?"

"Completely well, Your Majesty."

"I gather there was quite a fracas."

"Nothing I couldn't handle, ma'am."

The Queen smiled. "So I'm told. I'm glad to see this job has softened you up."

"Quite the opposite." Rozie grinned. "Bring it on. I did warn the man before I took action."

The Queen nodded. "Very considerate. Even so, I think you should be careful about going out, for a while."

"Don't worry—I will be."

"I mean, *very* careful. I'd like you to stay on palace grounds, if you can, unless you're on official business."

Rozie gave a rueful shrug. "That afternoon was my own fault. I went to see Masha Peyrovskaya. I knew her husband was dangerous, but I really had no idea how bad it could get. I don't think he'd try it twice, though, ma'am. It would be too obvious."

The Queen sighed. "I don't think this was down to Mr. Peyrovski. Why did you go to see Mrs. Peyrovskaya, by the way? I don't remember suggesting it."

"You didn't, ma'am; *she* did. I wasn't sure why, but it turned out she wanted marital advice. Things aren't going well."

"You didn't give any, I hope."

"Actually, I didn't. I have no idea how married people stay together."

"Practice. But good. The last thing one needs is to get caught up in another divorce. Stay well away."

"I planned to, ma'am. But he came after me anyway. Or at least, he sent someone." Rozie felt so relieved she hadn't seriously considered getting Fliss caught up in all of this. While she was perfecting self-defense drills at Sandhurst, Fliss was winning the freshers' prize for most tequila shots downed while J-Setting like Beyoncé. Fliss would win every time on the dance floor; not so much in a fight with a knife-wielding Russian heavy. But wait—hadn't the Boss just said Mr. Peyrovski might not be behind it? "I mean, I assumed it was him. Do you think it wasn't?"

The Queen gazed steadily from behind her bifocals. "This has nothing to do with Mrs. Peyrovskaya. Or at least, only very indirectly."

"But I thought . . ."

"You were asking questions about Rachel Stiles. At my request, I know. But please don't, anymore. Not for now."

Rozie thought back. "But I only asked about her contact lenses recently, or lack of."

"I know," the Queen said, "and that's what worries me."

THE LONDON HIGHLIGHT of the following week was supposed to be the garden party at Buckingham Palace on Tuesday, but sadly for everyone, it was a bit of a washout. Even the Queen was noticeably disappointed. She knew how special the day was for everyone who came to see her and she always wanted them to see the garden at its best, and not from under the dripping canvas of a marquee. So often, the first week in May was one of the finest, but this year it was benightedly unpredictable. Charles blamed global warming, of course, and one tended to agree with him.

The thing was, if it was raining hard in Westminster it was almost certainly raining just as hard in Windsor. The horse show was due to start on Wednesday, with a day of dressage and special access for local townspeople, who were always so accommodating about all the crowds and queues of horse boxes. It had been arranged a year ago, and hundreds of people had put in so much work. But the director was warning her that the day might have to be canceled if the ground got too wet.

And then, to cap it all, she thwacked her leg against a footstool while rushing to stop Candy from stealing a plate of biscuits from the tea table, and she had to spend an evening in bed with a cold pack on it, feeling thoroughly miserable.

It was Sir Simon who brought the next piece of news, which cheered her up tremendously and almost, but not quite, made up for the fact that the car parks at Home Park were indeed flooded, and "Windsor Wednesday" was canceled, for the first time ever, to everyone's dismay.

Sir Simon, who brought that news, too, was surprised by how much of a smile the other detail brought to Her Majesty's face that morning. He simply explained that Gavin Humphreys had asked him to inform her that the murder investigation was taking a new and unexpected direction. Sir Simon had thought the update would depress her further, because presumably it meant the whole thing would take even longer. This would give the tabloids ever more opportunities to find out about the purple dressing gown and humiliate them all.

And yet, she smiled and said "Oh, really?" and looked rather insouciant.

"I can ask him to give you more details, ma'am, if you'd like them?"

"No need. As long as he keeps us in the general picture. And tell him to let us know if there's anything we can do to help."

"Yes, ma'am. Of course. Although I'm sure he has it all under control."

29

ROZIE NOTICED that the Boss was looking more cheerful on Thursday, but that was only to be expected because by then they were all back at Windsor, her leg was well enough to walk on, and before doing the boxes she was ready to head out in the cool but sunny air and see the horses.

The rainstorm had passed. The car parks had recovered enough to receive the queue of visitors. The forecast was fair. And best of all, Barbers Shop was fully recovered and raring to go in the Ridden Show Horse Championship and the birthday pageant.

It was a grinning Queen who drove one of the Range Rovers down to Home Park, where the crowds had already gathered to watch the show. The championship was one of the opening events in the Copper Horse Arena. Dressed in a cardigan, a padded jacket, boots, and a scarf, she mingled with riders, trainers, and other horse fans, making jokes about the weather and miming her horror at the biblical flood.

Rozie had come down as well, accompanying Sir Simon. She was still advised against trips beyond the castle confines, but here she was as safe as she would ever be. They watched the competitors from a position opposite the VIP stand, enjoying a rare moment of relaxation together.

Rozie soaked up the feeble but persistent rays of sun; the reassuring gravelly tones of the announcer on the PA system; and the smell of horseflesh, wet sand, and fly spray. It took her back to her teenage days, on borrowed rides, nervous about the biggest jumps and keen to get out there.

"D'you ride, Simon?" she asked, realizing she'd never really heard him talk about it.

"No. My mother was allergic to horses. Wouldn't go anywhere near them. Funny, really, because she was allergic to dogs, too, and we had two terriers and a Labrador. And three cats. And a guinea pig." He shrugged.

"Maybe she just didn't like them?" Rozie suggested.

"I did sometimes wonder. We all wanted to ride, but my sisters were besotted. The younger one, particularly—Beaty. She knew everything there was to know, exactly how to groom a horse and braid its tail, what all the different breeds were, how to cure croup. This was just from reading stories about them. I think my mother was terrified Beaty would become irrevocably obsessed if we went anywhere near a real one. And of course we couldn't afford it. Not with the school fees."

Rozie nodded. For a moment, she imagined being the sort of girl who grew up having conversations with people about the day-to-day drama of choosing between owning a horse and going to boarding school. There had been a few kids like that at primary school in Notting Hill, but they had always lived in another world—the one of the pastel town houses, so close and always so firmly out of reach. She laughed, putting an affectionate hand on her boss's shoulder.

"Poor you! What a nightmare that must have been."

"It was!" He grinned back at her. "My troubled childhood."

Rozie possibly didn't know it, but her straightforwardness was what got her hired. All the candidates had been very clever, with stellar records in the Civil Service or the City, but many were brash and arrogant when you peered under the surface. Rozie was never that, and yet she had an inner confidence. You always knew where you were with her, even when she was gently teasing you. She managed to fit in because she didn't try too hard, and Sir Simon liked that. She also looked fabulous in those ridiculous heels, combined with the heartwarming grin she gave when she got a difficult question right, but he had been far too professional to let any of that influence him in any way. Besides, the final decision had been Her Majesty's.

Barbers Shop came into the Copper Horse Arena with a spring in his step and the look of a champion. His glossy conker coat had been groomed with mathematical precision that would no doubt have pleased Sir Simon's little sister. He had endless legs with black socks, powerful shoulders, and a head that moved intelligently, pricking his ears at the cheers from an appreciative crowd. Rozie watched the Queen grin with delight as soon as she saw him and carry on beaming as he powered his way through the jumps, combining sheer strength with a theatrical sense of performance. He knew exactly what was demanded of him and showed off outrageously, seeming to suspend himself in midair, before landing with the precision of an acrobat every time and tossing his head with satisfaction at a job well done.

Rozie loved the horse, but she found it hard to drag her eyes away from his owner.

"She looks so happy."

"Doesn't she?"

"But . . . she looks like she's always been this up, and you told me yesterday she was miserable as hell, and her leg was killing her."

"She has a talent for happiness," Sir Simon said. "Luckily. She was a happy child, much loved. I think that's what got her through the next seven decades."

"She must have been bloody happy."

"I think she was."

To no one's surprise, and his owner's absolute joy, Barbers Shop won the championship and the Queen got a fifty-pound Tesco voucher. She spent a while with the trainer and the horse afterwards, congratulating them both on another great performance and sharing a moment of glee. Then she was off to see the children on their ponies. A whole new generation of young riders were coming through. It was marvelous. How many carrots could you get with fifty pounds at Tesco? she wondered. She would have to find out.

LATE THAT EVENING, after a busy round of receptions and a dinner for forty in the Waterloo Chamber, General Sir Peter Venn called Sir Simon in his apartment and asked if he could come over. His friend readily agreed, so Sir Peter was surprised to find the APS there, too, with a tumbler of whiskey on the table beside her chair and her feet tucked up comfortably underneath her.

"I'm sorry, I didn't mean to intrude."

"Not at all, Peter. Rozie and I are just catching up on a few things. What can I offer you? Glenmorangie? Famous Grouse? Gordon's? Port? I've got some Taylor's ninety-six that's rather moreish."

"Yes, please," Sir Peter said gratefully. He made his way over to a spare armchair and sank into it. "God, what a day."

"I saw you earlier. You looked a bit green about the gills. Are you feeling all right?"

Sir Simon handed a small, cut-crystal port glass to the governor, glowing with the tawny red of the '96. Sir Peter took a sip, closed his eyes, and settled back into his chair.

"Better now. I had to see HM before dinner. Wasn't looking forward to it much, actually."

"Oh?" Sir Simon sat back, crossed his legs, and looked concerned.

Sir Peter cast a nervous glance at Rozie, then back to his host. *"Pas devant?"* he muttered quietly.

"Oh, Rozie knows everything. And if she doesn't, she ought to. We're all servants here. And she speaks French."

Sir Peter flushed briefly, but recovered himself. "Fine, then. It turns out that I introduced a complete impostor to the castle during the dine and sleep."

"We knew about that."

"Well, you didn't tell me you knew, and I wish you had, because I was having kittens imagining what the Queen would say when she found out. It was bad enough that the girl was in the castle at all, but that she stayed overnight at my personal request to the master . . ."

"You weren't to know she wasn't kosher, though, were you?" Sir Simon said gently.

Sir Peter took another sip of port. "I don't see how I could have been. It wasn't my meeting—I was just hosting it for a friend in the Foreign Office because we have such tight security here—ha!— and it's so useful for Heathrow. I was happy to do it, but I must say I assumed MI6 and the Foreign Office and the security team here were on top of knowing who was who. It turned out this girl was fairly new to this type of input. She had a PhD on Chinese naval infrastructure, which not many people do, as you can imagine, and she'd given a couple of papers at think tanks in London, but nobody at this meeting had actually seen her in the flesh. They'd emailed quite a bit, but that was all. And she had this thick, distinctive hair. To security, she looked like her passport photograph. It never occurred to anyone to double-check.

"Anyway, I'd got a bit worried recently that she was a drug taker. That's what the news said when she died, wasn't it? I suddenly thought—what if she'd taken drugs here? Can you imagine if that got out? So I talked to Chief Inspector Strong's team about it and the moment they showed me a recent picture of the girl who died, I knew it wasn't the person I'd seen. Obviously I told them straightaway, but I thought the Queen would be incandescent. It had been my idea to postpone the meeting to the following day, you know, to wait for this boy wonder from Djibouti. So my fault the impostor slept in the castle. My fault entirely." He sighed and drained his glass.

"Not at all," Sir Simon insisted. He got up, reached for the port decanter, and put it by the governor's elbow. "That meeting was extremely useful, I gather. It would have been a washout if Lo hadn't made it. You did well to persuade them all to stay on."

"You're very kind. And I understand that it *was* a good meeting. I didn't sit in on it myself, but it pushed our thinking on the Belt and Road strategy in some new directions. We'd always seen it as ambitious but essentially benign. And we'd focused on the Belt part— the land routes. What they're doing in Africa, for example, is on a scale one can hardly imagine. However, Lo had some fascinating insights into the Road part—the sea routes. That's where the Stiles girl came in. Kelvin Lo is interested in their financing of new ports in developing countries. He's concerned about the effect it will have on their naval capacity. You don't think about China being a naval power, do you? But more than that, he's concerned they're deliberately driving some of these countries into debt on these port facilities, so they'll essentially have a string of indentured bases around the Indian Ocean and the western Pacific."

"Rather the way we did in the nineteenth century," Sir Simon mused.

"Yes, well . . . We don't anymore. We haven't even got Hong Kong. It means they can put unfortunate pressure on our trade routes. Lots for the FCO to think about. And Six. Kelvin's information about the extent of infrastructure funding was a bit of a bombshell."

A thought was occurring to Rozie as he spoke.

"Was it China, then, that was spying? To find out what we knew about them?"

The governor, who had been increasingly animated as he spoke, sank back in his chair again. "With my personally invited, drug-addicted overnight guest, you mean? Quite possibly. I couldn't say."

"I'm sorry, Sir Peter. I didn't mean—"

"No, no, don't worry about it. Entirely my own fault. I should have got security to double-check everyone's credentials. But it never occurred to me the vetting wasn't up to scratch. The bloody thing was held in the name of national security, for God's sake!"

"Exactly," Sir Simon soothed. "You weren't to know. What did Strong say? He interviewed the girl, too, didn't he, about the murder? Did he make the same mistake?"

"Damned if I know. He won't tell me a thing because of course Humphreys thinks we're all working for the Kremlin. Even though I wrote the defense strategy for a Russian combined-forces attack through Scandinavia when I worked in NATO. Perhaps he thinks that makes me *more* of a spy. God knows. I can only assume the girls were in it together, though. Otherwise why didn't the real Rachel Stiles go to the police? They must have killed her because she knew too much."

"You think she was killed deliberately?" Sir Simon asked.

"Don't you?"

"I was beginning to wonder. So now that's two dead."

Three dead, Rozie thought.

"Anyway," the governor went on, "I went to the Queen this evening, ready to fall on my sword, and instead she was perfectly nice about it. Said of course it wasn't my business to go second-guessing the vetting procedure. Which I gather is being redesigned as we speak. It'll be upgraded once we've got time when the horse show's over. Don't talk to me about stable doors and horses bolting."

"I wouldn't dream of saying any such thing," Sir Simon assured him.

"You were thinking it."

"No, no, no."

"You're grinning."

"I'm just happy for you that the Boss didn't chew you out."

"Thank God Barbers Shop put her in a good mood." Sir Peter put down his glass and levered himself out of the chair. "Well, thank you for the port, Simon. Good night, Rozie. Christine's waiting for me at home. Kylie Minogue arrives in seventy-two hours and they've put her in one of our spare bedrooms. Honestly, Christine's task list for the visit puts my NATO defense strategy papers to shame."

30

As soon as the Queen heard that the investigation had taken a new direction, she had started to relax. Billy MacLachlan had dangled the bait, and Humphreys had taken it at last. At Thursday's brief meeting with an anguished Sir Peter, she had wanted to congratulate him on playing his part so well, but it was important to be quite innocent of all discoveries until one was officially told.

On Sunday, the phone call she had been expecting finally came. She had just finished a light lunch with the family, before a last afternoon of events and prize-giving down in the park, when Sir Simon informed her that Gavin Humphreys and Ravi Singh would like to arrange a meeting.

"Once you've recovered, ma'am. From the festivities."

"You know me, Simon. I'll be up bright and early tomorrow. Is it good news?"

"They wouldn't say, ma'am. But news, certainly. I understand there's been at least one arrest. But they'd like to explain it all properly."

"They don't plan to incarcerate any more of my servants, do they?"

"Not as far as I know."

"Find a suitable time. Now, if I don't go and see the horses, there'll be none left to see."

She went back down to Home Park, and it was delightful. From the Pony Club to the puissance champions, she was surrounded by passionate equestrians, ready for the ring in spotless breeches and gleaming boots, or grinning and spattered in mud from the driving course. Parents to whom she had granted rosettes many years ago now brought their little ones in their first tweed coats, balanced precariously on their rides. At the other end of the scale, there was a healthy turnout of stars who would be going to Rio soon, to compete for Olympic gold. If one could not follow them there, how nice that they could perform in one's own garden, on a sunny day, with the castle as a benevolent backdrop. And then it was time for the musical ride of the Household Cavalry, and who could fail to be thrilled by that?

But everything paled into insignificance beside the pageant that night. Anne and Edward had participated in the earlier versions on previous days. They had tried to tell her what to expect— one thought one knew—but nothing, *nothing* could quite prepare her for how special it turned out to be. So unlike some of those disastrous jubilee affairs. (The river barge in the rain four years ago had practically finished Philip off.)

She arrived at the Castle Arena at dusk, in the glass-roofed Scottish State Coach, with Philip beside her. There was an audience of six thousand waiting in the grandstands and five thousand more along the Long Walk outside, watching on giant TV screens. But it was the horses one had come for.

It took a great choreographer to make this sort of event go with a swing and get nine hundred horses to perform with split-second timing. Dougie Squires had utterly excelled himself. There was the Omani cavalry, of course, who had been rehearsing on-site for weeks; the Azerbaijani dancers; the truly exceptional horse whisperer, who was like a magician with those animals; and Shirley Bassey, Katherine Jenkins, and Miss Minogue in rhinestones and sequins, looking so graceful and filling the stadium with sound. But what made it so very moving was the way Dougie had based it around one's love of horses, and how very *personal* it was. If she was a weeper—which luckily she wasn't—it would have been easy to shed a tear. Especially when Anne and Edward entered the arena with little Louise, riding her own pony, just as she used to do at that age, and so composed.

On the way back, Philip asked, "Has that Humphreys johnnie been in touch about his idiotic witch hunt?"

"He has."

"I hope you put him right."

"In a way."

"Good. And I hope he was suitably contrite."

The Queen's head had been full of horses, but she brought it back to the matter in hand.

"I'm not quite sure yet. I'll have a better idea tomorrow."

"Tell me if you're not happy. According to the papers, I know people who could have him erased from this earth."

"I think he is those people," she observed mildly.

"Bugger," he said, and looked up at the floodlit castle.

She laughed.

THIS TIME, Gavin Humphreys was more ready than ever. He had planned. He had prepared. He had made excellent progress. He was certain, this time, that he would perform.

He wasn't entirely sure Her Majesty would be able to follow his thinking, that was the only thing. He would probably have to slow down in some places and go over certain things. He had asked Ravi Singh to look out for moments of confusion and give him the nod, just in case he got carried away with explaining and failed to notice when he lost her. It was complicated. Lots of intertwining strands. He might even need to draw it out for her. He would normally use his touch-screen notebook for that sort of thing, but it was a bit newfangled for Windsor Castle. Paper. Plain paper—that was another couple of *P*s. He got his secretary to find some to put in his briefcase before he left for Windsor in the official Jag.

At ten thirty on Monday morning the Queen's equerry showed him and the Met commissioner to the Oak Room, where their hostess greeted them before taking her usual seat near the window. The Queen seemed perky and relaxed, in a heather-hued twinset and pearls. Two of the dogs lay safely half asleep at her feet and a third jumped up to sit beside her. Her assistant, the girl with the high-heeled shoes, lurked in one corner, while the equerry, all starch and gold braid, stood to attention in the other.

Her Majesty looked in very good condition for a woman who'd been up until all hours, listening to Shirley Bassey and watching horses do tricks. Humphreys hadn't seen last night's pageant himself, but his wife had had the TV on in the background. The royals had all seemed very cheerful on-screen, and there were a *lot* of horses. He'd missed most of it because he had been busy practicing what he was going to say.

Now here he was, and Her Majesty was offering him and the Met commissioner tea or coffee. He asked for the latter, white with no sugar, and they indulged in a little polite small talk about the pageant, but soon she was asking the inevitable question.

"So tell me, Director General—who killed Mr. Brodsky? Do we know?"

Humphreys sat up straight, legs slightly apart without manspreading, the way he had been taught in media training.

"Yes, ma'am, we do," he said gravely—not entirely answering the question because he intended to build up to it. "And, I might add, dark forces have been at work."

"You told me." She nodded. "Putin's forces."

"Not actually those," he admitted. "At first we assumed Brodsky's murder was a brazen message. In fact, it was the opposite: something intended to be wildly misunderstood. For a long time, we were looking in the wrong direction."

"Oh dear. Were we?"

He nodded earnestly.

"How unfortunate."

For the briefest of moments, Humphreys was reminded of the time his ten-year-old self had had to explain to his grandfather that, in taking apart his gold hunter pocket watch to see how it worked, he had accidentally broken it beyond repair. But this time, everything was fixed! And he was fifty-four. He shrugged off the memory and went back to his story.

"Those forces might have stayed hidden a while longer," he went on, "if there hadn't been a storm over the Arab Peninsula, and if a young woman hadn't dropped her contact lens." He had practiced this part, and he liked it. The Queen's eyes lit up. Encouraged, he relaxed a little and said, "It's a bit like chaos theory, ma'am. A butterfly flaps its wings in . . ." *Damn*. It never paid to extemporize. Where did the butterfly flap its wings? Then there was a storm somewhere. But in this case a storm *was* a butterfly. He moved on swiftly. "The, er, Amazon. And as a result, three people are dead." He paused, dramatically.

"*Three* people? Goodness."

The Queen was suitably impressed.

"I must say at this point, there is one person who made the

whole discovery possible," Humphreys added generously. "Without them I think we might still be trying to pull the threads together."

"Oh?"

"Sir Peter Venn. One of his visitors was not who she said she was. You see, in this case the person we were looking for was a woman. *Cherchez la femme,* ma'am."

The Queen cocked her head slightly to one side. "Ah. *La femme.* Yes. Quite."

"It pays to maintain an open mind. Thanks to Sir Peter, we began to focus on an entirely different group from that of your dine and sleepover."

"Sleep," the Met commissioner interrupted.

"What?"

"Dine and sleep."

God, the last thing he needed was Singh correcting his vocabulary. With a deep breath, Humphreys kept calm and carried on. "They were here for a meeting that had been due to take place the day before Brodsky was found dead. It was all about a project called the Belt and Road. That's a Chinese strategy to—"

"I know about the Belt and Road," Her Majesty assured him.

"Oh. Ah. Good. Anyway, it was organized by MI6 and the Foreign Office, and kindly hosted by the governor. It might not seem connected to your little soirée, but bear with me. We're actually looking at three interconnected cases."

Thank goodness he'd brought the plain paper. He delved into his briefcase, took a few pages out, and stacked them on the coffee table in front of him in landscape format. On the uppermost page he wrote "Brodsky" in the middle near the top with a box around the name, then drew another box near the bottom right-hand corner and circled it with a swish of the pen.

Beside him, Mr. Singh couldn't contain himself. "The link to

Mr. Brodsky was *extraordinary,* ma'am. I'm still not sure how the director general did it. A real leap of the imagination—"

"Thank you, Ravi. I'll get to that. The purpose of the meeting, ma'am, was to share classified information on China's thinking and make high-level recommendations on the UK's response. The visitor in question—the one who was *supposed* to be here—was a young lady called Rachel Stiles." He wrote "Stiles" in the empty box. "She was an expert on the Chinese economy. In this case, ma'am, it was *China* that was of interest. Not Russia at all."

"Goodness," the Queen remarked levelly. "How fascinating."

"Isn't it?" He wrote "Belt and Road" in the bottom center of the paper. It was simplistic, but he could see the diagram was going to turn out quite useful. An image flashed into his mind of it framed, above his desk at home one day, and recounting to dinner guests how he'd used it to explain the Brodsky case to Her Majesty.

"The meeting drew together experts from various fields. All carefully vetted, of course—but they were forming a new group. It turned out that nobody at the meeting had met Rachel Stiles in person before. Dr. Stiles was in her twenties and had blue eyes and heavy, dark hair. So did the woman who arrived at the castle. She seemed to match the identity photo supplied on the vetting form. It wasn't until Sir Peter's subsequent revelation that we noticed some facial discrepancies, but these were quite small."

He paused, to see if the Queen was still following. She seemed to be.

"Dr. Stiles was unfortunately dead by the time we uncovered the deception. However, when we showed other participants a decent-sized photograph of her, they agreed: *it was not Rachel Stiles they'd met.* So the question was, who was she?"

"I do hope you found out." The Queen raised an eyebrow.

"Not to start with." Humphreys leaned forward and drew a third box in the bottom left-hand corner of his diagram. He considered writing a question mark inside it, but that would only mess the thing up later. He left it as it was—unfilled, glaring with possibility. Then turned the paper to face Her Majesty, and tapped it thoughtfully.

"For now, let us just call her the agent of a rogue state."

The Queen's voice rang with bell-like clarity. "Oh? Which one?"

Humphreys had been going to build up to this, too, but she obviously wanted the information, so he gave in. "This might come as a surprise, ma'am."

"Not Russia, then?"

"In fact, no."

"Or China?"

"Not China either. It was an ally of ours, would you believe?" He named it.

"Really?" She leaned forward, frowning. "And why were they spying on us?"

"There's a problem with the state in question, and actually, I believe it started with me." Humphreys thought he detected the faintest trace of a smile flit across the APS's face. But perhaps he imagined it. The Queen merely looked intent and curious. "Last year, as I believe you were briefed, King Zeid chose to make one of his young nephews the head of his country's police and intelligence services. We think he's testing the boy—young man, I should say—to see if he has leadership potential. I gather you know Prince Fazal quite well."

The Queen nodded. "*Quite* well."

"I understand he occasionally visited you here at Windsor and at Sandringham on holidays from boarding school and Sandhurst." She glowered. From what Humphreys had heard, she had treated the young man like a member of the family. "They spotted his lack of ideal leadership potential at the Royal Military Academy," he went on. "An excellent shot and tough as old boots, but constantly getting into fights in the town and sneaking off to London to gamble in the casinos. I gather he only lasted two terms. He was young. Our top brass put it down to hormones. Nevertheless, he wouldn't have been our first choice for head of his country's police service, or the intelligence side."

"Nor mine," the Queen agreed. From the tone of her voice, Humphreys suspected the lad had been nasty to the dogs, or possibly one of the horses.

"As you know, we considered his first few months in the job to be . . . unsatisfactory. There has been an increase in state-sanctioned torture in the prisons. Certain activists have gone missing, believed dead. There are rumors—nothing confirmed—that he likes to have people brought to his house so he can deliver the coup de grâce himself. He regularly argues for war in the region. When I took over as DG, I took the decision to limit intelligence sharing with his agency. I didn't think he could be trusted to protect our sources. Needless to say, he was outraged."

"I see."

"I thought his uncle the king might complain to you about it."

"He didn't."

"That in itself is interesting, ma'am. It suggests either the young man's power is quickly fading, or the older man's is. Anyway, it seems the prince decided to take matters into his own hands. If we wouldn't tell him what he wanted to know, he'd find out for himself. Since we've looked into it, it transpires that for several months he's been trying to target our intelligence on a whole range of topics. Including the Belt and Road."

"How?" the Queen asked.

"How what, ma'am?"

"Has he been trying to target it?"

"Ah. It turns out he had a source in the FCO."

"Oh," the Queen observed blandly. "So there was an insider."

"Yes, ma'am, and we've—"

"But not in my castle."

"Well, ma'am, I was going to get to—"

"I'm so sorry. Do continue."

Humphreys wrote "Fazal" on his diagram, near the empty box, and underlined it.

"Thanks to this person's information, the agent was able to insert herself into the intelligence group at the castle. She was quiet, but by no means the only one to appear somewhat shy at first." Humphreys had a thought. "Not that you would remember, ma'am, but you might even have met her that evening, at a reception in the governor's drawing room . . ." He broke off, to consider that extraordinary, unknowable possibility.

"I suppose I might," the Queen said meekly. "More coffee?"

"I—uh . . ." Humphreys realized he was parched. His original cup had gone cold, but was replaced by the silent footman. He drained the new one and felt a momentary wave of confusion.

"Where was I?"

"In the governor's drawing room," the Queen prompted. "With the spy."

Humphreys smiled gratefully. She was sharper than she looked. Which was useful, under the circumstances.

"Yes, of course. And that should have been it. They were all due to go home that night, but a key analyst at the meeting had been held up by a storm on his way here from Djibouti. This was the storm I mentioned at the beginning, ma'am. The one like the butterfly in the— Anyway, his connecting flight from Dubai was delayed by several hours, and the main meeting was postponed, so the governor arranged for the others to stay here overnight, unplanned."

"Yes, he told me about that."

"A generous decision. He wasn't to know the consequences. The group stayed up for a while, talking and drinking, including the so-called Dr. Stiles. The others said that by this point she was quite animated, joining in and making jokes. They liked her. Looking back, it's rather impressive, ma'am, in its way."

"Is it?" the Queen asked, somewhat briskly.

Humphreys backtracked a little. "Well, obviously everything she did was reprehensible. But you have to admire the enemy sometimes. Courage in the face of adversity and all that . . ."

"I prefer not to think of my hospitality as adversity, Director General."

"No, no, of course not." He took another sip of coffee. "Anyway, they all went up to their allotted rooms sometime before midnight. They were scattered around in various attic locations. Stiles, or rather, the agent, happened to be above the Visitors' Apartments."

Humphreys could see those apartments now, from where he was sitting, through the wide expanse of glass overlooking the quad— row upon row of Gothic windows set into heavy stone, with turrets and crenellations and thick-set towers. And he could imagine the panic of the unprepared young woman, trapped in the oldest inhabited castle in the world, surrounded by police and armed members of the Foot Guards. The Queen might not think the agent was brave, but he did. He had known of young women in similar situations, in other places, serving their country in difficult circumstances. He didn't underestimate what it took.

"At around half past midnight, one of the housekeepers saw her on her way back to her room from the shower. She was wearing a towel, with another around her hair. She was crouched down, looking for something. The housekeeper asked what it was, and she said it was a contact lens. This information seemed irrelevant at first, but then we realized it was essential. The lenses are important, ma'am, because as we subsequently discovered, the agent had brown eyes, and Rachel Stiles's were blue. So we now know these were blue contact lenses that she badly needed for the next day.

"The housekeeper offered to help her look, but she declined. Then, by sheer chance—and that's the thing about this whole sorry affair—it was just pure chance, ma'am—Maksim Brodsky came out of his own room, a few doors away. Yes, finally, we arrive at Mr. Brodsky. I was getting there, ha ha." He picked up his pen and tapped the "Brodsky" box on the diagram.

"He was on his way somewhere else. But the key point is, he saw this girl, saw her with her hair up, scrabbling around for something on the floor—and he bent down to help her. And that, ma'am . . . is where he made his terrible mistake."

This time, Humphreys's dramatic pause was positively Pinteresque. It was like waiting to announce the winner of the *Great British Bake Off.* Everyone held their breath.

Eventually, Mr. Singh couldn't take it any longer. He leaped in. "This is where Mr. Humphreys had his revelation, ma'am. It was a real leap of inspiration. I'm still not sure how he did it."

"Thank you, Ravi." Humphreys gave a self-deprecating shake of his head. "I couldn't have done it without you and your men. And women, of course. It was an absolute team effort."

"But to connect three totally separate investigations. It was a stroke of brilliance."

Humphreys had the grace to blush. Looking down at his thighs, he picked an imaginary piece of fluff off the knee of his trousers, then took up his pen and scored a line along the bottom of the paper, between the empty box and "Stiles."

"Not brilliance," he demurred. "Just luck. And teamwork, as I say. And—"

"And what was it?" the Queen interrupted. "This stroke of brilliance?"

Humphreys was too modest to look her in the eye. He found himself telling the story to Willow, or possibly Holly. One of the corgis, anyway, curled up on the seat beside Her Majesty.

"Mr. Singh mentioned three investigations. Six days ago, while we were already looking into the Stiles case, we received an anonymous tip-off through our website about a potential spy. The source was right—we quickly found a pattern of payments to an offshore bank account. Significantly, both abroad and at home this person associated with certain contacts who were already on our radar. Contacts who work for Prince Fazal, in fact. The desk officer flagged it to Director K Div, who immediately put a note on my desk with the file. I believe I was talking to you at the time, Commissioner, wasn't I?"

"Yes, indeed. We were discussing the Duke of Edinburgh's val—"

"It's not important. What matters is, in the Stiles case we were looking for someone who might have passed herself off as an expert on Chinese finance—an, er, a female, obviously. And here was a woman called Anita Moodie, who was born in Hong Kong and educated in England, spoke Cantonese and Mandarin fluently, and was about the right age and size. . . . Surely, I said to myself, we've found her. But there was something else.

"It was when I was looking at Moodie's case file, not long after you left, Commissioner, thinking about Stiles, that it all came together. It wasn't the money trail or the associates or the places she'd been. It was a simple detail—so small I'm surprised I noticed it. It was the name of Moodie's boarding school. Oh."

He looked up. The assistant in the corner had been taking a drink and was choking on some water that had gone the wrong way. She raised a hand apologetically. He carried on.

"Moodie went to this place called Allingham. The name rang a bell and I remembered—it was in the police files of course—

Maksim Brodsky went there, too. As soon as I realized, it hit me in a flash. *This* was our visitor. Moodie was here. And, quite simply—Brodsky recognized her from school, as he bent down to help with the lens. There she was, without the heavy wig and with at least one eye its natural color. He would have seen straightaway that it was her.

"I checked the dates: Moodie was in the year above Maksim Brodsky at Allingham. You know how you tend to remember the people in the year above you? Well, perhaps you don't, ma'am—you were tutored here, of course—but people do. More to the point, it turns out they had played music together. He accompanied her at various concerts. There was no question of her pretending he had got it wrong. He knew her as Anita, but here she was Rachel. He knew her as a musician, but here she was a City analyst. She had to fix this by morning, before he started talking about this schoolmate he'd met."

Humphreys stopped. The room was silent again. He realized he had been talking rather fast, and perhaps a little too enthusiastically, but he still remembered his epiphany as if it were five minutes ago. He often relived it, and always with a shiver of . . . one could hardly call it pleasure in the circumstances, but satisfaction, certainly.

"Gracious," the Queen said at last. "You're a very instinctive investigator, aren't you?"

"Yes, ma'am," he agreed, with more than a little pride.

She smiled, and in that moment, he thought she looked really quite attractive, for an old lady.

Glancing modestly down again, to avoid her sapphire gaze, Humphreys scribbled "Moodie" in the last, empty box on his diagram and drew a line between that and the "Brodsky" box at the top of the triangle, connecting them all at last.

"There it is, ma'am. The international influence of the British boarding school system. One unfortunate encounter and . . . there we are."

The Queen's gaze was still intense. "And are you sure it was she who killed him?"

"Absolutely, ma'am. Once we identified her, we immediately matched her DNA to that found in Brodsky's room. Even her fingerprints were there. But perhaps the commissioner can talk to that part better than me."

The man beside him looked reticent. "If you like."

"Go ahead, Ravi," Humphreys said expansively. He sat back at last, crossed his legs, and wondered if it would be rude to take the diagram with him when he left.

The commissioner addressed himself to the Queen.

"Miss Moodie didn't try to solve the problem straightaway, ma'am. In fact, she couldn't. Perhaps it was Mr. Brodsky's absence that gave her the chance to consider her plan. Because, you see . . ." He wasn't sure how to say this, until he remembered that it was the Queen herself who had alerted him to this side of things. "He had an assignation. With one of your guests." He checked her reaction and, to his relief, she didn't look like a woman who needed smelling salts. Even so, talking to Queen Elizabeth II about this sort of thing, he felt slightly light-headed himself.

"Mr. Brodsky joined this, er, person, downstairs in her suite and it all . . . went quite well." He felt his cheeks go warm. "And afterwards he went outside for a cigarette." He coughed. He was not making this easy for himself. "By the time he got back, Miss Moodie must have found an excuse to join him in his room. She was an old friend, after all. It's possible that she went in with the hope of seducing him, but he wouldn't have been very . . . He was probably quite . . . you know . . . tired. Anyway, at some point in the early morning, she overpowered him. Given the broken bones in his neck, we believe she strangled him manually before applying the ligature. He would have been relaxed in her company, so it would have been easy for her to surprise him. She was small, but strong. Trained, we assume, and desperate."

"How dreadful," the Queen said, in such a way that Singh felt for the first time that he was not recounting a case to a royal, but talking about an ugly death to a person who really cared. It took him back to his early days as an officer on the beat.

"Yes, ma'am," he said quietly. He noticed that she nudged her ankle against the nearest dog on the floor beside her. He wanted to reach across the coffee table and squeeze her hand. But he didn't, and the moment passed.

"And so now there was a body. There would be questions in the morning. She had to make it look like an accident. But, more than that, she must have been panicking that if there *was* an investigation, a public one anyway, we would quickly discover the real Rachel Stiles hadn't been here. She needed to make it as hard for us as possible. The question was, how?"

Singh had asked the question rhetorically. He was about to answer it, but the Queen did first.

"By bringing me into it," she said grimly. "By making it all so sordid that my reputation must be protected."

She was absolutely right. He was impressed by how fast she got it. It was almost as if she knew. "Exactly, ma'am." He nodded. "Miss Moodie staged a scene. She stripped Mr. Brodsky of his clothes and put him in the dressing gown provided by the castle. She put the cord round his neck and tightened it, then arranged him in the wardrobe with the other end of the cord tied to the handle. But she didn't pull it tight enough to—"

"I know about the second knot," the Queen reminded him.

"Yes, ma'am. Of course. At first, we were confused because there was a hair on the body, between the neck and the cord, that we identified as belonging to Dr. Stiles. I admit that derailed the investigation a little for a while. However, it must have come from Dr. Stiles's clothes, which Miss Moodie was wearing."

"Ah. Was she?"

"Almost certainly, ma'am. We know that she was using Dr. Stiles's bag."

"Oh, really?"

This surprised Singh a bit. Of all the things to pick, the bag seemed the least likely detail. But the Queen appeared genuinely interested.

"A cabin bag was taken from Dr. Stiles's flat that morning. It matched exactly the one Miss Moodie arrived with here at the castle. Judging from the shape and size, we believe it would have contained Dr. Stiles's papers for the meeting and her outfit for the evening drinks reception. It went missing afterwards, so we can't be sure."

"Yes." The Queen nodded. "Yes. I see."

She had an odd look about her. Sharp. Thoughtful. He tried to be helpful. "The bag doesn't play a very big part in the investigation, ma'am."

"No, I suppose it wouldn't. Do please go on."

"Returning to the hair, I don't think she put it there deliberately. She was careful to scrape Dr. Stiles's lipstick to remove the DNA. Then she covered it in Mr. Brodsky's fingerprints and left it near the body."

"As well as some pants, I seem to remember," the Queen added. "Where did those come from?"

Another unusual detail to pick up on, but Singh remembered how adamant Gavin Humphreys had been about them belonging to her page. She must have been rather cross about that.

"We think—" Singh's voice wavered slightly. "Um, from what

was found in Dr. Stiles's bathroom at home . . . er, that she had been . . . um, menstruating, ma'am. And I understand ladies like to pack spare—"

"Thank you, Commissioner. I see."

"And so Miss Moodie used them to try to make it look as if Mr. Brodsky had died mid- . . ."

"Ye-es." The word had several syllables, and the Queen's voice was weighed with melancholy. "Her old school friend . . . A rather special young man. I danced with him."

"I'm sorry," Singh said.

"Well, yes. So am I."

He wanted to lighten the mood, but he knew what was to come. "You might perhaps be wondering, ma'am, what Dr. Stiles herself was doing all that time, while Miss Moodie was busy taking her place?"

"Something like that," the Queen said, inscrutably.

"We can discuss it another time if you like."

The Queen sighed deeply. "No. Tell me now."

Singh sensed a certain reluctance. She was probably tired, after last night. But it was almost as if she knew what was coming. "Well, by the time Sir Peter discovered the impersonation, Dr. Stiles was already dead. We had assumed she must have been bribed or blackmailed into going along with the original deception, because, after all, she never reported it. However, it turns out that nobody had seen her alive since the day before she officially came to Windsor. DCI Strong thought he had, when he went to her flat to interview her as a witness, but after Sir Peter's revelation he realized it was Miss Moodie he had spoken to, not Dr. Stiles.

"So we looked at the CCTV footage outside her flat. The evening before the first meeting at the castle, it shows a tall, hooded man arriving. None of the other residents saw him in the building.

We believe he entered Dr. Stiles's flat without her knowledge and slipped a knockout drug into something she was drinking."

"In my day, we used to call that a Mickey Finn," the Queen observed.

"Yes, I think I've heard of those. In this case, it was almost certainly a tranquilizer called Rohypnol, sadly used in date . . . ahem . . . assault, ma'am. It lowers anxiety but can also cause the person taking it to forget what has happened. It can also make them feel pretty nauseous the next day. We think Dr. Stiles was out of it that night, and in the morning she thought she'd caught a bug. She emailed her contact at the Belt and Road meeting saying as much, but there was another thing—GCHQ discovered that her emails had been hacked. You know about hacking, ma'am? I see you do. She sent it, but he never received it.

"According to the CCTV, the hooded man was still inside. We think the plan had been to keep an eye on her while Miss Moodie was playing her part at the castle, but afterwards to let her recover from her woozy symptoms and go back to her normal life. The body soon metabolizes Rohypnol from the bloodstream. Dr. Stiles would have had confused memories, but otherwise have been OK, physically, at least. However, after Mr. Brodsky's death they changed their minds. It's ironic, really. Miss Moodie did what she did to the body to stop Rachel Stiles hearing about the murder and telling someone she hadn't been here that night. But that was never going to happen. Are you all right, ma'am?"

"Quite all right, Commissioner. I might just have another cup of tea. Thank you very much." The Queen nodded to the footman as he poured it.

Singh was worried. She was looking a bit grey suddenly, and he hadn't even got to the really nasty part. "So . . . and stop me if this is too much . . ."

"No, please go on."

"Ma'am." He waited while she took a sip. "The intruder left Dr. Stiles briefly, but soon returned. As they feared, we quickly suspected murder at the castle. We believe he kept her tranquilized in her bedroom until Anita Moodie could do her bit in the living room when the police visited. But by now they were stuck. Strong's team could come back at any time and ask more questions. They couldn't keep Dr. Stiles out of it indefinitely. Besides, it had already been three days. When she came to her senses, she would know it was more than a bug. She might remember at least some of what he'd done to her. So he waited. For three more days. We think he kept her drugged up while they used her email and social media to tell friends and work that she was under the weather. They wanted to leave a long enough gap that what happened next wouldn't ever be connected to the castle. GCHQ pointed out that the hackers didn't bother to divert the messages anymore. They knew Dr. Stiles would never read or check them."

The Queen pressed her ankle more firmly against the warm body of the sleeping dog. "How did she die, in the end?"

"Vodka, ma'am," Singh said baldly. "Mixed with more Rohypnol. The bottle was still in her apartment. She would have been too out of it to refuse. He also rubbed cocaine into her gums. Enough to give her a heart attack."

The ormolu clock ticked. The dogs snuffled. The Queen looked bleak.

"One must . . . I would like to . . ." She coughed and recovered herself. When she spoke again, she was sitting ramrod straight and the bell-like clarity was back. "Dr. Stiles was killed in public service. *My* service, really. I hope that when I contact her family to offer my condolences, I can assure them that we've done everything we can to get justice done."

Humphreys had been quiet for longer than he intended. He decided that now it was time to cheer Her Majesty up.

"The cocaine was their mistake, ma'am," he interjected. "A bit like Anita Moodie, they were too theatrical. If they'd just plied Stiles with alcohol and tranquilizers, the death would have gone unremarked. But City workers use cocaine, they thought, so that would look more natural. Instead, it made the news. It meant that Sir Peter Venn heard about it and was thinking about her when he talked to DS Highgate, and . . . Well, it brought us to where we are now."

"And where is that, exactly?" the Queen asked.

Humphreys gestured towards his diagram.

"We mentioned three cases. Anita Moodie, too, is dead, ma'am. She died before she was brought to our attention. Her body was found two days after that of Rachel Stiles. It was supposed to look like suicide, but we happen to know she was in fear for her life."

"Oh?"

"An old friend rang the police to say so. The same man, presumably, who gave us the anonymous tip-off about the spying."

"Mmmm."

"And Moodie was right. She had messed up. She knew she might be punished, and she was. CCTV footage outside *her* flat shows a tall, blond male entering her building the day she died, and leaving it thirty minutes later. There was no sign of forced entry into the flat, no useful DNA, no absolute proof that it wasn't suicide, but we're certain she was killed. She had caused a lot of trouble for her handlers and in the end, they took care of her, ma'am. I think they had an idea of poetic justice. She'd hanged Brodsky incompetently. They hanged her, too, but more professionally."

The Queen's look suggested she didn't see this as justice of any sort. "How ghastly."

"Yes. But there was one critical development. The CCTV proves that it was the same man who was with both women at the time they died."

"Ah, I see." At last, Her Majesty seemed slightly brighter.

"And the footage from outside Moodie's flat is much clearer. He wasn't wearing his hood up then. We identified him as Jonnie Haugen: a small-time hardman hired by Fazal's intelligence office to take care of things in London without putting them in the frame. Except, we know they use him, so it *does* put them in the frame. We've got Haugen down at New Scotland Yard, charged with Stiles's murder. We found his DNA at her flat. He'd tried to clear up, but it's hard to be somewhere that long and leave no trace, without making it look as if you've steam cleaned the place. I'm not sure we'll get him for Moodie's death, but the police are working on it."

Singh nodded his assent.

"And the person who came to collect the bag from Stiles's flat and give it to Moodie is a driver at the embassy," Humphreys went on. "Because the prince is much more amateur at this than he thinks he is. The driver's being deported tomorrow. Having spoken to you, I'll inform the prime minister. The prince is back at home, and of course we couldn't touch him anyway, but it'll be made very clear to the king that his nephew is a dangerous fool who has brought his country into disrepute. If you might reinforce the message, ma'am. He might listen to it, coming from you."

"He might. One can try. And what happened to the insider, may I ask? The one in the Foreign Office?"

"Caught yesterday, trying to get a flight out of Heathrow," Humphreys said. "By a nice irony, his flight was delayed by several hours because of a storm over southern France. We were already on our way to get him. It saved us a trip and some paperwork."

"Good. And now, I think I must rather get on."

The Queen smoothed her skirt and stood up. Humphreys and Singh leaped to their feet. She adjusted her handbag strap over one arm and smiled at them both. "Well done. Three murders . . .

how very clever of you to solve them. Please thank your teams, too, for all their hard work. We've all been rather unsettled by this. It's nice to think one can sleep easily again."

"It was an honor, ma'am," Singh said, with a little bow.

"An honor," Humphreys agreed.

Talking of honors . . . *Sir* Gavin Humphreys . . . The words repeated freely in his head as he bent down and picked up his little diagram. He'd thought the honor would come, but not for another five years or so. Sir Gavin Humphreys. His wife would be thrilled to the core. He had found a spy and single-handedly solved three murders in the process. What else, quite honestly, could Her Majesty do?

She walked out, with her equerry behind her and the dogs at her heels.

31

T HE QUEEN WAS in her private chapel, sitting quietly, when she heard a noise at the door and Philip came in, pausing just inside.

"Mind if I join you?"

"Please do."

He walked slowly towards her and sat down in his favorite chair nearby.

"Tom told me you had your meeting with the idiot from Box." He paused and she said nothing, so he went on. "He said they sorted everything out. Found out who did it and so on. Not a sleeper."

"Not a sleeper, no. There was a mole."

"It's like living in a le Carré. That or a stuffed-up lawn."

He grinned at his little joke, but she didn't. He didn't take it personally, though. He knew this would be a hard conversation.

"He said there were three of 'em, Tom did. All in their twenties. All died rather unpleasantly."

"Yes, they did."

He looked towards the altar, where a Renaissance painting showed the Madonna with her baby. "You'd think they'd still have three score years and ten ahead of 'em."

"I'm sure they thought that. But . . ." She trailed off. She didn't do that in front of most people. She always found her backbone from somewhere and carried on. But she didn't mind so much when Philip saw her struggling. One wasn't made of stone; he knew that.

"Tom said Humphreys solved the whole thing," he said. "Wouldn't have thought he had it in him."

"Yes, it was rather surprising."

"Bloody shocking, I'd say. D'you know, I think he had someone feeding him information."

"Do you?" She frowned at her husband sharply.

"God, yes," he said, with an emphatic nod. "Some underling, no doubt. Brainy as hell but quite passed over. Doing all the work and giving him all the kudos. Don't you think?"

She relaxed a little. "Something like that."

"He'll still get a gong, though, won't he?" Philip made a face.

"I think he rather must."

"It'll make him even more insufferable, of course."

She merely smiled at this. It was probably true, but if anyone was trained to suffer the insufferable, she was.

Philip reached across and put a hand over hers. His skin was cool and soft. He squeezed her knuckles, briefly. "Well, at least they found the truth. Have they got the men who did it?"

"Not all were men. But, yes."

"Glad to hear it." He squeezed her hand again.

She didn't tell him about Prince Fazal. Not yet. She was still too furious to say his name, both at what he'd done and at the thought of him escaping proper justice—though the humiliation of having been caught out would cause him significant anguish. At least, she hoped it would.

"I'm off. Having dinner in town tonight. Few things to do before I go," Philip said, rising.

"Wait. I'll come with you."

He offered her his arm and they walked down the aisle together, towards the window. His window. It showed timelessness, and recovery and hope. It didn't stop her feeling terribly for the young man in the attic room and the innocent girl in her flat, and even the other one, who suffered such terrors before she died, but it gave her the strength to walk calmly and capably back into the busy castle, where she was the center of its turning world.

In two days she and half the Household would head back to London to prepare for the State Opening of Parliament. Life very much went on. One did what one could. Right now, it was absolutely time for a little gin.

"DID YOU FIND OUT if the hardman was the same one who tried to kill you?"

Aileen Jaggard was visiting the castle at Rozie's invitation. They stood at the top of the Round Tower, away from prying eyes.

Rozie's mouth twisted into a smile. "Billy MacLachlan found out for me. The guy in the cells had a broken nose and a damaged hand. Three broken fingers. Giving him a lot of pain."

Aileen met her eye. "Poor thing."

"What I don't get," Rozie said, changing the subject, "was why Gavin Humphreys? Of all the people. I thought the Boss hated him."

"She doesn't hate anyone. She might have been a bit infuriated."

"But when you think of the misery he caused," Rozie persisted.

"Everyone could feel it. She *knew* he was wrong about the Putin thing, right from the start."

"She must have decided he was the right man for the job. She wouldn't let personal feelings come into it."

"How could she not?"

"Practice. Loads and loads of it. She's a brilliant politician— how d'you think she's coped all these years? She thinks long term. *Was* Humphreys the best man for the job?"

Rozie looked out at the horizon. In the far distance you could see all the way east to the Shard. Without meaning to, it marked twenty miles from here to the Tower of London, from fortress to fortress, as William the Conqueror had planned it, with London in between. She considered the question. "Perhaps," she conceded. "I mean, the Boss worked out who did the killings, but I don't think she could ever prove who was behind it. Once she'd worked out that it *was* a question of spying after all, MI5 were the best people to deal with it, I suppose."

"There you are."

"But why not tell him how far she'd got? I saw her in practice. She just, kind of . . . seeded these little ideas. He didn't even know she was doing it. *She* told *him* about Allingham. *She* got MacLachlan to make the anonymous tip-off about Anita Moodie. She let Humphreys take all the credit, even to himself."

Aileen grinned. She pulled a wisp of hair out of her eyes. "Yup, that sounds like her. Gave me a bit of a shock the first time, but the more I saw her do it, the more it made sense. She doesn't want to be seen as interfering."

"But it's her own castle!"

"She's not head of the investigation, though. Imagine if she'd said what she'd found, and you'd found. It would prove she was basically second-guessing him all along, which of course she was. That would hardly puff up his self-esteem."

"So it's all about his ego?"

"Think about it, if she'd proved him wrong and made him feel small, what would happen the next time there was a problem? He'd constantly be worrying she'd do it again. He'd stop trusting her. Trust is *everything* to Her Majesty. Much more than petty point scoring. He'd stop telling her things. What good would that do?"

"So he gets a knighthood, and he goes on thinking she's a dim old lady who lives in a nice castle?"

"A dim old lady he works his guts out for, right or wrong."

Rozie shook her head. "I still can't get my head around it. I mean, who has that much . . ."

"Self-discipline?"

"Yeah."

"One person in the world, I'd say. Enjoy it while you can."

They took a last look at the panoramic view, from the Long Walk to the southeast, to the town to the west and the river behind it, slow and stately, heading from Oxfordshire to the sea. Above them, the sky was sapphire, flecked with cirrus. It was nearly June and soon the castle would be gearing up for Ascot.

"I assume she thanked you, by the way," Aileen added on the stairs on the way back down. "Did you get the box?"

Rozie grinned. "Yep. I did."

A week ago, the Queen had asked her to come and see her in the Oak Room. This was more formal than their usual private meetings. When she got there, the Boss was freshly coiffured, in her favorite skirt and cardigan, and beaming with that delighted smile that went straight to Rozie's heart.

"I owe you money," she'd said.

It was true, but Rozie was still shocked to hear her say it. "Oh, Your Majesty, don't—"

"You thought I'd forgotten, but here it is. Lady Caroline told me how much."

This must be repayment for the Fortnum's hampers. They had cost a fortune back in April and Rozie had paid out of her own pocket because she didn't know what else to do. She wasn't going to say anything.

And yet the Queen wasn't proffering an envelope. Instead, she handed Rozie a slim, blue cardboard box from the table in front of her. It was surprisingly heavy.

"Open it."

Inside was a smaller box made of silver and blue enamel, about the size of a narrow clutch bag, with the royal cipher engraved below the clasp. Rozie opened it to find a Coutts check for the correct amount inside. But it was the box itself that held her attention. Rozie had noticed one just like this one on a side table in Aileen's flat in Kingsclere. Hers now sat on her bedside table, at whichever royal residence she happened to be working. She imagined she was the first person to use such a thing for storing spare shea butter for her skin.

"She doesn't give you one for every case, does she?" she asked.

Aileen laughed. "No. But she always thinks of something. Now, didn't you say you were going to take me for a hack in the park? I brought my riding togs. Let's go and enjoy this weather."

$$\textbf{32}$$

A YEAR WENT BY. Another Easter Court, another birthday. In the New Year's honors list, Sir Gavin Humphreys had indeed received the good news he didn't dare (but nevertheless did) hope for. So, somewhat to his surprise, did Sir Ravi Singh. DCI Strong was pleased with his OBE. Now the horse show approached again.

Before all the festivities began, the Queen had a couple of visitors she wanted to see in private. First was a young man Rozie had taken a while to track down. She had eventually located him at a hostel in Southend, where he was doing occasional work as a laborer. He had been in and out of rehab, unable to hold down a job. His mother's death when he was in his teens had hit him hard, Rozie had established. His father had died when he was only seven. His older sister had done what she could to stop him going off the rails too badly, but now she was dead, too.

When Rozie told him about the invitation, his first concern was that he had nothing appropriate to wear.

"Don't worry about that," she'd assured him. "She doesn't mind. Just make sure you borrow a jacket of some kind. It'll make things easier."

He was terrified approaching the castle. Scared of the police in the road outside the gates, scared of the troops he knew were inside. He was used to being scared of authority in all its forms by now, and this was like all of it, concentrated in one spot, in a bloody *castle*. But when he showed his invitation, he was escorted past the general public in the queue like some sort of VIP. The lady who had written to him (who was hot, and tall, and black, and not what he'd expected at all) came to meet him near the gate and took him a special way up the hill, avoiding all the public places, until they came to the bit where the Queen actually lived. He could hardly believe it.

The tall lady took him along one side of a massive rectangle of grass in the middle of all these grey stone buildings, into a corner one they called the Brunswick Tower. Then she accompanied him upstairs and he thought he'd be waiting for ages in some kind of holding area—whatever, he didn't know—but instead, she knocked on a door and someone said, "Come in," so they did, and inside was . . . the Queen.

The real Queen. Right there. In person. Like, on her own, or nearly, with just, like, some dogs and this guy in gloves standing near a table with drinks on it. And the room was not big, and quite dark, and full of the kind of furniture you would expect the Queen to have—like, old and very, very expensive looking, like she'd got it all from a museum—and through the window he could see a long row of trees in the distance and people walking between them, ordinary people, just kind of doing their ordinary thing, not knowing that he, Ben, was standing in a room with Her Actual Majesty.

It was an out-of-body experience. He was really, really glad he'd let the manager of the hostel lend him some leather shoes. Trainers just wouldn't cut it on this carpet.

"Good morning, Mr. Stiles. Thank you so much for coming. I hope your journey wasn't too difficult?"

"No, Your Majesty," he said. The tall lady, who was standing there, too, had told him to say "Your Majesty" the first time, and "ma'am," to rhyme with "ham," not "marm" to rhyme with "farm," after that, and to bow—which he hadn't done. Bloody hell! So he did, too late, but whatever. And Her Majesty smiled. She looked really nice when she smiled. She was tiny, though. She looked bigger on TV. But she kind of glowed. He didn't know how she did that, but it was awesome.

"Rozie, could you ask Major Simpson to join us in five minutes?" she said.

The tall lady disappeared and the Queen sat down and pointed at this other seat, so he did, too, and then the guy in gloves came over and asked him what he'd like to drink. He had this soft, Scottish accent and he looked really kindly, and Ben liked him straightaway. He had no idea what to say, though, so he just blurted out "Whatever," and the guy came back with a glass of cold, fresh water with a slice of lemon in it, which was OK.

And they talked—he and the Queen did, the guy in the gloves didn't say anything else, just kind of hovered in the background— for what could have been a minute or half an hour, Ben had no idea. Nor could he remember afterwards a single thing they'd said, exactly. Except that she was really nice, and they'd talked a little bit about his sister and his dad, and she'd said how hard it must have been growing up without his dad, which it bloody was, and how brave he'd been, and how sorry she was about his sister. And he felt it was true. She really meant it. And at some point he stopped being terrified and he just felt kind of . . . at home. Like, this is just what you do on a Tuesday morning. And it was OK.

Then the tall lady came back with this other guy in the most outrageous uniform you've ever seen in your life—all red and black, with gold braid everywhere and medals and shiny shoes, like a costume drama, and the Queen stood up, so Ben did, too, and she walked over to this table with a cushion on it, and uniform guy picked up the cushion and handed it to her, and on it was a small, black box, lined with black velvet, with two silver crosses inside, one medium-sized and one small.

The Queen looked at Ben and said, "You stand here," pointing to a spot just in front of her. She sounded kind of strict, but not mean with it, and Ben did as he was told, and she said, "Mr. Stiles, I know the version of this award that was given to your mother went missing last year. I was sorry to hear that. Your sister, too, died serving her country, and I would like to say how very grateful I am for her service, and your father's sacrifice. And how sorry I am about your mother." She reached out to shake his hand, then turned and took the box from its cushion and gave it to him.

He looked down, and in the process two of his tears landed on her thumb, which was embarrassing. Ben hadn't been able to hold it in since his mum died. One of those things. But the Queen didn't seem to mind. She just made sure he was holding the box securely. And when it was done she took a step back, and smiled at him in a friendly way, and Ben didn't know what to say, so he said, "Thank you. Er, ma'am. Appreciate it."

And he realized that what she'd given him wasn't really the replacement cross and its miniature so much as the time spent in this room, with her, which could have been ten minutes or two days for all he knew—it was like being in a time warp. But he was properly crying now so it was probably best just to go. She said something else that he didn't really hear and then the tall lady was showing him out, and as soon as they were out of the room he just turned to the tall lady and hugged her tight—which you're totally not allowed to do and he knew that, but sometimes you just kind of have to go with it—and she hugged him back for a moment, and asked if he was OK. Which he said he was, because there was the long version and the short version and the short version was always easier. But she squeezed his arm as if he'd given the long version, and held on to it as they walked down the corridor, saying something about a scroll he'd get, too, but he'd worry about that later.

And that's how he got the Elizabeth Cross back and the whole thing was weird. He'd vowed he'd never wear it after his mum died. Rachel was happy to, but she was more into that sort of thing; Ben was sure he'd just lose it. He knew he wouldn't lose this one, though. Not ever.

THE OTHER VISITOR was Meredith Gostelow, whom the Queen invited to see the headstone she had designed, at the Queen's personal request, for a very unusual grave.

They met at the castle and the Queen drove the architect down through Home Park, towards Frogmore House and its grounds. It was here that many members of the Royal Family were buried, including Victoria and Albert, who had chosen the spot specially, and the Queen's uncle Edward VIII, whom the family could hardly put anywhere else.

The royal graves were neatly tended, in the shadow of Queen Victoria's mausoleum, but the spot the Queen took Meredith Gostelow to was somewhere a little distant, half hidden by trees, just to the north of Frogmore lake. If you weren't looking for it, you would hardly know it was there. A patch of grass among the flowering bluebells was marked by an asymmetrical slab of white marble, set with brass lettering that simply read MAKSIM BRODSKY. MUSICIAN. 1991–2016.

The architect looked at her work with a critical eye. This was the first time she had seen the finished piece in situ. It was extremely simple, and far from her usual style, but a tremendous amount of work had gone into its simplicity: choosing the exact shade of white, the perfect block of marble, the most pleasing asymmetry, the right style and size of lettering with the most attractive spacing, and the best sculptor to achieve it. It had taken days of work on the design, and weeks of thinking.

"Do you approve?" she asked.

"I think it does very well," the Queen said. "Don't you?"

"Oh, there are always things I'd change." Meredith sensed this wasn't the answer the Queen was looking for, so amended it. "But overall, it does what I wanted. I think it does him justice. I hope so."

"I hope you didn't mind me asking you to do it," the Queen said.

"I must admit, I was rather surprised."

"We admire your work. It's why we invited you that night, of course. And you knew Mr. Brodsky."

Meredith felt a hot flush coming on. "You might say that."

They both stared at the headstone. "You danced with him, too," the Queen said, to take the heat out of the other woman's cheeks. She didn't mean to embarrass her.

It seemed to work. Meredith smiled. "Didn't I just? And wasn't he a dream?"

"Yes, he rather was."

"I was kind of told, on the low-down, that they found the man who did it," Meredith offered.

"Ye-es," the Queen agreed. "I gather your name was brought into the investigation. That wasn't my intention."

"Please, don't apologize." Was it an apology? It had sounded like one. "As long as justice was done."

"Up to a point."

They stood in silence for a while. "I like the bluebells," Meredith said. "The whole place. It has a real sense of peace."

At that moment, a 737 roared overhead, causing them both to look and Her Majesty to hoot with laughter, but it was true—planes aside, it was the most tranquil, private spot in this patch of woodland. The Queen had taken her time to find the best location.

"How come he's here?" Meredith asked. It was the question she'd been asking since she first received the commission for the headstone and nobody would tell her. It was as if they were as mystified as she was. This kind of thing wasn't done. It didn't happen. There was no precedent.

"There was nowhere else for him to go," the Queen said, with a wave of her hand.

Nobody had come to claim the body from the morgue. The embassy would have collected it eventually, of course, but she wasn't sure what would happen to it then. He had no one at home to mourn him. She thought he deserved better, after all that Rachmaninoff.

"I think he'll be happy here," Meredith announced. She crouched down—with some strain—and leaned forward to pat the stone, under which Maksim's ashes were buried. "Or maybe unhappy-happy, in the Russian style. I mean, wow, I'd love to be here. Who wouldn't? It feels . . . safe, doesn't it?"

Birds chirruped from the trees. There was a dull, insect hum and a distant sound of horses. They stayed there for a while, soaking up rays of sun that interspersed the dappled shade. But for the white marble, and one contrail in the sky, it seemed as though this spot among the trees could have looked and sounded and felt this way at any time over the last millennium.

The Queen turned down the path eventually. "Shall we go?"

Together, they headed back towards the castle.

Acknowledgments

THANK YOU, above all, to Queen Elizabeth II, for being a constant source of inspiration, both literary and otherwise.

My parents, Marie and Ray, for the precious gifts of a love of detective fiction and a lifetime of anecdotes about the British Royal Family.

My fabulous agent, Charlie Campbell, sine qua non. Alongside Charlie, I'm eternally grateful to Gráinne Fox and the team at Fletcher & Company as well as Nicki Kennedy, Sam Edenborough, and the rest of the team at ILA. I write this four months after we first encountered each other, as the copyedits for the UK and US editions are being finalized. How far we've come together in that time.

My editors, Ben Willis in the UK and David Highfill in the US, and the teams at Zaffre Books and at William Morrow, who have been a delight to work with from the moment we first spoke. That happened as lockdown started, so we haven't met yet, but I can't wait until we do.

For their friendship and generous insights: Alice Young, Lucy Van Hove, Annie Maw, Michael Hallowes, Fran Lana, Abimbola Fashola, and those who prefer to remain anonymous.

Mark and Belinda Tredwell, and Otis, who hosted me on the writing retreat when I was supposed to be writing another book but got a little obsessed with the idea for this one.

The Place, the Sisterhood, the Masterminds, and all my students and fellow writers. You know who you are. A huge thank-you to Annie Eaton, who shares a love of art, history, fashion, and books, and knows some great agents.

The National Health Service, which kept Alex and me alive last year. An eternal thank-you.

The Book Club, with a special mention to Poppy St. John, whose early enthusiasm kept me going when this story was still an idea and a few paragraphs that didn't work.

Emily, Sophie, Freddie, and Tom, who put up with benign neglect when I was in the writing shed. And to Alex, my first reader, love of my life, the man who told me the first version wasn't good enough . . . but the second one was.

P.S.

Insights,
Interviews
& More...

Meet SJ Bennett

About the author

KT Bruce

SJ Bennett holds a Ph.D. in Italian literature from the University of Cambridge and was a strategy consultant at McKinsey & Company before turning to writing. She has published ten books for teenagers, winning the *Times*/Chicken House Competition for *Threads* and the Romantic Novel of the Year Award for *Love Song*. She lives in London. ❧

Reading Group Guide

1. Before beginning any discussion of Queen Elizabeth II, the character in *The Windsor Knot* or the real woman, it's helpful to understand her legacy and where she comes from. Discuss how she has carried on her family name from her father, King George VI, and how that has influenced the woman she is in the novel.

2. Having an eighty-nine-year-old main character presents both advantages and disadvantages, even for a queen. Discuss both as they relate to a protagonist who is attempting to solve a crime.

3. What qualities does the Queen bring to the role that make her a good investigator? Would she be good at solving mysteries outside her royal palaces?

4. The "dine and sleep" event held at one of the Queen's favorite palaces, Windsor Castle, is a unique and very civilized occasion. What role does the Russian soirée play at Windsor, and how might this ►

3

have factored into the murder of the young Russian pianist Maksim Brodsky?

5. What was it about Brodsky that fascinated Queen Elizabeth? What did he remind her of?

6. Both Brodsky and his father, decades earlier, died suspiciously. Are their deaths connected, and what role did international relations play in each event?

7. One of the Queen's assistants, Rozie Oshodi, plays a pivotal role in the novel. Why is it that she seems unaffected by the Queen and her royal position? What is it about her personal background that makes her such an ideal investigator? What kind of relationship does she have with the Queen?

8. It is obvious that the title, *The Windsor Knot,* has multiple meanings. Discuss both the physical and symbolic interpretations.

9. Those holding the highest royal positions are often looked at as merely figureheads. How does this make Queen Elizabeth feel? How do you feel about the royals?

10. *The Windsor Knot* is set in the year 2016. Why do you think author SJ Bennett chose this time frame?

11. Queen Elizabeth fondly recalls one of her all-time favorite films, *Brief Encounter.* Discuss the irony of Bennett's decision to name the final part of the novel "A Brief Encounter."

12. How does Rachel Stiles fit into the story? Did her eventual death make it more or less likely, do you think, that the Queen would solve the crime?

13. Which of the following do you think was the ultimate driving force that led Queen Elizabeth to involve herself in the murder case: lack of faith in the investigators assigned to the case; the involvement of MI6; the effect on the morale of her household; the potential for it to be part of an international incident involving Vladimir Putin; or something else? ∽

Behind the Book

On a drive one English spring evening, I found myself thinking about an episode of *The Crown*. The young Queen Elizabeth II had picked up a painted soldier from a model battlefield and absentmindedly returned him to the wrong place. Her punctilious private secretary corrected the mistake. And I thought to myself that, while it made a nice observation about the private secretary, it was something the Queen—the woman I knew—would never have done.

I haven't met her, but my father has, many times. In the course of a long career in the army, he's cohosted an event with her at the Tower of London, drunk cocktails on the Royal Yacht *Britannia*, and been awarded medals at Buckingham Palace. The woman my father knows is funny, engaged, well informed, and good company. She would have understood that it's impolite to fiddle with someone else's model battlefield, and if she'd ever moved a soldier it would have been to put him in the right place, not the wrong one.

That got me thinking: here's a woman with a lifetime of learning, who is often thought of as not very clever. But she's recognized as a world expert on horse racing, and there are many other fields besides, such as military history, that she knows extremely well. Also, while we're all looking at her, she's looking out. She must spot things all the time that others don't see. What a perfect setup for a detective. The woman I know could do it brilliantly.

The last half hour of my drive spooled by in a dream as I considered the possibilities. I've been a fan of the Queen since 1977—her Silver Jubilee year—when I was eleven and somebody gave me a book called *The Queen's Clothes* by Robb and Anne Edwards. It was about how the Queen developed her signature style, making sure she was always hard to copy and easy to see. Poring over this book, I began to tune in to the complexities of her life: the glamour of the designer clothes, certainly, but also the myriad constraints on what she can wear. Skirts can't fly up in the wind, or rub, or crease, or look too sexy or too bland, or too ostentatiously fashionable, or not fashionable enough. . . . It's harder to be her than it looks.

As a detective, she could have access to any information she wanted, but she must never be seen to interfere. Total freedom, infinite constraints . . . I wanted to write about this woman a lot. Not just one book, but a whole series, following her around all the familiar locations and delving back into her long life.

I've always written books with a feminist element to them, and I'm fascinated by the idea of a "little old lady" surrounded by men, someone who is deeply respected, but not always taken seriously. In this series, the Queen (my Queen) has learned she can trust only certain women to keep her secrets. They are her assistant private secretaries (APS), a role I interviewed for myself after a brief career as a strategy consultant with McKinsey. I'll never forget walking across the forecourt of Buckingham Palace. I didn't get the job in the end; it's still the one that got away.

The latest APS to work for my Queen is Rozie Oshodi. It is 2016, and she's a Nigerian Londoner in a multicultural, postcolonial world, where a Black woman can work with the Queen at the highest level. In fact, the real Queen's last equerry was Lieutenant Colonel Nana Kofi Twumasi-Ankrah, a Ghanaian-born British army officer. Like Rozie in the book, he's a veteran of the war in Afghanistan. The world is changing and at the heart of the plot is the UK's shifting position in it. The Queen is as likely to Google something on her iPad as to ask for someone to research it. And when President Obama asks difficult questions she must, in the parlance of Prince Harry's generation, "style it out."

I tell my writing students that a good plot, like a good martini, should always have a twist. There's a twist to the telling of these ▶

stories, because the Queen's uniqueness as an investigator is that she can't take the credit for solving the crime. And so the reader watches Her Majesty piece together the clues, pick out the red herrings, and find out what she needs to know, but each time, she arranges it so that someone else—usually a senior man—thinks he's solved it for himself. The denouement is all about how he explains it to her. In *The Windsor Knot,* he even gets knighted for it.

I had fun picturing the Queen behind the scenes, but in an affectionate way. President Obama called her "an astonishing person and a jewel for the world" after that visit in 2016. Back then, in her ninetieth year, things were going well for her and her family. Four years later, her life, like ours, is more complicated. The Pantone shade of 2020 (Classic Blue) was chosen because, "We are living in a time that requires trust and faith." Perhaps that's why I wanted to write about someone solid and dependable. When she was twenty-one, Princess Elizabeth declared to the Commonwealth "that my whole life whether it be long or short shall be devoted to your service." She has tried to do that ever since. She is the sort of the person I like to imagine quietly in charge of things, working courageously to make sure good prevails. Isn't that what we hope for, in detective stories and in life?

SJ Bennett, London, May 2020

SJ Bennett's Guide to Windsor Castle

April 2021

Windsor is special to me—but perhaps not in the way you might imagine. Alex, my husband, took me there on our first date away from home. We stayed in a hotel near the river and lay on the grass beside the Long Walk looking up at the sky, while he taught me how to recognize the jets landing at Heathrow by silhouette and sound. This is the reluctant party trick I gave to the Queen many years later. I don't know if she was taught by a former naval helicopter pilot as I was, but I imagine it's something she can do.

Years before, in 1992, I had been driving with friends from Cambridge to Wales for a weekend away from our research, when traffic ground to a halt on the M4. We eventually discovered why: Windsor Castle was on fire. From the road, we could see it lit up against the night sky as we crawled by. This was the Queen's "annus horribilis," and the blaze looked absolutely devastating, but as I learned in my later visits, the project to put it back together gave skills to a new generation of craftsmen. The interiors, which had become a bit shabby—by royal standards—were returned to their pristine Regency and Victorian splendor. Some spaces were changed, and the beautiful Lantern Lobby was created where the old chapel had been. With time and patience, new achievements grew out of sadness and failure. It's one of the abiding themes connected to the Queen's life I wanted to capture in this book. And as I happened to be writing it the year before a pandemic was about to strike, it's a lesson I've since been keen to learn.

When our children were little, Windsor mostly meant Legoland. It always struck me as strange that the Queen's thousand-year-old castle sat within a stone's throw of the Jolly Rocker and the Viking River Splash. When Prince Philip retired in 2017, they added a "Gone Fishing" sign to the Buckingham Palace in Miniland. ▶

SJ Bennett's Guide to Windsor Castle *(continued)*

At around that time, I visited the castle with our youngest, to make up for a missed school trip. He was keen on the weaponry and armor displayed in extravagant patterns on the walls; I was more interested in a passing comment by one of the wardens. We were in the State Dining Room, which is more intimate than it sounds. The table was laid as if for a dinner party and when asked why, the warden said, "Oh, this is as it would be for a dine and sleep." He described what they were and from that moment, I dreamed about being able to spend the night at Windsor Castle as a guest of the Queen. When I looked them up later, the first one I found online mentioned Tim Peake, the astronaut. Others have included Helena Bonham Carter and Helen Mirren. Did they talk about *The Crown* or the film of *The Queen*? I'm dying to know.

Things you may not know about the castle:

- William the Conqueror built the original fortress as one of three along the Thames to deter Anglo-Saxon rebels and to guard the western approach to London. He started construction in 1070. The location was attractive to monarchs because it was near a royal hunting ground and not too far from the capital. Good for riding and for popping into town. From that point of view, not much has changed.

- I describe some of the interiors as "gothic style" and by that, I mean the architectural gothic revival of the nineteenth century. But the castle buildings were jazzed up in the original gothic style by Edward III in the 1350s. It has been "gothic" for a long time.

- Sir Geoffrey Chaucer lived there. In 1390, Chaucer was appointed by Richard II to superintend repairs at St. George's Chapel. Odd to think he did other things than write—but in fact he was very busy. In the St. George's Chapter Library, paw prints have recently been found across the "Man of Law's Tale" in a sixteenth-century manuscript of *The Canterbury Tales*. The prints look like those of "a very large cat or small-medium sized dog." Yes—Corgi-size. Nobody is quite sure when they were made.

- Sir Christopher Wren was an inhabitant, too. His father was made dean of St. George's Chapel in 1635 and young Christopher spent part of his childhood living in the Deanery next door and playing with the future Charles II. It could have been Christopher Wren's dog, or very large cat, who made those paw prints. You decide.

- Prince Albert died there in 1861. Queen Victoria believed his death was caused by typhoid—perhaps not surprising, as the castle sat on fifty-three overflowing cesspools, "too primitive and abominable to bear elaborate description." Ten years later, their son Edward, Prince of Wales, fell ill with typhoid at Sandringham. It seemed all the royal residences had a similar problem that risked killing them off. At Sandringham, the Appleton Water Tower was built to provide fresh water to the estate, and I mention this because you can stay there if you want, courtesy of the Landmark Trust. The views of the Norfolk countryside are reported to be amazing. By the way, today, the historian Helen Rappaport believes Albert didn't die of typhoid after all. Her theory, described in her book *A Magnificent Obsession,* is that he had Crohn's disease and a perforated ulcer. Albert's life had not been made easy by Victoria, who insisted on no heating and open windows at all times. He used to work on his early-morning papers at Windsor wearing a wig and wrapped in a fur-lined coat. (Those cesspools are begging for a murder mystery, aren't they?)

- Many decades later, Princess Elizabeth and her sister put on plays and pantomimes at the castle to raise money for the troops during the Second World War. With echoes of Kate Middleton's fashion show appearance at St. Andrews University, Prince Philip watched Lilibet play Aladdin in ▶

December 1943, while he was on leave from the navy. She was seventeen at the time, and had been keen on him for four years already. They would marry four years later, when she was twenty-one.

• One of the minor problems for any public visitor to Windsor Castle used to be food and snacks. This always constitutes a key part of my days out at big attractions, and inside the walls of the castle—which takes ages to explore properly—the only venue seemed to be an ice-cream stall. But recently it opened its first visitors' café, in the medieval Undercroft. This grand cellar beneath the State Apartments was originally built by Edward III (of gothic tastes) to store beer and wine. Now it serves scones and vegan chocolate cake. What would Edward make of this, I wonder? It's another thing that fascinates me about Windsor: it's the oldest continuously occupied castle in the world and it's constantly evolving. Built a thousand years before I was born, it hasn't finished its story yet.

I get some of my research ideas and updates on what's happening at the royal residences from the Royal Collection Trust. I recommend their website, www.rct.uk, if you want to explore some more. They have everything from 360-degree views of some of the rooms to the royal recipe for scones. You can access some of the links from my website, too: www.sjbennettbooks.com. ᴖ

Map of Windsor Castle

Learn more about rooms featured in *The Windsor Knot*

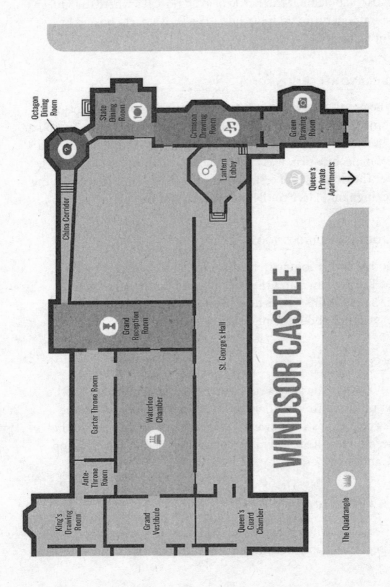

Map of Windsor Castle *(continued)*

THE WATERLOO CHAMBER

This large room was decorated to celebrate the victory of the allies against Napoleon at the Battle of Waterloo. It's where the Queen celebrates her ninetieth birthday, at a lavish party hosted by Prince Charles.

THE GRAND RECEPTION ROOM

In the novel, the Queen is on her way to the Grand Reception Room when her private secretary asks to see her, to give an update on the body. This ornate room, with gilding, chandeliers, and a huge malachite urn, was once used as the ballroom of the castle. After the fire, costs of restoration were partly funded by opening Buckingham Palace to the public each summer.

THE OCTAGON DINING ROOM

A gothic-style room with crimson curtains overlooking the East Terrace Lawn and the park beyond. In the novel, the Queen entertains guests here before lunch one day and quizzes the governor about the night of the murder.

THE STATE DINING ROOM

This is where the guests eat dinner together, and breakfast the next morning (in the book), at the dine and sleep where the story begins. It's where we first meet the main suspects in the case, along with Sir David Attenborough and the Archbishop of Canterbury.

THE LANTERN LOBBY

This space is where the fire started in 1992, in what was the old chapel. The chapel was moved and the Lantern Lobby, with its impressive modern fan vaulting, now forms part of a castle tour of the State Apartments.

THE CRIMSON DRAWING ROOM

After dinner, the Queen entertains her guests with music and dancing in the Crimson Drawing Room. Like all the rooms around it, it was badly damaged in the fire of 1992 and has since been beautifully restored. It is where the Queen meets and dances a foxtrot with the victim, Maksim Brodsky.

THE GREEN DRAWING ROOM

This room forms a stunning contrast to the Crimson Drawing Room. Like the others, it was restored to its nineteenth-century appearance after the fire using the original designs supplied to George IV. It was used as the backdrop for the official wedding photographs of Harry and Meghan, the Duke and Duchess of Sussex, in 2018.

THE QUADRANGLE

This area of grass is overlooked by the Oak Room, where the Queen meets visitors, and by the Visitors' Apartments where some of the suspects spend the night. It is where the Queen knighted Captain Sir Tom Moore in 2020, in recognition of his efforts to raise over £30 million for the National Health Service during the pandemic. ◡

Read on

A Sneak Peek at the Next Book in the Series, *All the Queen's Men*

Available in hardcover Spring 2022 from William Morrow

October 2016

Sir Simon Holcroft was not a swimmer. As a trainee pilot in the Royal Navy, about a thousand years ago, the Queen's private secretary had endured being dunked in the water on various training exercises. He could, if necessary, escape from a sinking helicopter in the Atlantic Ocean, but plowing up and down an indoor pool held no allure for him. However, as he approached the grand old age of fifty-four, his trouser waistline was two inches larger than it should be and the palace GP was making noises about cholesterol levels. Something needed to give, and it wasn't just the button above his fly.

Sir Simon felt tired. He felt flabby. On yesterday's long, uncomfortable car journey back from Scotland he had come to the conclusion that here was a man who had eaten too much Dundee cake and not offered to accompany the Queen on enough cross-country walks. His first thought on arriving back at his cottage in Kensington Palace was that he needed to jolt himself out of this slump.

Those last few weeks in Balmoral had been bloody. It was as if the midges had been staging a Highland games of their own. He had been busy most mornings with Prince Philip, discussing the details of the impending Reservicing Program, and then up most nights on the phone, conferring with fellow courtiers about the Duke's latest suggestions and questions, as well as adding several of his own. If they hadn't done all their homework by the time they presented it to Parliament, the proverbial ordure would hit the fan like a fireworks display.

Vigor was what he needed. And freshness. Despite his lack of enthusiasm, the Buckingham Palace swimming pool seemed like the best solution. Staff tended to avoid it when the royals were in residence. The problem was, when the family were away, he tended to be so, too, and vice versa. However, catching sight of himself in an ill-advised full-length mirror in the bedroom at KP that night, he made the decision to take a risk and nip in early. He prayed that, with his midge-bitten body stretching the seams of his Vilebrequin trunks, he wouldn't encounter a super-keen young equerry in peak physical condition or, worse, the Duke himself, fresh from a royal dip.

Sir Simon walked across Hyde Park and down through Green Park—one of the few forty-minute commutes you could make through Central London that was entirely green—in time to arrive at the palace by 6:30 A.M. He had stupidly put his trunks ▶

on under his trousers, which made both uncomfortable. He parked his briefcase on his office desk, hung his suit jacket on a wooden hanger on a hatstand, and took off his brogues. Neatly rolling his silk tie, which today featured tiny pink koalas, he placed it safely in the left shoe. Then, shouldering the backpack containing his swimming towel, he walked the short distance to the northwest pavilion in his socks. By now it was 6:45.

The pavilion, attached to the North Wing that overlooked Green Park, had originally been designed as a conservatory by John Nash. Sir Simon always thought they should have kept it that way. His mother was a plantswoman and he saw conservatories as paeans to the natural world—whereas heated swimming pools were a little bit naff. Nevertheless, the Queen's father had decided to convert this one in the 1930s for his little princesses to swim in, so there it was, with its Grecian pillars outside, and its somewhat-the-worse-for-wear art deco tiles within, as much in need of updating as so many nooks and crannies of the palace that the public didn't see.

The pool area was reached from inside the main building through a door papered with instructions for what to do in case of fire and reminders that nobody should swim solo, which he ignored. The corridor beyond was already uncomfortably humid. He was glad he'd left his tie behind. In the men's changing room, he divested himself of his shirt, socks, and trousers and draped his towel across his arm. He noticed a cut-crystal tumbler abandoned on one of the benches. Odd, since the family had only arrived back from the Highlands last night. There must have been a homecoming celebration among the younger generation. All glass was banned in the pool area, but you didn't tell princes and princesses what they could and couldn't do in their granny's home. Sir Simon made a mental note to tell Housekeeping so they could deal with it.

He showered quickly and walked through into the pool area, with its windows overlooking the kissing plane trees in the garden, bracing himself for the shock of coolish water lapping against this too, too solid flesh.

But the shock he got was quite different.

At first his brain refused to register what it was seeing. Was it a blanket? A trick of the light? There was so much red. So much dark red against the green tiled floor. In the center of the stain was a leg, bare to the knee, female. The image imprinted itself onto his retina. He blinked.

His breath came short and punchy as he took two steps towards it. Another two, and he was standing in the gore itself and staring down at the full horror of it.

A woman in a pale dress lay curled on her side in a puddle of darkness. Her lips were blue, her eyes open and unseeing. Her right arm reached towards her feet, palm up. All were soaked and stained with congealed blood. Her left arm was stretched towards the water's edge, where the dark puddle finally stopped. Sir Simon felt his own blood pulse, pounding a one-two, one-two rhythm in his ears.

Gingerly, he knelt down and placed reluctant fingers against the neck. There was no pulse, and how could there be, with eyes like that? He longed to close the lids but thought he probably shouldn't. Her hair lay fanned around her head, a halo soaked in red. She looked surprised. Or was that his imagination? And so fragile that, had she been alive, he could have easily scooped her up and carried her to safety.

Rising, he felt a sharp pain in his knee. As he tried to wipe some of the sticky blood from his skin, his fingertips encountered grit. Examining it, he could just make out small shards of thick glass. Now his own blood, seeping freshly from a cut on his leg, was mingling with hers. He saw it then—the ▶

A Sneak Peek at the Next Book in the Series, *All the Queen's Men*
(continued)

remains of a shattered tumbler, sitting like a crystal ruin in the crimson sea.

He knew the face, knew the hair. What was she doing here, with a whiskey tumbler? His body didn't want to move, but he forced it back outside to seek help. Though he knew it was too late for any help worth having.

1

Three Months Earlier . . .

P HILIP?"
    "Yes?" The Duke of Edinburgh raised half an eyebrow
from the folded *Daily Telegraph*, which was propped up against
a pot of honey on the breakfast table.

"You know that painting?"

"Which painting? You have seven thousand," he said, just to
be difficult.

The Queen sighed inwardly. She had been about to explain.
"The one of *Britannia*. That used to hang outside my bedroom."

"What, the ghastly little one by the Australian who couldn't
do boats? That one?"

"Yes."

"Yes?"

"Well, I saw it yesterday in Portsmouth, at Semaphore House.
At an exhibition of maritime art."

Philip stared pointedly at the editorial page of his paper and
grunted, "That makes sense. For a yacht."

"You don't understand. I was launching the navy's new digital
strategy and they'd put up a few paintings in the lobby." The
digital strategy was a complicated business, bringing the Royal
Navy up to date with the latest technology; the art exhibition had
been more straightforward. "Mostly grey things of battleships.
A J-Class yacht in full sail at Southampton, because there's always
one. And next to it, our *Britannia*, from sixty-three." ▸

A Sneak Peek at the Next Book in the Series, *All the Queen's Men*
(continued)

"How d'you know it was ours?" He still didn't look up.

"Because it was *that* one," the Queen said sharply, feeling suddenly and vertiginously sad at his lack of interest. "I know my own paintings."

"I'm sure you do. All seven thousand of 'em. Well, tell the staff johnnies to hand it over."

"I have."

"Good."

The Queen sensed that the *Daily Telegraph* article was probably about Brexit, hence her husband's more than usually prickly mood. Cameron gone. The party in disarray. The whole thing so fiendishly botched . . .

A single painting by an unremarkable artist, presented long before Britain joined the Common Market, was hardly important. She glanced up at the landscapes by Stubbs, with their wonderful horses, that adorned the walls of the private dining room at the palace. Philip himself had depicted her here, reading the paper, many years ago. And he had done it better, one could argue, than the man who had painted *Britannia*. But that picture had once been very precious to her.

It had become a favorite in ways she had never shared with anyone. She intended to get it back.

A COUPLE OF HOURS LATER, Rozie Oshodi arrived at the Queen's study in the North Wing to collect the morning's red boxes containing Her Majesty's official papers. Rozie had joined as the Queen's assistant private secretary a few months ago, after a short career in the army and then at a private bank. She was still relatively young for the role, but so far had performed admirably, including—and perhaps especially—in the more unconventional aspects of it.

"Any news?" the Queen asked, looking up from the final paper in the pile.

Yesterday, Rozie had been tasked with finding out how the painting of the ex–royal yacht had ended up where it was and organizing its swift return.

"Yes, ma'am, but it's not good."

"Oh?" This was a surprise.

"I spoke to the facilities manager at the naval base," Rozie explained, "and he tells me it's a case of mistaken identity. The artist must have painted more than one version of *Britannia* in Australia. This one was lent to the exhibition by the Second Sea Lord. There's no plaque on it or anything. It's from the Ministry of Defence's collection and it's been hanging in his office for years."

The Queen eyed her APS thoughtfully through her bifocals.

"Has it? The last time I saw it was in the 1990s."

"Ma'am?"

There was a belligerent glimmer behind the royal spectacles. "The Second Sea Lord doesn't have another version. He has mine. In a different frame. And he's had it for a long time, you now tell me."

"Ah . . . Yes. I see." From the look on her face, it was clear that Rozie didn't.

"Go back and find out what's going on, would you?"

"Of course, ma'am."

The Queen blotted her signature on the paper on her desk and put it back in its box. Her APS picked up the pile and left her to ponder. ▶

2

"THIS PLACE IS a death trap."

"Oh, come on, James. You're exaggerating."

"I am not." The Keeper of the Privy Purse glowered at the private secretary across the latter's antique office desk. "Do you know how much vulcanized rubber they've discovered?"

"I don't even know what that is." Sir Simon's raised left eyebrow managed to convey curiosity and amusement. As private secretary, he was responsible for managing the Queen's official visits and relations with the government, but he ended up taking an interest in everything that might affect her. And the death trap status or otherwise of Buckingham Palace most definitely fell into that category.

His visitor, Sir James Ellington, was in charge of the royal finances. He had worked with Sir Simon for years and it wasn't unusual for him to make the brisk ten-minute walk from his desk high up in the South Wing to Sir Simon's spacious, high-ceilinged ground-floor office in the North Wing, so he could complain about the latest fiasco. Behind every stiff upper lip lies an Englishman bursting to share his withering irritation in private. Sir Simon noticed that his friend was unusually exercised about the vulcanized rubber, though. Whatever it was.

"You treat rubber with sulfur to harden it," Sir James explained, "and use it to make cable casings. At least, they did fifty years ago. It does the job, but over time it degrades with exposure to air and light and so on. It becomes brittle."

"A bit like you, this morning," Sir Simon observed.

"Don't. You have no idea."

"And so . . . what's the problem with our brittle vulcanized rubber?"

"It's falling apart. The cables should have been replaced decades ago. We knew it was bad, but when we had that leak in the attics last month, they discovered a nest of the blasted things that practically disintegrated on contact. It means the electrics around the building are being held together by a wing and a prayer. A hundred miles of them. One dodgy connection and . . . *pffft*." Sir James made a gesture with his elegant right hand to suggest smoke or a minor explosion.

Sir Simon briefly closed his eyes. It wasn't as if they didn't know the dangers of fire. The Windsor Castle disaster in '92 had taken five years and several million pounds to put right. They had opened Buckingham Palace to the public each summer to help pay for the repairs. Unfortunately, when they'd done a survey of *this* place, to be on the safe side, they discovered it was even more hazardous. Plans to fix it were underway, but they kept discovering complications.

"So what do we do?" he asked. "Move her out?"

No need to specify who may or may not need to move.

"We probably should, pronto. She won't want to go, of course."

"Naturally."

"We ran the idea up the flagpole last year and she didn't exactly salute," Sir James mused glumly. "I don't blame her. If she did go, it would have to be to Windsor, so she could keep up her schedule. We'd clog up the M4 with ambassadors and ministers and garden party guests zipping up and down. The castle itself would need to be reconfigured to cope. She'll soldier on as is if she possibly can. If it ain't broke . . ."

"But it is broke, you say," Sir Simon pointed out.

Sir James sighed. "It is, as you rightly remind me, broke." He raised his eyes heavenwards. "Buckingham Palace is broken. ▶

If it were a terraced house in Birmingham, the experts would stick a notice on the front door and forbid the family to return until it was fixed. But it's a working palace, so we can't. We were just finalizing the Reservicing Program to work around her—this will add another million or two, no doubt. Oh, and I almost forgot. You know Mary, my secretary? The efficient one who always answers emails on time and knows everything in the Reservicing planning agenda and is a bit of a genius?"

"Yes?"

"She's just handed in her notice. I didn't hear all the details, but she was in floods of tears this morning. So—"

He was cut off by the arrival of Rozie with the boxes, which she placed on a marble-topped console table by the door, ready for collection by the Cabinet Office later.

"All good?" Sir Simon asked her.

"Mostly. How do I find out if we loaned the Ministry of Defence one of the Queen's private paintings back in the nineties?"

At this question of negligible interest, Sir James stood up and took his leave.

ROZIE OBSERVED his departure with curiosity. Leaning forward, meanwhile, Sir Simon steepled his fingers and focused on the matter in hand. He was good at leaping from one problem to another—like a gymnast on the asymmetric bars, Rozie had often thought, or a squirrel on an obstacle course.

"Hmm. Talk to the Royal Collection Trust," he suggested. "They look after her private art as well as Crown stuff, I think. Why do we care?"

"The Boss saw it in Portsmouth," Rozie explained. "The MOD say it's theirs. The thing is, she says it was a personal gift from the artist. You'd think she'd know."

"She tends to. What's the MOD's excuse?"

"They're suggesting there must be two of them."

Sir Simon whistled to himself. "Brave move on their part. Can you ask the artist?"

"No, he's dead, I checked. His name's Vernon Hooker. He died in 1997."

"Did he paint a lot of boats?"

"Hundreds. If you Google him, you'll see."

Rozie waited while Sir Simon duly typed in the artist's name to Google Images on his computer and instinctively recoiled.

"By God! Did the man ever sail?"

Rozie was no expert on maritime paintings, but Sir Simon's reaction didn't surprise her. Vernon Hooker liked to depict his subjects in bright colors, with exuberant disregard for light and shade. The images featured more emerald green, electric blue, and lilac than you might expect for scenes that were largely sea and sky. But then, one of the Queen's favorite artists was Terence Cuneo, whose paintings of trains and battle scenes were hardly monochrome. And to Rozie's surprise, when she looked up Hooker online yesterday, it turned out that his work generally sold for thousands. He was quite collectible.

"They're probably right, aren't they?" Sir Simon concluded, peering back at his screen. "The Ministry, I mean. There are dozens of the bloody things. I bet this Hooker would get more money for a Day-Glo royal yacht than a bog-standard seascape. He probably did loads of them."

"She's adamant. And actually, he didn't do any others of *Britannia* that I could find."

"As I say, talk to Neil Hudson at the RCT. See if we loaned it. Twenty years is long enough for the MOD to hang on to it."

"OK." Rozie changed the subject. "Why did Sir James look so uncomfortable just now? I hope I wasn't interrupting anything."

"Only existential despair. It's the bloody Reservicing Program. ▶

His secretary's leaving, and they've discovered vulcanization or something. Dodgy electrics, anyway. The palace is a death trap, apparently."

"Good to know," she remarked breezily, heading for the door. "It sounds expensive."

"It will be. The budget has sailed past three hundred and fifty million already. We need Parliament to sign it off in November, and they can't even give themselves a pay rise."

She paused at the threshold. "Yeah, but this is the second-most-famous house in the world."

"But . . . three hundred and fifty million." Sir Simon folded his shirtsleeved arms and stared despondently at his computer. "When it was only three hundred, it didn't sound so bad somehow."

"Over ten years," she reminded him. "And it'll come in ahead of time and under budget, like Windsor Castle did. And the bill for the Houses of Parliament refit was four billion, the last I heard."

The private secretary brightened slightly. "You're absolutely right, Rozie. Ignore me, I need a holiday. How d'you stay so chipper?"

"Fresh air and exercise," she said decisively. "You should try it sometime."

"Do not cheek your elders, young lady. I'm very fit for my age."

Rozie, who was very fit regardless of age—hers happened to be thirty—threw him a friendly grin before heading back to her office next door.

He tried not to show it, but her remark rankled. She was a tall, attractive young woman, with a short, precision-cut Afro, an athletic physique, and a fitness level that had hardly dropped since she left the Royal Horse Artillery. He, meanwhile, was a quarter century older, and his knees were not what they were. Nor was his back. As a young helicopter pilot and then a diplomat at the Foreign Office, he had been reasonably athletic: an ex–college rower who was handy on the rugby pitch and a demon at the wicket. But over the years, his consumption of good claret had increased in inverse proportion to the time spent wielding an oar, a ball, or a cricket bat. He really ought to do something about it. ▸

BACK AT HER DESK, Rozie clicked on a series of images stored on her laptop. She had asked the facilities manager at the naval base in Portsmouth to send her a photo of the *Britannia* painting, so she would have some idea what she was talking about. The image he'd sent showed the royal yacht, flags fluttering, surrounded by smaller boats with a flat blob of land in the background. She wondered briefly why the Boss was so attached to it. This was a woman who owned Leonardos and Turners, and a small, very lovely Rembrandt at Windsor Castle that Rozie would have cheerfully sold her Mini for.

The facilities manager had been quite firm. The Second Sea Lord—a vice admiral in charge of all "people" matters in the navy—had a variety of paintings in his office, all legitimately sourced from the Ministry of Defence. Any loans from other places were quite clearly recorded and always returned shipshape and Bristol fashion. This wasn't one of them. There must simply be two paintings.

And yet the Boss was equally certain there were not.

Rozie made a phone call. The artist's dealer in Mayfair wasn't aware of any other paintings of *Britannia* by his late client, but suggested she talk to the son.

"Don's the expert on his father's stuff. He's in his late sixties, sharp as a tack. He lives in Tasmania. It'll be evening there now, of course, but I'm sure he won't mind talking to you."

Rozie considered what a generous offer that was, then remembered on whose behalf she was calling. No—the artist's son probably *wouldn't* mind talking to her about the Queen's little problem. People were usually fine with it.

Don Hooker was everything the dealer had promised.

"The royal yacht in Hobart, for the regatta? Oh yeah, I know the one. It was 1962 or 1963—something like that, and Her Majesty was on one of her tours. I remember Dad telling me the story. He was so proud of that painting! He was a big monarchist, was Dad, and there she was, this beautiful lady, traveling the world on her boat. He followed her on all the news broadcasts and made us listen, too, even though, to be perfectly honest with you, Rozie, I was a callow youth at the time and I didn't really care. But Dad loved the whole thing. He had a map on the wall and he marked off where she went with little green pins. Collected postcards, mugs, the lot. He said she looked so happy on that trip and he wanted her to have something to remember it by. 'A piece of that joy,' that's what he said. He copied the picture from a newspaper photo, added the colors, you know . . . And he got a proper pommie thank-you on palace notepaper, with a big, red crest. It said the Queen had never seen *Britannia* look so colorful. It was the only one he did. We've probably still got that letter in Dad's archive somewhere. I can look it out if you want . . ."

When Rozie rang him back, the facilities man from the Ministry of Defence was much less confident about his multiple-paintings theory.

"Perhaps ours is a copy?" he suggested. "I agree it's very unusual, but I can absolutely assure you it's not a loan from the palace."

Sir Simon was due to see the Queen next, and at Rozie's request, he updated the Boss while he was there.

"She says it's not a copy; it's her original," he informed Rozie on his return. "Find out how they got it and tell them to stop stalling. She's pretty pissed off."

"How can she tell it's the original?" Rozie wanted to know. ▶

A Sneak Peek at the Next Book in the Series, *All the Queen's Men*
(*continued*)

After all, the Queen had only seen the painting for a couple of minutes in bad light in a makeshift exhibition at a naval headquarters building on a visit about something else.

"No idea. But she's certain."

If she was certain, Rozie would get the job done.

"JUST A LITTLE CLOSER towards the light."

The Queen adjusted the tilt of her neck, which was getting stiff. "Like this?"

"Lovely, ma'am. Perfect."

She closed her eyes briefly. It was nice and peaceful in the Yellow Drawing Room. Beyond the heavy net curtains, sunrays gleamed off the golden statue of Winged Victory on the Victoria Memorial—or the Birthday Cake, as the guardsmen called it. Warm shafts of light fell on her left cheek. If only one didn't have to maintain this wretched pose, one could quite easily fall asleep.

But she did have to maintain it. The Queen opened her eyes sharply and rested her gaze on a Chinese pagoda in the corner, which was nine tiers high, reaching almost to the ceiling. Her third great-granduncle George IV did not do things by halves.

"Are you getting what you need?"

"Absolutely. Won't be long. You can roll your shoulders in a couple of minutes."

Lavinia Hawthorne-Hopwood, who stood at an easel making preparatory sketches of her, was a considerate artist. She knew what her sitters went through and tried to minimize the trouble. It was one of the reasons the Queen liked to work with her. This wasn't their first rodeo, as Harry would say. (What a marvelous expression. The Queen was delighted by rodeos. She had always thought that, under different circumstances, she might have been rather good at them.)

"Which bit are you working on now?"

32

"The eyes, ma'am. Always the trickiest."

"I see." Through the window, she watched several people posing for photographs outside the palace gates. One seemed to be doing dance moves. Was this for one of those social media crazes Eugenie had told her about? The Queen craned slightly forwards to get a better view.

"If you wouldn't mind, ma'am . . ."

"What?" The Queen was jolted out of her thoughts and realized she had changed position. Lavinia had stopped drawing. "I'm so sorry. Is that better?"

"Thanks. Just another minute or so and . . . There. That one's done. Phew! Would you like a glass of water?"

"A sip of tea would help."

A porcelain cup and saucer appeared at the Queen's elbow, proffered by Sandy Robertson, her page. After a welcome hit of Darjeeling, she stretched discreetly and rubbed her stiff knee, while the artist reviewed her sketches.

Nearby, two video cameras on tripods and a boom microphone on a stand recorded the session. A small team of three, dressed in practical T-shirts and trousers, moved softly between these and their assigned chairs against the far wall. A lanky young man in the red and navy blue Royal Household uniform stood by to help or corral them, as appropriate. A documentary was in progress: "The Queen's Art," or something like that—they hadn't finalized the title. Not just what she owned but also what she contributed to.

Today they were filming the making of the latest artwork she had agreed to sit for: a bronze bust. There really should be someone recording the filming, the Queen mused, just to round the whole thing off. Or someone to write about the recording of the filming of the sketching . . . ad infinitum. She was used to being watched, and used, by now, to being such a source of fascination that her watchers were watched, too. ▸

"Is it going to be life-size, the bust?" she asked Lavinia.

She knew the answer to this question, but also knew the need to make small talk for the cameras and the need for that small talk not to be about Lavinia's recent, horrendous divorce, or her son's arrest for drug dealing at boarding school. The poor woman was entitled to some privacy.

"Yes," Lavinia said, peering at a group of sketches spread out on a table near her easel. "Actually, slightly larger. They want you to stand out at the Royal Society."

"Mmmm. Was the last one larger, too?"

"I think it was, ma'am, from memory. Did you like it?"

"Oh yes. I thought it was rather good. You managed to avoid making me look . . ." She puffed out her cheeks and made Lavinia laugh. "Too much like my great-great-grandmother." Heavy. Jowly. Old.

Lavinia went back to her easel. "My aim is to make you shimmer. Even in bronze. Right, are you ready, ma'am? If you can turn your head to look at my hand, here. Just a bit more. That's lovely . . ."

The artist kept up a gentle patter of conversation while she worked. She got more from her subjects when they talked than when they stayed silent. The Queen's face, in particular, lit up when she was animated. At rest, it could look grimly forbidding, which gave quite the wrong impression of her.

"Have you been to any good exhibitions recently?" Lavinia asked, and then regretted it. She should have asked about racing.

But the Queen didn't seem to mind.

"We're opening one next year that I'm looking forward to," she said. "'Canaletto in Venice.' We have rather a lot of Canaletto." By which she meant the largest collection in the world. "Bought in bulk by George III from Joseph Smith. He was the consul to Venice at the time. A dull name for a rather interesting man, I've always thought."

Lavinia gulped. "Goodness."

The Queen smiled to herself. She'd had a lively chat on the subject with her Surveyor of Pictures recently. After several decades of living with them, she knew her Canalettos very well, although she preferred her own impressions of the place. Sailing from Ancona to Venice onboard *Britannia* in 1960—or was it 1961?—visiting the ancient little island of Torcello with Philip, and taking a moonlit gondola ride . . .

She thought back to those early royal tours on the royal yacht. Italy, Canada, the Pacific Islands . . . *Britannia* had been fitted out after the war, in another time of austerity, and its interior was practical, rather than extravagant. It suited the Queen's temperament better than the gilt and grandeur that surrounded her now. How *happy* they had been, she and Philip and the "Yotties," visiting the farthest corners of the globe together. So many marvelous memories. The "ghastly little painting" uniquely conjured some of them in particular.

"I saw one of my personal paintings at an exhibition by the Royal Navy recently," she said aloud. It still rankled.

"Oh, that's nice," the artist said absently.

"It wasn't really. I hadn't lent it to them. The last time I saw it, it was hanging opposite my bedroom door."

Lavinia's head jerked up in shock. "Oh dear."

"Oh dear precisely," the Queen agreed.

"How did it get there?"

"That's a very interesting question." A minute later she added, "There. I think we're done."

Her tone was friendly but firm. The artist looked up, then glanced at her watch. The hour was up, precisely, and her subject was already removing the diamond tiara she had kindly agreed to wear for the sculpture, which had looked delightfully over-the-top above her shirt and cardigan. The documentary team took charge of their cameras, watched by the eagle eye of the lanky young man from the Household. The Queen's equerry ▶

was already hovering in the doorway, ready to accompany Her Majesty to her next appointment.

"Thank you very much, ma'am," Lavinia said.

The Queen nodded. "I look forward to seeing the shimmer." Her tone was dry, but there was a twinkle in her eye. ❧

Discover great authors, exclusive offers, and more at hc.com.